RUBIX APOCALYPSE

RUBIX APOCALYPSE

Vladimir M. Mavar Jr.

GSH

ISBN: 978-1-956074-93-2 (Paperback Edition)
ISBN: 978-1-956074-94-9 (Hardcover Edition)
ISBN: 978-1-956074-92-5 (E-book Edition)

Book Ordering Information

Phone Number: 315 288-7939 ext. 1000 or 347-901-4920
Email: info@globalsummithouse.com
Global Summit House
www.globalsummithouse.com

Printed in the United States of America

CONTENTS

"To my deceased parents, Vladimir Sr. & Iva."

Introduction

This is a writing of science fiction, with elements of verifiable history, that may contain components of a given future reality that could materialize if humanity were ever posed with the question of what is more important, territorial dominance or the survival of a species. It may not come into play at all, in the very least, in our lifetimes, but is something to ponder at the beginning of the 21st century while we are experiencing something of a contemporary day Renaissance in all aspects of our daily lives, including those advances made in computer networking, advances in healthcare, genetics, physics, biology, astronomy, nuclear sciences, as well as various social sciences, such as sociology, economics, history, all with an accompanying deterioration in the recent global economy. It seems as though these economic hardships are an inescapable fact of historic reality necessary for contemporary progress to be refreshed at a given level until socioeconomic circumstances and this said progress are on the same page. Until something like this even occurs, many people will be preoccupied living with problems within their daily existence, some of which they could barely deal with, such as losing loved ones to natural death or that inunexplained circumstances, jobs to a turbulent economy, global viruses like H1N1, serious illnesses, homelessness, divorce, prejudice, just to name a few. If fact, for many of us, it may not be wise to ever contemplate or give a second thought as to what would happen if humankind was really faced with this predicament of a choice. The best thing any person could do at this point is to be prepared for something even our respective governments cannot shield us from, and ironically, may have even contributed to. We have always seemed to come out ahead in past recorded history, or at least those who were lucky enough, intelligent enough, or in some other way capable of surviving major cataclysmic events such as volcanic eruptions, horrific tsunamis, hurricanes, and global conflicts, to name a few. even. if you didn't believe in luck, you may be in a position to involuntarily change your opinion. My scenario is not that much different in some ways from others in that it attempts to combine the best elements of the human instinct to survive with some of the most innovative ways of thinking that have allowed us to do so. As a species, we have had some good fortune along the way considering that we have never quite mastered our respective environments even at this point in history. With all of our courage and veracity, we come closer ever day to fully securing ourselves against those events and catastrophes that could endanger our collective survival and endanger our existence on earth. Our scientific methodologies, approaches of trial and error, along with any accompanying statistical margin, and pursuit of knowledge at an ever increasing rate are testaments of our need not only to survive, but to dominate ourselves, each other, and our surroundings. The question is: would we be able to drop whatever dominant activities that we are preoccupied with at a given time in the present and act as one unified human race if many of our lives were at stake, if at the very core of the problem was our potential annihilation? After all, were are as much free radicals as we are constituent members of the same life force that has allowed us to do these wonderful things for millennia. each of us has a will, a will to do and a will to think. We can also potentially function as a willing, doing and thinking collective. This doesn't need to be a reference to socialism, but could we be unified enough to stop what some for centuries already have called inevitable? Once again, do not let me distract you from a quieter afternoon reading a romance novel, watching your favorite soap opera, jogging in the park, or bathing your dog. This could concern all of us one day, if not tomorrow, then a few decades from now. The book is not meant to be a series of alarming statements, but something entertaining, gripping and food for thought. It is based on my experiences and contemplations from beyond the grind and realities of my own everyday life. It may also involve epistemological inputs that I have attained in no logically explicable way (just as a vivid dream may come to represent an unexplained reality). As many people, I look forward to a day when our survival as a species is entirely guaranteed and we are truly in a position to live happily and peacefully, free from most encumbrances or threats, regardless of what our future social systems hold in store for us. I see it as a day when we can continue to explore the finite and the infinite and continue to give credence to those who came before us and sacrificed for the future, which is why I propose not to view the scenario in this book as completely necessary or morally valid. I also see it as a time of greater understanding of one another and the need for greater morals to prevail than certain leadership initiatives of the past. The one aspect of this picture I am not so sure of is our own unity.

Can we ever be truly unified as brothers and sisters of all nations, ethnicities, creeds, colors, persuasions, and religions to overcome the seemingly inescapable without turning to our primal warring instincts? The ending can be a blissful one, but it depends on all of us. It may also depend a little on the next revolutionary invention that puts us one step ahead of clear and otherwise unavoidable danger.

A Paradox Unresolved

Is it madness that motivated us in our pasts, that certain fervor to materialistically out-do or achieve our neighbors, to catch the eye of that special someone, their affections, to achieve and to twist fame beyond recognition, or to simply know more? Or was it perhaps necessity combined with twists of the human condition? The necessity to recognize that we are happier if our neighbors are happier and we are healthier if our neighbors are healthier is more than just a sign of the times. In the 21st century, many countries are truly starting to live the global village concept to the fullest; in some cases, because many of us don't have a choice. In most cases I can only wonder and not assume to know better. We all know how many hardships there are today and, however many more there were in the past, history only knows. History is something almost akin to Nature's diary. We can pick up on bits and pieces, but we seemingly are never allowed to know too much of our own pasts. Nevertheless, it is recorded through our ancestries, our past lives, our evolutionary development, and space-time itself. This record of history can never be changed or altered in the slightest. It is our past and our past existence. It is our planet's past and the history of our Solar System. As immutable as this record seems, it could be the Diary of Nature Herself. If only we could just see excerpts from this Diary to have something to refer to in the case of a cataclysmic emergency. We now have that opportunity, but how do we copy what was once our past onto an appropriate medium, in other words, what do we use for this elaborate scheme? We are on the verge of many new creative computer technologies, some of which are very futuristic, are already available, and have manifested themselves in the form of newer video game technologies, long-distance surgeries by way of the Internet, and previously unimaginable computing power which allow us to "look before we leap." In addition, more than a decade ago, we were presented with news that a rough draft of the human genome had been completed in the year 2000. With the completed map of the human genome within reach of my own generation (specifically a customized one of a consenting rational individual), a detailed and advanced understanding exists of the fundamental particles and forces that keeps these particles glued together for human life to simply exist and subsist, as well as the eventual ability to transfer these particles as virtual DNA data packages through a network of time backwards and forwards at will by using background cosmic radiation (discovered in the 1950's) as a natural guidance system, a sort of chronological GPS; humankind could potentially achieve safe time travel for the purpose of fact finding research and survival. This radiation could provide the constant within the span of human history that would provide the necessary guidance in propagating through this Diary, much like the cursor on a computer screen functions. The variable factors in this case would be genetic factors and the ancestry of the traveler, as well as unpredictable effects on individual human psychologies and physiologies.

The fixed component would be the boost attained from the superluminal jump and the visualization of the occurring environment. Just like a wireless networking beacon, a traveler could find his way to his respective point in space-time through the use of frequencies and his unique genetic characteristics. Technically, one cannot be expected to remember something that he experienced out of this time frame once in his own chronological environment, but the futuristic virtual database stored within their DNA would record it accurately regardless of the person's recollections). Could Virtual Time Travel (VTT) pose a paradox on a global society threatened by a loose asteroid, from the Kuiper belt or from elsewhere in space, while impending doom from a global warfare was looming and well underway Does morality ultimately dictate that one put himself or herself in the situation of traveling back in time as a series of DNA data packages (much like ethernet_II frames travel across intranet networks & the Internet itself to deliver data)? Or does one ultimately make peace with dying in some fashion or form, whether by potential conflicts or an asteroid rendezvousing with earth? It follows that one attempt Virtual Time Travel; the proper scientific methodology can ensure within an infinitesimal margin of error that it can succeed if one is only there to witness history as it happened, much like running an old educational library movie. Of course, the drawbacks are tremendous, one of which is that one travels back through his or her own ancestry, since the genome is closely related to human ancestries through the connecting links of natural and social evolution; for the traveler, it would be as though he is regressing in time through his own parents, grandparents, great grandparents, great great grandparents, and so forth. One's DNA (dubbed virtual DNA signature— VDNAS—during travel) is what allows him to exist in a parallel sense within a particular ancestor (male or female, or vice versa), without being detected by the flow of history or without making alterations to the Book of Time.

Deoxyribonucleic acid (DNA), statistically and mathematically speaking, is an imperfect guide for time travel if only because it is corruptible by the very experiment. It is literally impossible to travel this precisely in today's terms because it is scientifically impossible to pin-point the here and now without a grid system. However, one can travel to any point of recorded history as a virtual enigma (a virtual representation of genetic fact that is more representative than a hologram), passing through the bodies and co-existing with ancestors until the genetic variations between the enigma and that person were distinct enough to naturally disallow use of the lineage. The assumption then is that the cosmological background radiation is the constant, the guiding mechanism. At that point, one would return to his or her present or continue as the Virtual enigma (somewhat like a sophisticated mathematical encryption, a virtual enigma, which by means of preserving the original DNA sequence would be able to assume as many virtual DNA sequences as is allowable and imposed naturally by the aggregate DNA set of living people within the original subject's time frame and evolution itself until the grid is developed and built). The net effect would almost be to invade the privacy of someone else's ancestry by being in the body of another without permission, equating the real with the virtual. Other unintended consequences might be to assume the body (and coexist with) someone of the opposite gender in the past flow of space-time. While this might conjure up visualizations of out-of-body experiences, it is nothing of the sort. Ultimately, the goal with this series of DNA packet information traveling backwards through history is not to be noticed in order to avoid a potential paradox and to return safely so that apocalypse can be averted, all while managing to collect specific information for the present; this is the very reason virtual representations are necessary in this scenario. Scientifically, these technologies could be used for further fact finding and research. It may ultimately be the only thing that prevents detection from the side of Nature.

We may otherwise never know what lies beyond the delineating moment of our past existence. The Virtual enigma (an enigma in itself) would allow the subject to continue traveling even in the event that, historically, a bloodline was wiped out in the past due to a catastrophe such as war or and it would allow safe passage back to the present as the original subject with largely unaltered DNA. The enigma would theoretically resolve any quantum conflicts of information from having identical things in two separate points in time. Unfortunately, the traveler is never quite the same person afterward.

The modern analogy that comes to mind almost immediately is

hacking a computer. In order to be a "good hacker", one must know how NOT to leave a trail of evidence that anyone was there. It is almost like hacking Chronology's personal records. Now, would that not be a valid impetus to attempt the thing that has fascinated readers of science fiction for over a century? I think not, but it may be achieved eventually. What better time than right now? Necessity need not be the only driver of progress, nor should improvement. It is natural to be curious, the love of being endowed with knowledge is a good justification to seek out our environments in ever- changing ways; this is why we should seek out all truths, even if we have to be cautiously curious about our surroundings. Our lives may never really depend on reading the scripts of the past in order to survive future calamities since no two closely identical calamities are the same in any way. Would you take that plunge into the unknown with me?

The Reverse Evolution & Virtualization of Saved Processes

All processes occurring in a human subject at the time would cease and reverse in order to be precisely captured and recorded at the DNA-level by the employed technologies. All levels of organic functioning at the molecular levels will be recorded, saved and virtualized. When the enigma emerges within a newly found host, these processes would resume in the ordinary direction again as the thermodynamic arrow of time, only upstream, in an undisclosed fashion. Thus the summation of organic and inorganic processes would be captured and made readily available within the human subject, leading to a co-habitation within another human existence. The summation of chemical reactions would be accounted for within the "virtual cloak" as a localized chronological phenomenon.

The Chronology Labyrinths of Human History

History as perceived in modern times has consisted of many series of continuous events that have led from present time to their future, with human memory left to pick up the pieces of understanding and fragments of reality to form experiences for this struggle called life. Our very existence and wellbeing depend upon time itself flowing in a certain verifiable direction.

Our notions of the Divine as well as scientific fact stem from these perceptions. Modern songs sometimes make mention of love continuing if time stood still. Time is the reel that our ancestors' memories are woven around, as well as the force that guides our everyday decisions. It is one of the most complex concepts and phenomena humankind has ever had to tackle and under most circumstances has taken its time to fully understand and record the results of its discoveries. Chronological history is like a labyrinth, with the door to many records permanently sealed and the database key completely secured. As far as we know today, there is no going back. It is also said that history is recorded by those who are triumphant and dominant in past eras to be able to have written it in a favorable way to them (many times somewhat skewed versions compared to what might have actually happened in respective points in history). Unlocking the pathways to the hallways of history's labyrinth may also provide the gateway to survival if something of the magnitude of a super volcano ever occurred in our time. From time to time, historians and others have pointed to the fact that certain facets of history are false. Unlocking the key to past time flows may be as dangerous as opening up Pandora's Box. Normally undertakings of this magnitude take much time, years or even decades. What would you do if we had to act much sooner?

A Fact Finding Mission Aimed At Preserving Human History

You might wonder what sort of solid facts one hopes to gather from a sort of time travel mission into human past that would be useful for not just survival, but for less stressful times as well? How about a framework for the verification of recorded history? As one might guess, many historical dates are not completely accurate or, in some cases, are just approximations. The further one goes back in time, provided the ability to, the more variations in accuracies there may be. The mission could be looked upon as having the broad scope of providing genuine and verifiable data to a revised history, constructing as detailed and specific of a genomic map to allow for this travel (akin to building roads where needed), and accomplishing this in ample time to divert disaster. Its secondary mission is to preserve global historical culture and human traditions as well as possible in an all-encompassing virtual database. The tertiary mission is for personal peace and enrichment of the mind.

Pandemic Viruses of the 21st Century

One only need turn to 21st century global media to find out the burdens and plagues that devastate humanity on a daily basis. Some of those include the avian flu (H5N1), swine flu (H1N1), HIV/AIDS, weather disturbances such as monsoons, tsunamis, and hurricanes such as the more recent Katrina in the Gulf of Mexico, tsunamis in places like Bangkok, or earthquakes in places such as Haiti. There are always those that state vehemently that these events happen because of human negligence, as well as those who claim that is it the punishment and wrath of God himself that are manifesting themselves before our very eyes. Of course, it is of the utmost significance to stress that those affected can do little more than simply adapt to these changes and dynamic cataclysmic events. Could it be that Albert, a young man in contemporary Australia, knows the secret to saving the earth's population but doesn't know how to extricate himself from complete obscurity that surrounds him in his native Melbourne? It could be that Afrim from Tirana, Albania has a different take on the matter and wishes to preserve his homeland for his fellow countrymen but may not care that much about what happens in Kazakhstan or Namibia. It is our belief systems that dictate how we are to react even more in some cases than our natural upbringings or our natural tendencies. even if we do not readily admit this, history is a bond that enslaves as well as gratifies because it offers belonging while it punishes perpetrators, sometimes inadequately and sometimes excessively. In many cases, it rewards the perpetrators excessively. While it may not offer much more than a general overview of what was, it offers different realities as to what it could have been and never shall be in the grand scheme of existence. It is time for other paths to reality to emerge and help liberate those who still feel enslaved.

The Enigmatic Voyage

Only when the conditions are appropriate will the process occur. A protective bubble is needed to survive the process of planned de-moleculisation within the body and just outside of the protective area itself, a bubble which houses the experiment of reverse abiogenesis. Where is the detachment from euclidean geometry, or even multidimensional space-time realities? The assumption we are working from is that there is a quantum trace that identifies individual genetic signatures. It has proven by several prominent scientists that the thermodynamic arrow of time, analogically speaking, maintains the flow of time itself from one direction (from the course of The Big Bang itself, which is the origination point of the known Universe) to what we know and perceive of as the split of our current state of conscious awareness in present time relative to its progression from the past into what we know as the future. This arrow is an implied result of the Second Law of Thermodynamics, which states that entropy (natural state of disorder) evolving to organization in the universe tends to increase with time flowing in a certain direction. With respect to the thermodynamic arrow, the causal arrow of time deals with the manner of how an event's effect is preceded by its cause, while the radiative arrow deals with how matter was created in the early part of the Universe. Certain subatomic reactions violate the conservation of both parity and charge conjugation and are directly related to the particle physics (weak) arrow of time. Our bodies are held together at the molecular level by the strong nuclear force. Would it be possible to reverse the arrow of time for the traveler within the bubble and for the arrow to remain unaffected? It would only be possible if the perceptual (psychological) time flow would not be affected. Psychological time is the process of maintaining or cataloging an ever increasing number of items of memory from continuous changes in perception. With correct timing and planning, it is possible to send a cybernetic organism or cybernetic person equipped with a different type of memory than organic memory—virtual memory. This virtual memory cannot easily be erased and would survive traversals of the arrow of time in either direction. The effective set of databases in virtual form would include a linguistic database based upon every known dialect of any recorded or imaginable language, as well as variations of the known ones, that one would or possibly could encounter on her way through her genome, as well as variations in the language until the first transformation occurred. It would include a comprehensive database filled with known human history and what might be the best estimates if the traveler encountered situations where uncertainty loomed. It may only take a tiny fraction of a second before contradiction (or a potential paradox) kicked in. Any related epistemological discipline that could be necessary or that has occurred in contemporary academia is included. It would eventually be linked to the Internet in order to monitor radio waves (specifically cosmic radiation at a wireless frequency) from the past using statistical regression techniques. The most significant part of the process are virtual messages in the form of data packets which, much like RNA molecules in the human body, serve as messages guiding the traveler, then can be made to travel faster than light not only in the holographic sense, but in real-time, thus enabling time travel. If one has to wonder why this is even practical or beneficial to humankind as a whole, one need only consider a Doomsday scenario such as the Cold War. It might be too late to stop further occurrences, whether planned or accidental. Perhaps information from the past wouldn't just need to be looked upon as another way to rape and pillage Nature. It might need to be looked upon as humankind in general contributing to at least a partial healing of Nature. It heralds the way to a forward-looking society and, finally, a simultaneously backward-looking one. In this case, it would be beneficial to know what lies in the past, even if the morality of the process and the end result are not entirely ethical.

Virtual Virtuoso in a Mind of Her Own

A virtuoso is considered someone who is far talented in measure and movement from most others and far removed from her peers in a discipline such as music, art, or even a branch of science that he is on a plateau of his own. This definition also refers to the technical skill, fluency, or style exhibited by a virtuoso or a composition. Do such individuals deserve the exorbitant amount of attention that they are attributed in their chosen fields? It is impossible to say without raising general questions of social value and equity with respect to social intangibility, at least at times with respect to the meaning of sociological concepts of such as meritocracy (one is rewarded in this type of theoretical society based proportionally to their very merits), as well as individual worth in the context of a democratic society or less fluent concepts such as that of friendship and love. Modern society recognizes the value of a virtuoso by what one might say is her tempest, the driver of this instinct to perform. The faucet of virtuosity could be the valve that releases socioeconomic and human tension that is built up behind the facade. What does this have to do with a virtual device of any sort, might you ask? History is sometimes as random as it is exact and punishing to those who write it as well as to those who are simply its bystanders. It permeates other links like a wind of omnipotence. Fortunately, the objectively veritable and verifiable force that is the virtual virtuoso, or time traveler, can never truly find the most neutral starting point simply because it does not exist. Objectivity has to be assumed and, in all honesty, every place on the continuum has its own objective and neutral starting point that must be unknowable. Where are those simpler days when Nature was treated with much dignity, kindness and respect, when the skies adhered to no man-made aircraft with the lethal potentiality of being used as weaponry to entice fear and preeminence of death, when Nature was almost untouched like a virgin?

Revolutionary Progress Achieved

Has it ever been called progress to kill an innocent life, in order to achieve something motivating, something that helps that sense of order or reduces the appearance of entropy to a single human being? For the sake of scientific inquiry, one must truly relate the importance of anything, including a single insect, to the aggregate ecosystem in which the person lives. Temporarily, the entropy is increased; the tendency toward chaos rises in response to a violation of the natural laws of physics, chemistry, as well as biology. Does it necessarily mean that progress is achieved if we affect the natural flow of history and time within our own existence and the existence of both living and non-living matter at the same time? Is it possible for two beings to visibly exist within the exact same spatial co-ordinates and both remaining unaffected? A different type of progression is very probable. Humankind is literally swimming in an ocean of technologies that many may never know about let alone ever use. Man and Nature might have once been in closer Harmony with one another, but something happened, something even cataclysmic. The Virtual Time Travel machine could never reverse that evolution or dampen the effects of such a tumultuous relationship. It is a genomic time machine.

Human History Preserved

Virtual miniaturization is the process of preserving past living and non-living materials in the form of quanta packets for the purpose of obtaining and the process of comparison between current data and specimens from our contemporary time. It is more accurate than radiometric dating that is used to date materials, usually based on a comparison between the observed abundance of a naturally occurring radioactive material and its decay products, usually know as decay rates. In this sense, magnitudes of information can be preserved in one single miniaturized database that can hold millions of times more information than the most advanced database in the early 21st century. Precisely for reasons of preparedness must we utilize this technology? We can collectively and individually move the bar of scientific and human progress into the next century by knowing what is contained within the chronological records within the earth and from within the atmosphere itself. We are breathing history in the making. We are walking on past mistakes and past achievements. While one might wonder about the needs and the risks of preserving human history in such an unconventional way, there is no way to avoid the resulting margin of error due to the statistical regression that ensues in obtaining past's information. Preservation of the genetic code of humans—as well as other species on earth—is not the same as preserving the essence of all life. Man must know before he can manifest himself in another form just what he is made of; he mustn't even make a movement of viol indecision because everything else that is planned may be hinging upon it. Were it not for this, human progress would be dynamically reduced and drastically scaled back. Humanity can never wipe the slate clean of the animalistic past. It may never be possible to completely bridge that gap.

Humanity's Clean Slate

Could it be that the Virtual Bubble, which is needed to achieve genomic time travel, can initially be achieved without detrimental health consequences with respect to memory, mood fluctuations, sleep disturbances, or emotional variabilities related to transition? It might appear that in order for virtual genomic time travel to occur, the slate must also be wiped like a computer hard disk in order to avoid paradox from a recent memory or event. There is no way to defragment human memory or pain.

The Road to Somewhere

The notion that a road need lead to something or to a particular place is not wrong—it is chilling and horrifying. It is a notion of our fear of the unknown and the unknowable. But is it unknowable because there are no means or methodologies to make this phenomenon more knowable, or is it unknowable because it is not in our place to know? The history database goes on filling in the missing pieces of local and global histories as they have happened whether they were originally preserved or not. It is just like the act of retrieving, processing, and recording data. These particular databases are meant to update themselves. The main question is how to record and update something that already exists in a secretive fashion? How is it possible to make a copy of something that only Nature and Time can synchronize and create together?

Databases of Fear, Injustice & Torture

Armed with databases from our past and present, we can concede that we know a little more and are not in a position to impact the course of historical annihilation by much more than the margin of error or a statistical curve that would be needed to achieve in order for us to maintain our realness and to avoid the unknown consequences of a direct hit, including massive tidal waves and earthquakes. Advanced virtual technologies are no longer optional, they are mandatory. To reiterate, this is a scenario posed as a fundamental basis for a hypothetical situation that may arise on our planet one day. It is not completely independent of others' works or the thoughts of others in places I have never even visited. It may very well be a simple attempt at independence. Would we be able to step up to the plate for one another and would that plate be of the correct shape? It always is, if our nuances and measurements are correct. They are symbolic gestures and readings that would indicate caring as well as interdependence. Do we expect Homo Sapiens to act alone or to make a split decision in helping itself in the context of these potential events? Do we expect individual or collective organizations to save the day, to have that handful of heroes or a singular hero that saves us from certain disaster as they always tend to do in 20th century and 21st century film medias? It is difficult to say since human will is not factored into the set of equations. Free will is a tenet of modern history.

Human instinct is predetermined and is the part of our genetic make-up that is measurable and attributed our personalities, our genealogies, our ancestries, and our evolution. Human will is a synergistic unraveling of the preface that those individual parts collectively can create tangible value. Human volition therefore transcends time, shape, and many different forms. If one could travel through time into the past virtually, what language or even what script would initially power the virtual database that controls the traveler's memory? Would it be Chinese, english, Spanish, German, French, Russian or maybe even esperanto?

The First Fully Conscious Cybernetic Time Traveler

Because of the emotional and other barring conjectures of sending a live subject, a human traveler, to the past for the fact finding mission, the idea for several years has been to send a cyborg, cybernaut, or a cybernetic traveler to travel through time in a virtual sense. Only a being such as this could withstand the pain and have enough endurance to manage the travel due to its part-human and part-cybernetic brain. The brain would be less dualistic and have the tendency to act as a human, yet to think, process, and warn its human host as a computer functions to warn a PC user of different things in its environment, such as an inadvertent download of a computer virus. The model that most greatly impacts virtual time travel still must be the model of Velocity Reversal and the Arrows of Time (reference abstract "Velocity Reversal and the Arrows of Time", by John G. Kramer). The only perceived arrow of time that does not directly link up to the kaon arrow of time, thermodynamic arrow of time, electromagnetic arrow of time, and cosmological arrow of time is the subjective (psychological) arrow of time.

A More Realistic Tomorrow

One might say that there is not only a way this method of gathering and preserving historical records would fail due to its limited scope because of lacked resources and modern- day human emotion and conflict getting in the way, but also because there is not a set way this newly found information could actually help humankind in a tangibly beneficial way, such as setting social goals for the remainder of this century and the following century, reducing the probabilities of war and conflict globally, resolving issues of hunger and unrest, as well as preparing and saving us from the apocalyptic or cataclysmic event that may await. The primary purpose of any Virtual Time Travel research would be dedicated to the improvement and progress of global society as well as the eradication of any major problems that may be facing us at the time. It would be dedicated to promoting better ways of powering our vehicles, powering our homes, feeding our global population, eradicating hunger, being better prepared for events such as massive blizzards, hurricanes, and tsunamis, dealing with mental and physical illnesses in a more humane way, as well as dealing with the questions that have never left our minds, including the question of whether intelligent life exists elsewhere in the Universe, whether there any other nearby planets in neighboring galaxies that can harbor life, or even those than contain the conditions that would allow us to answer these questions from further away, by proxy. It may be that we might not fully know until the 22nd century how to handle this resource. For the time being, for the scenario given, it may not be immediately possible to have access to any "new" information resulting from this addition to the World Wide Web without prior allowance.

Cataclysmic Event to the Yoctosecond

Suppose that a cataclysmic event could take place and we discovered its occurrence through one of the many telescopes and satellites that we have circling around the earth. It is valuable to be able to calculate things to a miniscule fraction of a second, as small as a septillionth of one second (yoctosecond), not only for the survival of a population, but also with regard to any potentially material or immaterial paradox that would normally occur if an expedition through time was attempted. Could we truly stop destruction on the face of the planet itself by having information beforehand about what might happen by a few milliseconds to a few days? It might be plausible if we employ the method of Virtual Time Travel.

Prediction Pinpointed and Global Disaster Researched

When astrologers and predictors made announcements in prior years and centuries about expected events in the past, they used a number of questionable methods, those methods that most people living in today's time would normally discount if presented with enough information to do so.

Nostradamus is a good example of one such prophet, the best known of any doomsday prophet. Many of his prophesies dealt with disasters such as plagues, earthquakes, wars, floods, and the comings of three antichrists. If there is a supernatural reason that any of these predictions need to come true, it has done a weak job of manifesting itself. The clues and signs that are exhibited are not as related to each other as the prophesies that Nostradamus wrote in "quatrains", which was a style of poetic writing in 16th century France. Unfortunately, modern scientific methodologies cannot realistically pinpoint certain disasters. Virtual Genomic Time Verification is an update to existing ones.

DNA Configurations and Customized Virtual Files

Our time is one of global computer networks, global positioning satellites and space research, cloning, cryogenic freezing for futuristic preservation, human genome research and solutions, exploration and implementation of alternative fuel sources, as well as the virtualization of global technologies as a whole.

Virtual technologies of genomic time travel, as all virtual technologies (which might include future military technologies such as cloaking & shadowing), have the capacity to adapt to the flow of space-time in that sense. In genomic travel, the virtual particles have the capability to "deceive" time in the way that they flow or are perceived to flow. The customized model of the alpha subject's DNA configuration is what is converted to virtual packets along the "cosmic radiation network", which has given us insight into past atmospheric conditions; further details on how the dinosaurs may have become extinct, a more accurate occurrence of the next ice age, as well as overall climatological changes may emerge. The human genome draft sequence, as encoded in 2003, has mapped roughly 30,000 genes. The human genome consists of roughly 5,000 million chemical nucleotide bases (A, C, T and G), with almost all nucleotide bases (99.9%) being exactly the same in all people. In actuality, humankind differs in its diverse genome by variations in a little less than 30 genes (0.1% of 30,000). If we hypothesize on the number since the time Homo sapiens started to walk the earth, the number of genes may increase.

Difficulties with Virtual enigma Travel

The activation of the Virtual Genomic Time Machine is almost a purely random process for the first time. It has been extraordinarily difficult gathering the necessary information, as well as processing and crunching the information in a furious attempt to allow the project to live, as well as to enable it to outlive its usefulness and to outperform the utility of its cost/ benefit analysis scenario. The conditions necessary for the human enigma to materialize have been next to impossible to conceive of, but my staff and I have been working to bring this project into the realm of the possible and plausible. The machine is built upon the benevolent need to allow equal and unequivocal access to information in the realms of the past. Scientifically, it is built on the principles of closure of perpetual motion that is the sole impetus that drives the Virtual enigma into the initial human past. I believe I have stumbled upon a way to unite my hope with a technological breakthrough. In a world where nothing is yet universal, a hope for a better idea of progress is what unites us.

Backwards To The Future And Forward

One might wonder if there is an exponent by which history would increase in overall improvement if the Virtual Time Travel experiment is a success. One of the first variables that must be mentioned is credibility in the invention and credibility garnered in the experiment itself; any degree of faith itself or lack thereof must be coupled with a conclusive guarantee that less than a slim margin of error (0.0000000000005%) exists in the interoperability of the working softwares involved. eventually, for an invention to be globally and universally recognized and accepted, it need be accepted in its premise to provide a utility for the improvement of life and the progressiveness of human society as a whole. While Virtual Genomic Time Travel may provide a multitude of answers, it does not provide a way to correct the injustices that have been committed in the past, even just prior to the 21st century. Another solid question to ask is would there be at some point in the initial super- collision smasher event, which brings about virtual time travel into the past, a way to open up avenues into potential future time travels from the first instant of backwards travel on? Another question has to do with whether or not these parallel future realities can ever be experienced as we experience the linear flow of time. In other words, it would be possible to live in a reality created that happens to encompass a certain futuristic detour, until that alternate road or loop meets up with the main branch.

Mimicry of Space-time

The mimicry of space-time events happens in order for certain artificial events that conflict with the natural laws of space-time to occur. For Virtual Time Travel to take place there must exist mimicry of an ancestry's DNA in order for a traveler to achieve Genomic Virtual Time Travel. The continuity of space-time itself allows for this to happen, while mimicry disguises the natural processes of evolution and ancestral flow in order for the Virtual enigma to initially leave the traveler's body. Without this function, the Virtual Time Traveler's particles in transit would be made to look like alien DNA or alien particles that did not belong there after all and that needed to be flushed out.

Virtual mimicry is an extension of natural evolutionary mimicry that occurs in many living plant and animal organisms, such as insects that mimic twigs. In addition to the backwards and statistical regression analyses, mimicry poses the only challenge of a successful Virtual Run even as it is a solution to a resolvable paradox problem that I have encountered at the beginning of this simulation.

Paradox Solved

Virtual Genomic Time Travel solves the paradox of time travel into the past, but does it create other types of paradoxes in the process? It hypothetically raises the overall level of global progress by an exponent that invariably relates to the underlying change, for which there is no benchmark. It may create the paradox of perpetual progress, as was mentioned earlier, as genomic travel is defined within the context of these passages. A paradox could also arise in reality because of a poorly decoded DNA sequence on either the paternal or maternal side of the Virtual Traveler. If that sequence belonged to either parent, it may cause a continuous paradox which could only be closed by reversing the effects of the Virtual Genomic enigma.

Though for matter there may be an equivalent amount of anti-matter that annihilates it, for a virtual particle there is less probability of creating an antiparticle that would equalize the particle itself. Could we be absolutely sure that these experiments wouldn't require the loss of a single human life or anything else in the vicinity of this gaping wormhole while attempting the perfection of the Virtual Genomic Time Device?

Biological Altruism

Would the Virtual Genomic Traveler have to possess much of a sense of biological altruism in order to be careful that his journeys do not affect the biological environment, plant, animal or other wildlife? One must be selective when it comes to preserving information that has never been recorded before or at least be in a position to verify what has already been transcribed as history, or etched into stone. This change is only the beginning. It is time to embrace the future, real and virtual. It is time to be virtualized.

A Complete Theory of Everything

Is it possible to conceive of a complete theory of everything while in the midst of such valuable information, a theory that would explain all human knowledge from history's past, into the present, or even begin to predict the not-so-near future? Is it possible to find just what we are looking for in order to solve everyday problems as well as make a grand headway into the next scientific advances? Would it grant us detailed information into something that is referred to in particle physics as the Grand Unification Theory, or GUT, or would it provide an additional dimension to scientific inquiry?

Leaving Planet Complacence

A seal of scientific credence depends on a threshold that needs to be passed. Neil Armstrong left planet earth years ago to become the first astronaut to walk on the moon. We are leaving the realm of the complacent logic, the realm of obedient and subservient premises. We make the call and create the countdown before it is too late.

Super Atom Collider

It is time to let the God particle out of the box so that it can fend for itself. The particle for whom some doubt its very existence nevertheless simmers, awaiting a time when it can be released from its chamber of torture and possibly seek revenge upon those who trapped it there. At 7:16 in the morning on March 6th, 2011, I grabbed my 256 GB flash drive, my jacket, and my eGSI technician's lab manual, and bolted through the door. That traffic on the border of France and Switzerland was never mediocre and it usually took a while to access the train that headed toward the facility. I had landed my first job at the site of the Super Atom Collider as a temporary technician and did not want to be late for any reason whatsoever other than the opening of a massive black hole on either side of the border. It has been said for this facility that it translates Doomsday work into a reality and that the risks to the global environment from the potential opening of even a tiny singularity on earth are great. The one thing I was not so sure whether to bring today was my flash drive. I needed the manual from which to study procedures as I learned the techniques of this massive installation. My flash drive contained something that I did not want anyone there knowing about, yet it was compact enough to fit on less than the total allotted hard disk space. It was my customized DNA virtual file—which contains the molecular breakdown of all of my DNA sequences, recombinant and non-recombinant, in virtual format. I have an idea that might just baffle even the General engineer Monsieur Dr. Jacques Hourdeau at Super Atom Smasher. However, if I didn't live up to par with expectations, I could also get terminated from the first real job of my life. As I waited to access the train, I read from the technician's manual and formed an opinion of how the installation could work better, as well as how well it works and how it is secured. I hold a Master's Degree in Theoretical Physics from M. I. T., with a minor in Applied Genetics in conjunction with Yale University and happened to be in europe at the time the position was announced. I already have reference letters from three senior professors from both institutions, so I was already well established in the eyes of the employer. From a logistics standpoint, I never could understand the need for so many checkpoints at either side of the border until I got a good idea of how many people would accept monetary and other forms of payment in order to try to sabotage operations at Super Atom Smasher. As I turned to page 24, the train arrived and I boarded. It was 7:34 a.m. By 8:15, I was in the conference room with the interviewers for the announced positions and the two other candidates who had applied for similar positions in engineering and Thermodynamic Maintenance Operations. We greeted each other in english and French and proceeded to introduce ourselves in our native languages. When it came to be my turn, I told them my name and who I was, what town I was from in the United States, and where I had graduated from. One of the interviewers was intrigued about my minor in Applied Genetics and wondered if this might be the reason why I chose to accept the position. I nodded, stating that it was a part of the reason; the main one being the opportunity of a lifetime to be able to work with such lovely people and with such state-of-the-art machinery in making science for the 21st century. I thanked them at that point once more for extending me the opportunity. The trainers smiled and proceeded to interview the other two candidates in the room with us. I had never been to Paris prior to learning of this job and had taken extensive language training courses in French. The French language is somewhat like the diverse culinary styles of this beautiful country: descriptive and elaborate at times, at other times relaxed in a prosaic sense. I understood as well as any newcomer to the country, but what I happened to be struggling with (which almost got me in trouble) is the slight nuances in dialect between traditional French and the dialect spoken near the border with Switzerland. It goes without saying that there are certain things newcomers to a French or Swiss firm would not bring up on the first day on the job. Having finished our first day rounds, we had a 20-minute break for brunch, which consisted of green tea and bagels, freshly made and brought from the bakery down the street. At 10:00 a.m., our first routine testing started where the newcomers simply watched and recorded procedures for later regurgitation. I recorded fifty pages by noon and another forty eight by 3:00 p.m. The hierarchy of the installation outlay became clearer by the end of the first work day. Nothing was given to chance and nothing was taken for granted (which answered my previous query about the number of checkpoints). After arriving to my flat near Geneva, the famous site for Super Atom Smasher, I turned on the telly. My musings that the world could potentially become unstable due to hostilities of the West toward countries such as Iran and North Korea, summarized in part by alleged uranium enriching capabilities of Iran, as well as the capabilities of other countries in achieving the same end goals, might not be based in reality. While acquainting myself with French and Swiss programming, something I had not had a chance to do as of then, I fingered my 2.90-inch flash drive. I was only going to get one shot at this; therefore I needed to make it last for a good long while. If in my studies of applied genetics there was a way to create a reverse and forward flow of organic processes that could allow the re-creation of the human body and mind from virtual file, I could create an individualized time machine from within Super Atom Smasher that would allow me to travel back through my ancestral genome as far back as the statistical variance would allow. With the right settings on the collider, I could return the same way, or more precariously, as a Virtual enigma, traveling down a path never trudged by my ancestry due to my ability to change my customized virtual DNA files and adapt to any pertinent ancestry. I would soon know if, within a few days, I could gain access to the main super atom collider at eGSI. In fact, it would be several minutes before anyone even realized I was not there anymore. In the next 11 days, I would learn all that I could, in addition to my technician's procedures manual, about the world's largest particle physics laboratory and the adjoining installation (Super Atom Smasher). This personal experiment is very dangerous and could mean the end of my life, as well as the pursuit of my quantum physics prowess. To me, the risk was well worth it. On day two, I arrived 15 minutes early and was warmly greeted by the laboratory staff. So far, I feel I have left a good impression. I clocked in, registered my name in the staff 's register, and then proceeded to go about my routines. I checked the functionality points of each internal stage, and then proceeded to check the individual parts and to conduct a holistic check of the equipment itself. So far, the only thing out of the ordinary that I detected was a user access account not protected, but I assumed these may occasionally be left that way in order to test the honesty of the new technicians, as well as the overall security system. I reported it immediately. After lunch at 12:15 p.m., I continued my rounds and my note- taking. Within three more days I had gotten the procedures memorized. I had a convenient time planned during lunch break during which I had requested that I analyze the working of one of the inner collider parts, which were cybernetic. The fifth day of my employment with eGSI's Super Atom Smasher was to be my trial date with my concept of genetic time travel. Soon I would see if it worked and if my virtual recordings would bring me somewhere I had never before been and if it would be worthwhile. My stunt would make the news; I'm sure, whether or not my flash drive survived me. I would wash thoroughly tonight and feel as clean externally as I would internally. After all, if I was successful, God only knows the next time I would be able to shower in such lovely quarters.

Virtu Al Genomi C enigma A At eGSi

After a salami sandwich, a Caesars salad, and a tall glass of iced tea for lunch the day before my "little experiment", I started to make preparations while still at work about things I had to have done before I started co-existing with persons of the past within the next 24 hours. It did not seem unusual, or enigmatic, or mysterious, that what my host would be eating would necessarily bother my digestive track back in the 21st century. This is what I had predicted. After all, my own birth will not have occurred for some years into that future. It would only be I in virtual form and my spiritual essence traveling around from person to person. I have a pretty good idea now how much quantum energy induction I would need to induce a jump to the next host and about things I would not be able to tolerate while in any previously living host. What I am more afraid of is taking "steam away" from everyday events, perceptions, and actions of the host I am currently in. even though I was born in 1975, I could be experiencing in real time what my host might have been experiencing in 1878. in the normal flow of time. The one thing that will allow me to experience the words as they are spoken to my host is the virtual linguistics database that is saved as a sub-routine in the customized language file of the Genomic Virtual enigma. This database contains all versions, dialects and accents contained in all historical and all contemporary global languages in use as of March 17th, 2011. It contains a database of the english language from as far back as the writing and establishment of the Magna Carta in 1215. It contains a set of historical and contemporary databases of Slavic languages from before the 7th century A.D. In addition, it contains a database of Latin languages including Spanish, from the travels of Christopher Columbus to the contemporary 21st century

Spanish and its dialects that hundreds of millions of people rely on and use in daily communications. The co-existence factor is 1: 1.000000000000121, which means that, to the host, having my essence in his or her body is like having a mild cold or a sweet summer breeze blowing through her hair and not even noticing that anything unusual is amiss. What would have had me worried is the lingering thought of why I am doing this and if it is the correct reason or the one of the grandest moral standard. I decided that risking my life was the least I could do for the science that has been guiding me since I was 4 years old. It has been my compulsion, even an unwavering obsession that drives me toward the ultimate truth of this universe that I reside in. Life is another mystery that I could only previously fathom from my own body and has the originality to realize in a sense of fight-or-flight intellectualism. I am fighting that which I am not well equipped to conquer or sometimes fully comprehend; therefore I am fleeing the scene of this confrontation between myself and my own fears, myself and my own twisted understanding of my own purpose and existence. God is the only driver of my hopes in the very sense of victory over that which subdues me. I turn to pray for all of those who had passed, and then I pray for myself, my abilities, and my own sense of responsibility in the event that something goes disproportionately wrong in this world and I cannot return. I am departing and a particle smasher/ reconfiguration device holds the key to my destiny; it holds the key to my journeys through the historically defined human genome.

the trip through the Genomi C Void

Is there a quantum void in the gaps between the family genealogies that bridge the history of people, those people that we meet in our everyday lives, our family members, our spouses, our employers, our friends, as well as total strangers? That void is filled with tachyon dust, with sprinkles of existence. What might seem like a hundred million miles traversed could actually be no more than the separation between two or three generations. What on earth bridges the gaps between people's genomes and that distinct yet intangible thing called intermolecular love? Love is one of those phenomena that could be described in many different ways; it is often a mystery when people try to make it into something tangible. Love is one of those phenomena that I couldn't even begin to describe on next day's lunch break, two hours before my timed experiment, when I noticed the beautiful young assistant eGSI had hired in lieu of expecting a vacancy from one of the daily engineers. Her name was Petra and her beauty defied the laws of gravity and electromagnetism. She was someone I couldn't help but notice. I said hello in French and she replied with a greeting in english. She gazed around stunningly as if she was distracted by the sheer size of Super Smasher left wing. When I offered her some assistance, I had not forgotten my own schedule and she said she might take me up on the offer in a few minutes. I wondered if I had done the right thing considering how tightly my own project needed to run. I didn't regret it. I only helped her with a checkpoint explanation for a few minutes, during which I noticed my heart starting to bob up to my mouth like an apple during an apple eating contest in Florida.

She made me glow for several minutes, but I immediately resumed my own schedule. It was time to show the world my own invention, even if I had to do so in an unconventional way. If I could make myself resistant to the charms of Petra, I may have found the ideal way to exit this thing I called exo-reality. Perhaps the ideal way back into it is a different time and a slightly different place. In an unusual way, I almost wish she was going with me. I double-checked the contents of my flash drive and the technician's manual one more time. I prepared to access checkpoint #56 by the left side of the atom collider. I logged into the computer itself with a generic technician's user name and my own password after having verified that nobody was observing me. eGSI was about to find out the full potential of this multibillion euro installation, a conservative estimate of the value of the Super Atom Smasher.

departure From eGSi

I had to temporarily disable the security cameras surrounding the checkpoint and set the encrypted timer by way of wireless adapter for two minutes before I stood on the podium. It was a bit easier than I had expected. The enigmatic technologies

I employed in doing so have bridged the gap between existentialism and the surreal world of virtualism. I had added additional database files to the flash drive which was plugged into the mainstay by #56, including the virtual one that would record the very journey for me. The original copy started to virtualize my physical DNA. I had to return to this location even at the risk of getting apprehended. I had planned it out that way for the past month, even before receiving the job offer in Paris. Having my customized DNA file virtualized took almost eleven months by itself. Now I would find out the outcome of functionality of something I had invented, but not yet tested. I would find out how well the virtual device held the structures of my DNA sequences. I conducted this as safely as possible and had every angle mapped out and every check mark on my list from memory marked, including locking the log-in screen on the mainstay. At sixteen seconds on my countdown clock, one of the senior engineers approached the mainstay and issued an alarm. Sirens rang out in the entire installation. I was about to be made or broken. I programmed the log in screen to be locked to outside intervention until the countdown was done. There was nothing he or anybody else could do; they would not have had sufficient time. The look on his face was one of concern and of someone who appeared to be observing a planned suicide, as well as someone who was genuinely concerned for the fate of a fellow worker. The look on his face seemed to angrily indicate the phrase “I hope you know what you are doing, you idiot.”

The rest of what happened after the final second on the clock was history and couldn't be recreated by the best sketch artists money could buy. I said a brief prayer to myself for my own life before the blinding flash.

the Journey Begins

As soon as the collider beam hit me, I felt nothing but an intense tingling sensation from the soles of my shoes to the hairs on the top of my head. For one to one and a half seconds, the only other feeling amounted to the perception of blindly being picked up by an invisible force, a very powerful one. At that point I simultaneously started to perceive that the surrounding lab was disappearing from view and swirling in a counterclockwise direction as the thermodynamic arrow of time started to flow in the opposite direction from its usual course. It felt afterwards like I had slept for an eternity; when I awoke, I felt as though I was looking out of a set of eye sockets that were not my own, stimulated by organic senses that were not my own, and talking in a male voice that was a tad more masculine in tone than my own voice. I didn't even know for the next ten hours who I was nor was I supposed to be. At any rate, it wasn't until I looked at myself in the mirror that I knew who or what I looked like. My name was Ricardo Johanes and I was 28 years ago. To Ricardo himself, who had suffered from a heart attack inconveniently when I "lept" into him, it felt as though he had become a few years younger and couldn't explain why given the fact that he had just experienced a cardiac arrest. Why was he so agile and full of energy, he thought? But how did I happen to know this? I lay dormant since it was about all I could do and collected information about my situation. I did not know how I was to emerge from this body into my own again or if anything was even left of it. I was genetically embedded into his psyche in virtual fashion. If only one could imagine the horror I felt! I believe that there is now and that I can prove it, but not inside of the mind of Ricardo. even though my thoughts are independent of Ricardo's own, I have been spending much of my own consciousness in and out of my host's mind. He is otherwise not aware of my consciousness or presence. He is a professor in Meyrin at a private high school roughly 32 kilometers from the site of the eGSI installation. In fact, while he was reading the paper I was able to ascertain that from the front page of the International Herald Tribune that there was an incident at the Super Atom Smasher and that a perpetrator was incinerated. I learned that any private possessions that the "perpetrator" had were kept to be studied further. The situation was also being kept quiet in the overall flow of global media because of the private nature of work that goes on at eGSI. The question was now would I ever be able to launch into my own body after the thermodynamic arrow of time was reversed. I had been declared dead and had no idea whether the impetus of the blast was going to transcend the body of Ricardo and if I would remain inside of him until further notice or until his natural death. To the best of my knowledge, without even thinking about it in virtual form, Ricardo and I are not genetically or otherwise related. The fact that I jumped into his body in virtual format with almost perfect correlation in order to function, without the ability to impede him, told me that my invention works, but that there were obvious structural mistakes made. The Virtual enigma turned on immediately on the first attempt, but it functions randomly. I perceived Ricardo's thought as to how far away he was when this went down, as casual of a set of thoughts that they were. He was over 40 kilometers away. Now that eGSI directors had my flash drive, the main question was how to get back into a body of my own. Something had to happen randomly that would allow me to move from my host's body. It might be an even more random move.

From random to An Cestrial

How would I have known what was going to happen? My ancestry is Southern Slavic; my roots are Dalmatian. I am a Croatian-American and I had virtualized into a Frenchman. Although, in a general way, my ancestral history is not entirely removed from someone who is French, our genealogies are quite different. Is my next move on the Virtual Genomic spectrum going to lead me somewhere closer to what I have gotten used to? early the next morning Ricardo showered as I involuntarily moved in tandem with him and independently thought in troubled silence. I knew he knew something was mildly amiss, but at least he didn't suspect he was a different person and he was happy that he was feeling in much better condition to return to work after having been hospitalized and on sick leave for a total of less than three days. It made him feel healthier that he did not have to miss as much work as he had originally thought. In a way, I felt a bit guilty that I was not planning on being there for more than a few more days and that, with me out of the way, part of his health would diminish soon thereafter. Overall, this was the most awkward situation I had ever found myself in and needed to get out of sooner than the end of the week; otherwise, I was probably going to be stuck residing there in this body for an indefinite period of time. The name of the game was virtual quantum energy. The object of the game was to have some, even limited, control of the Virtual enigma. The Virtual Genomic enigma that I would become depended on dramatic events that were to occur within Ricardo in the next 36 hours. Until then, I took notes through my own virtual memory, knowing that I had a backup for later viewing, for when I would be in a position to sit down at a computer in privacy to view what I was seeing. I had to leave his genealogy and the way to do this was a random sub-routine that calculated how much time I could reside in a dissimilar body, or ancestry. For all I knew, I could easily have virtualized into the body of someone belonging to any other descent. I essentially have 8.333 THz of processing power (which allows me independent thoughts from my host) and 1500 TB of virtual RAM and I am ready to complete some research and to benefit humankind. I sincerely hope that I will not be labeled as a fraud if I am back in my own flesh and blood. I have worked exceedingly hard and will hope at least that this scientific research that I yield may benefit humanity in a sense of what has historically been missed, in part on purpose, in part by complete accident. I am a living breathing time machine and, although my research was never quite completed, I have the initial potential to return, provided that I return in one piece, and to completely finish my research studies and experimentation on cybernetic Genomic Time Travel. I have predicted that forces beyond my control may be looming, that invariably could lead the world to the brink of a third global conflict, which would ultimately benefit nobody and no country, particularly not the human race. In this case, cause-and-effect could and would ultimately lead to sequences of events that could require the use of any remaining stockpiles of nuclear weapons that were not destroyed in the 1990's and the first several years of the 21st century. Could my venture lead to the prevention of conflict or another apocalyptic impetus that could end human life? What if the apocalyptic event involved runaway asteroids or comets with exceedingly long tails? The bulk of my work has largely been in quantum mechanics, theoretical physics, and applied genetics. I do not and have not ever predicted the sequences within human nodes that create aggregate human behavior in everyday living and dying. I have created models of particle behavior that are realized in the event of certain precursor causes. Had I thought that it was previously possible, I would have teamed up with other scientists in exchange for due credit. I do not have the real means, methodologies, or even abstract theories that lead to predicting such cataclysmic cause-and-effect scenarios.

This is the reason for my journey, this collection of information and past data that was never previously harvested. This journey is my reason for being a scientist and the impetus of my desire to seek out and understand how to help create benevolent solutions to complex problems.

SlAViC Metamorphosis

It happened out of the blue as accidents tend to happen. Ricardo was watching the evening news when he went to reach for his raspberry juice- filled glass; he hit his knee fairly hard on the coffee table and almost immediately started to feel dizzy and weak. He was having trouble breathing. Within a few seconds of his first gasp, I started having the same spinning expects as before, as I started feeling my own presence to myself within his body for the first time in six days. Before I knew it, the thermodynamic arrow was turning counterclockwise and the room began to swirl. I closed my eyes and blacked out. In the same instant, I felt the same excruciating effect as being painfully blown to smithereens. I didn't know if I would make it. What seemed like another eternity became the embodiment of a fruitful jump into a body that I wouldn't soon forget, never as far as I am concerned. It took me over 49 hours to discover the newly found identity and I was eventually able to find out whose it was. The man's name was Branimir Dragišić and he hailed from Makarska in the Republic of Croatia. He is a small business owner, a manager of his own convenient store. At the time this happened, I virtualized into his body while he was sleeping on a train from Slovenia to Split, Croatia (the historic capitol of the Dalmatian empire). Of the few words I did recall from my parents, who are both Croatian but chose to raise me to speak exclusively english, I was immediately able to surmise that Ivo was on his way from visiting a friend in the Slovenian capital of Ljubljana whom he had not seen in over a decade. Branimir is 29 years old. I began to wonder if I would frequently have to leap into people who are in their mid to late twenties. He spoke little to no english and, among other items of interest, did not care for any global news from the West but those concerning politics. He was liberal-minded and had two children, a ten year old boy and a six year old girl. They were beautiful children. To my dismay, the linguistics database did not activate until the day following my virtualization, when we were almost in Split, after which he took a local bus down to his hometown of Makarska. It seems as though it required an update that wasn't available until 9.2 hours later (my only connection to the Internet exists through a latent wireless connection directly through background cosmic radiation that opens only periodically when it is least likely to be obscured by satellites and encumbering weather conditions). Once it was updated online, this virtual on- board database enabled me to focus on what Ivo was saying. He felt very little in anything of my presence in his body. What he felt as equally as I do is an occasional tingling of the little toe on his right foot, which he attributed to fatigue and riding extensively on trains and buses. Now what should I do? The main virtual database continually records details about my environment, events in the host's lifetime and his experiences while I am residing in him or her, the host's bodily temperature, blood pressure, overall health, as well as the exact time based on the closest atomic clock available through the Global Time Satellite and its cosmic frequency. What more could I ask for? What about global providence for a mission so inexplicable! If you are trying to save the world from itself, you need all the information you can get, including some information that you couldn't get. I was thinking of Petra and the stunning effect I received from her right before I virtualized for my first time. I needed to acquire info that was relevant, albeit not regarding a potential relationship between random variables. I was patient with the virtualization procedure for, as far as I knew, no other person had even attempted what I was doing, at least not through genomic means. I also wasn't quite sure what I had gotten myself into or if I knew how to voluntarily get out of it. The next virtualization may not come up this week or the week after. I resolved to acquaint myself with my host and his surroundings to the best of my knowledge and recording skill. He held a very tight ship and had a very organized store; his bookkeeping skills were immaculate and his organization skills pristine. He reminded me in many ways of my own father. He rarely had a lapsed moment and he treated his customers with the utmost respect, even if he was having a bad moment, or what most of us are most likely to have from time to time, a bad day. The date he arrived back home to Makarska was June 21st, 1989, at 19:18 (7:18 p.m.). This had been a historic time for his country, from what I have read and know about subsequent and fixed historic events, such as the symbolic fall of the Berlin Wall in Germany as well as the breakup of the U.S.S.R. It was the time leading up to the nationalist/liberation movements in the Balkan wars between Croatian and Serbian forces, as well as Croatian, Serbian, and Bosnian forces in Bosnia. It was the year when Croatia, Slovenia, Macedonia, and Bosnia & Herzegovina opted out of the political entity that granted those countries global recognition, especially Croatia and Bosnia & Herzegovina, as well as deliverance from several decades of political torment and persecution. The words ethnic hatred and travesty almost take on an entirely new meaning in these times, as well as a few years from now in real-time. I have much to learn and I know that this might yield more intangible information to sift through in the virtual databases later on. even as a first generation American, who has been born, raised and educated in the West, I knew I was going to have to make a metamorphosis analogically equivalent from one of a butterfly to a caterpillar.

My own transformation would allow this journey to be worth the transformation into a genetic virticon just several days into my recorded virtual memory. In reality, I had already traversed through two people and virtually lept twenty two years into the past. It is hard to estimate how much more is left of my total journey or if I have enough say-so to bring it to a conclusion when I feel that I have had enough and that I have gathered sufficient evidence to prove my new technique useful. I may be traveling more than half of my natural life and, as for how quickly or how slowly I age is going to be more than just a function of my correlation factor of covariance with my current host, or more than just an issue of temporal dilation. It will be a slew of nameable and indeterminate factors that will determine my ultimate fate here in the book that God himself rarely seems to take a peek into. The book of Recorded History is the void through which my journey stems and how my trip will end. I am striving that my trip has a happy ending, no matter how anguishing it may be or how difficult for the travel it may prove. After all, I am not alone on these past roads. I have memories, some of which I cannot ever escape from.

Crises of Humanity

Humankind has come to many crossroads in its history. The one I am encountering is surely not that different than many others from past centuries. The Greeks, the Romans, the Confucians, and many others, all experienced epiphanies that sometimes seemingly led them in the opposite direction of conventional wisdom, for some into the direction of war, famine, and suffering. This is my ultimate goal—to prevent that which was previously not preventable—the accompanying suffering singularly. Progress needs to continue, as it always will in some form or another. Does humanity have enough will to prevent what comes next and will others have the ability as I currently have to find meaning of this in past travels? I hope that this is the case since what I have to offer humanity is an experiment that has currently yet to reach critical mass, incremental value perhaps, but not that significant in the grand scheme of things. What I am hoping to provide to myself and others is an example, a reason why something can be done, not why it shouldn't be done. I have taken this project into my hands not because it only provides scientific impetus, but because it provides hope as well as reason that current reality can be deterred. It can't be stopped altogether, but perhaps one day evil can and will be deterred for the sake of good. By the way, what are good and evil and why do they seem so arbitrary at times? I am not trying to purify the process in which reality, life and existence all merge to create what we see when we wake up in the morning. I am trying to read the scrolls of past history (recorded space-time records) and to discover things that may have been forgotten about, disregarded, or left for granted. Since I resided inside of Ricardo Johanes virtually, I have not only felt what it is to be a different person, but what it is to not fully feel like myself (even if my essence was fully there). Tracking what comes next is not the exhilarating part; the process of giving and gaining in return is what is fascinating and the fascination does not die. I could not begin to emphasize how important this journey is to me. For the sake of my own humanity, I need to find a way back. For humanity's sake, I need to find a way back in order to share with the world and scientific authorities records of the past that transcend well beyond their own time and, perhaps, understanding. So far, the health status of an ailing teacher as well as a man's bookkeeping records and the tidiness of his small business are my primary value, but not of any direct significance in saving the world from itself (and possibly from me) unless our directly studied variables happen to be healthcare and bookkeeping methods. I continue to gather information that I will sort through with all available database functions when I return.

Whenever that is, I will need to go back the same way I came into this game, from checkpoint #56 at eGSI's Super Atom Smasher. Would I be arrested, at this point, I don't know; I just might and I will find out soon enough. I might be detained even if there are people who are holding vigils day and night for me (and I sincerely doubt that anyone is). I am not seeking to make the sort of media splash that someone might when they claim they have found a new treatment for an old incurable disease. My discovery will hopefully be more comprehensive and land me back where I need to be. I am not looking for martyrdom either. That sort of destiny seems to suit terrorists of all colors just fine or perhaps anybody else for whom this is normal. As far as I know, I am symbolically not a terrorist even though some might consider this venture espionage and what I bring may be looked upon and scrutinized in the same fashion. Now that I am a caterpillar, I need to become a butterfly and spread my wings. I need to try to bring beauty where beauty is sorely needed and a smile where one is not unwelcome. The issue that I have is lack of patience and not knowing who this person is who may need my help. Perhaps that person is me. Perhaps the person who needs reassurance in his country at a time of prestigious cultural learning is I. I have a once-in-a-lifetime opportunity that I would not have received in any other set of circumstances. The cultures of Croatia predate the 15th century A.D. It is very difficult to find a similar set of cultures, a similar set of historical events, or a similar set of crossroads that could have led down to the beautiful landscape that this country of just over four and a half million residents has to offer in the 21st century. The historical record keeping mission continues, and I need to absorb as much information as possible about my host, Branimir. He is currently preparing supper for his children while they are watching a Croatian soccer game between Hajduk and Dinamo. Like many American households, they are allowed to watch TV while they dine. Like my own household, there is no talking during supper. After supper, dishes are washed and put up immediately and scraps are cleaned up or thrown away. As I observed through my virtual database, my host's temperature is 98.6 degrees Fahrenheit; his blood pressure reading is 124/80, while his other vital sounds appear stable. He is talking to himself in a way that is clearly related to my weaving in and out of his consciousness and understanding everything. So far, I am understanding every word of his language, thanks in part to a second update to the linguistics database. Another key person of interest in the country of Croatia was one of the main writers that lived here in the 1700's by the name of Ruđer Boškovic after whom a scientific institute was named. I am currently reviewing records that may be helpful to review while I am here, as well as any records available about the Croatian scientist of Serbian ancestry who drew much acclaim in the United States, Nikola Tesla. He was credited with "lighting up Niagara Falls." Other historic issues I have decided to study through Branimir's body and mind are the empires that resided here and controlled the territories at large, such as the Ottoman empire, Austrian-Hungarian empire, Byzantium, Illyrian Kingdom, 19th century Napoleonic empire, Italy before September 1943, among others.

Branimir seems to be much healthier than Ricardo was at the time I virtualized into him; I wonder what will be the stimulus instigating my next leap. I surely hope it doesn't come to him as a newly found health issue, or even as a threat to his life.

Hopefully the engineers at eGSI have a better understanding in March 2011 of what is going on and that they haven't entirely left me for dead. If this is the case, perhaps I can still send them a message to tell them the truth about what has happened. Of course, it may not be that simple to find a computer in this part of the world even in the late 1980's. Many people do not use or own a personal computer. Still, I may need a connection directly from the world's largest particle physics laboratory and its related installation Super Atom Smasher. I will try to send them a message as soon as I can muster up the will to force Branimir or the next host to use a computer for me. I am already responsible for a temporary bout from schizophrenia that I am causing Branimir, but he is otherwise well and is as good of a host if any that I could have asked for had I had the time to ask. I definitely asked for all of this whether I realized the full consequences.

trudging An Uncertain past

Ancestries are a funny thing; with as much variability that results from studying them comes a tangible feeling of belonging to something fixed. Although they are not fixed or set in stone due to human will, they are set into a space-time constant that we all depend upon to live, regardless of what that particular ancestry may be or to whom we belong to. It seems as if it may be something like moving up a stream while you are still downstream; in my case. I am finding out that it is possible to travel one's genome and that it is definitely possible to "jump into another ancestry." These leaps into another ancestry can be difficult and dangerous; it is very similar and analogical to an explorer going down an uncharted path. If one is successful, the rewards are very well worth it. My jump into Ricardo was very fruitful, yet I did not find what I was looking for in a sense that it might warn the world of an apocalypse. I found things of personal interest and how health issues can impact a person's global perspective, especially if those issues counter with one's ability to work and to function. I learned tangible and intangible things those several days that I resided with Mr. Ricardo. In order to get back to eGSI's Super Atom Smasher, I will have to take a similar route; of course, I have not the exact co-ordinates to do so. In order to make my presence known, I have composed a message and calculated that it must travel at 0.42c (0.42 times the speed of light), which is considerably slower than what existing networks connected to the Internet a decade later can handle. In the virtual world, the constraints are different and the problems are slightly less challenging. The need for my belongings and my flash drive to be saved is what part of the message reads. Fiber-optic lines can handle this speed very easily, but can it deliver the message clearly? What I don't know is that Dr. Jacques Hourdeau can handle receiving a message from me from the past by way of virtual e-mail, even though all computers currently functioning in his time provide some measure of virtuality and some measure of IPv6, with fiber-optic connections to networks. In the time I feel I am about to end up in, there are no computers or computer networks (with fewer ways to send a message back to the checkpoint that teleported me, my next jump will send me elsewhere to another person living in the Balkans, or to Austria, or perhaps Italy). My ability to direct or guide myself through the aggregate global genome will be encumbered, I think to myself, as my host continues to sleep. My presence is able to guide him through the stages of R.e.M. sleep. It will happen any hour now. In fact, the random effect is kicking in and I am getting sleepier than I have been in the last 4.3 recorded days. I hope the next host fairs well and is healthy. I also truly hope that she is willing to receive me.

Notes from Poland

I feel as though I have slept for two days straight up, or perhaps, straight down. I am awakening in a café to the smell of fresh donuts and coffee. Someone yells to me in an unrecognizable language: "Ivan, Ktora godzina?! Poranek! Powstac bezposrednio!!" While the linguistics database translated what the person had said (Ivan, what time is it?! It is morning! Arise immediately!!), I arose in the weathered body of a man whose consciousness I was already taking on. He is detecting nothing of my presence. It was July 27th, 1969. The city was Warsaw. evidently, I was 42 years old, my name was Ivan Bajek and I was out of work and homeless for the past four days.

His family had all but given up on him. I had just been ordered to rise from my slumber because the guests would be arriving soon. From the tone of the manager's voice, he was in a hurry and was starting to get upset with my sluggishness. This is not something I was immediately expecting. If I could stay here long enough, perhaps I would eventually have the momentum to compose and send a message. Wait a second; there are no modern computers in this part of Poland at this time. According to the virtual history database, in less than two days from where I was, there was to be an economic summit from all of eastern europe. I had to be out of this body by then, preferably somewhere more northern, otherwise I would probably meet my final resting place on the street. eventually I needed to return closer to Switzerland to see if there is a computer that I could use to either send myself a message or to my boss on March 5th, 2010. I didn't know a word of Polish, so I am relying entirely on the host that I am currently in, in order to get my message through. I am trying to incentivize Ivan to somehow get closer to a place where there may be something that would suffice. I was genuinely terrified of the reality I was in. If I am not careful, I may become a victim of the streets. My situation looked bleak for a number of reasons. It's for the best that I take any action, I deduce, since I would otherwise cause a genetic paradox. What is not for the best is that I have come fairly close to calculating my next virtualization, somewhere in 1916. without the spatial co-ordinates. My next step involves access to communications that are a precursor to the development of instruments of spying in the Cold War. This message of mine can travel in a unidirectional way until it reaches someone at the Super Atom Smasher installation or someone at Meyrin, France. I realize nobody will believe me initially, but what I am doing is trying to load the virtual historical database to test the validity of the data upon returning. If I could just raise more awareness of the nature of this experiment, I might have just won half of the battle. Ivan himself has several hours to go before he finally obtains housing and food at a time in history when many go ignored simply because of a lack of affiliation.

Coffee with the Bosnians

I temporarily lost my train of thought while Ivan was entering a shelter and awoke to find myself in a much different setting than I had hoped for or imagined. These genomic jumps are beginning to be more routine and less memorable. According to the history database, I was in today's Bosnia & Herzegovina. At first, I thought I was having coffee with the Ottomans, the last standing empire in World War I in a region that was astonishingly warlike, yet cultured and phenomenally musical. Actually, it was the aroma of something I perceived as a certain type of eastern coffee, perhaps Turkish. In a conversation between four men squatting around myself, I gathered I was in Bosnia in the city of Zenica and the year was truly 1916, much as my virtual database had predicted. It would be time to go to the mosque very soon, as I had just heard. I was petrified, imagining myself turning purple at some of the things I grew up watching on news media. I remembered that Muslims worship in mosques, but what I could not remember is why they pray in the certain fashion that they do. I had to somehow simulate something suggestive to the host. It hit me in a few seconds and something inexplicable happened. He suddenly started to vomit. His peers led him away to recover in the fresh air. His name is Behram Ademović and this was Bosnia & Herzegovina, sometime before the creation of the neighboring Kingdom of the Serbs, Croats & Slovenes. Times were trying and the country itself was in the middle of what would be considered a recession, while it was relatively not affected the same way by World War I as its surrounding neighbors. My bouts with virtually residing in the bodies of Ricardo Johanes, Braminir Dragišić, and Hans Schtengzer have taught me not to resist subconscious will even if something was simply not engrained in my essence to be doing.

Going to a mosque to bow is not something I have ever done nor have I planned to, primarily since I have been raised Catholic (many years later relative to the time I am co-existing in) and because this simply was not my faith. It was something I was going to have to do in a remote sense because, fifteen minutes later, my host was resting at his residence. I did not consider myself to have invoked this reaction since he obviously became ill. I wasn't certain as to how it happened. I just relaxed and tried to learn something from the experience of Behram as he was talking to himself while he lay on his back. In my time, there was a pyramid discovered in Bosnia in the town of Visoko not long before I graduated from M.I.T. It had something to do with an ancient culture from 12,000 years ago, in the theory of the discoverer and archeologist Osmanagić, who led an expedition in uncovering the walls. I felt that love of exploration was in my midst and was affecting me much like the pollen swirling around in the summer countryside air. In their traditions and customs, men in Bosnia typically marry within their cities and have high fidelity rates. There were even some marriages between people of other faiths. I was not here to get married, although I was not so sure about Behram until I knew for sure that he had a wife. My virtual linguistics database could not read his subconscious language that well, in part since his dialect was not that slavicized nor was it present in that many global linguistic databases. It felt very powerful to be here because of my ancestry and knowing some of the legendary things I have heard about this territory. Muslims are people of devout worship. What exactly was I doing in Behram's body I could have entirely attributed to the workings of advanced probabilities. However, there is an element of faith that I haven't overlooked and it resides in me personally, in my essence. I felt desperately that I needed to send that message by any means necessary; in some way to let my employer at eGSI know that I am alive and, more importantly, that this is not a publicity stunt. I have no reason to seek publicity. What I had was a motive to unlawfully use equipment that did not belong to me to prove a point while an employee of eGSI's Super Atom Smasher installation. I am seeking data that could benefit people in my time in a relative future, something that could stop the next apocalypse in my own time—the 21st century. I am actively seeking myself and the secondary and tertiary reasons I wish to continue doing this. As in this case, I do not always know what it is that I am looking for or what my virtual databases are recording in the meantime. I am still gaining valuable information regarding the mapping of the Virtual Genome and the Archives of History. In a mapped-out 4-Dimensional Matrix of Historical Space-time, there will always be those who will feel that others should not be given the right to learn from their mistakes and their past battles and losses. I agree with this, up until the point where they proclaim that this information is not useful to humanity as a whole. To me, it has enormous potential for usefulness and utility. Additionally, according to my calculations during this journey, I will have aged 9.45 days with the respective length of the journey being 11.22 days, meaning that I have aged 9.45/11.22 (0.842245990) day in relation for each day I have been residing inside of hosts' bodies. After his friends' visit to the mosque (in Bosnian, džamija), Behram was visited at home for lunch, where veal awaited him and his guest. His vital signs were stable and, if he felt anything of my presence, he certainly knew how to hide it. His blood pressure was 122/84, his internal temperature was 98.9 degrees Fahrenheit, his breathing is normal, and his pulse rate as could be expected usually. I wanted to see more of his village on the outskirts of the city of Zenica, but it looked like he was in for much of the day to worship. He was a very calm and gracious man, without children as of yet. Although he did not seem to be suffering from financial problems as some of his neighbors, the virtual database predicts that he will be living a similar fashion for a good part of his life, with potentially two children arriving within three years of each other in the next six years. I studied his communications with his wife as she was cleaning up after lunch and wondered why it is that Muslims themselves are misunderstood in this world today. The Ademović family communicates as regular people do and it does look as though they have metropolitan tendencies, regardless of what certain media in the 1990's and 21st century West might lead one to believe. What it did not look like I would be achieving while he was hosting my Virtual Genomic enigma was sending that message to my place of employment in the year 2011.

A Mission Forth e holy

Many of the people here in Zenica were laid back in their language, in their bodily gestures, but stern in terms of their livelihoods. They took advantage of the fact that the industrial economic stressors of World War I had not affected them as they affected some of the other parts of the Balkan Peninsula because they were very reliant on agriculture as Bosnia is, and they continue to make a healthy living in agriculture. Behram owned ten goats, forty sheep, and eighteen chickens, making a pretty mark in lucrative livestock farming in his time. It might be the equivalent of owning more like one hundred goats, two hundred sheep, and eighty chickens in the 1980's, with the exception that this was the time during which World War I was going on. In a subsequent time, a few decades from now, Bosnia & Herzegovina joins Croatia, Slovenia, Serbia, Monte Negro, and Macedonia into filling out the territories of the former Yugoslavia into what many later call an artificial state, which was formed in 1945. and dissolved in 1990. Behram is a man of faith and prowess of character in this village, but there is still something he is lacking. In three years, he will father a son and, three years afterward, a daughter.

They will be taught all of the virtues that my virtual history database is recording and picking up every nanosecond of. One of them will eventually join the Freedom fighters in Bosnia & Herzegovina. In fact, he will be one of the oldest ones there at the time to witness some very gruesome acts. It is true that there are elements of intolerance throughout the 20th century committed against people of different nations who are simply preserving their own cultures (or even subcultures) from dying out in the face of that late 20th century wind of change. If nothing else radical happens, I will have resided within Behram for a total of

2.38 days, trying to get my bearings in such an intricate culture, making peace with the fact that I have virtualized and resided in someone of another ancestral faith to which my own faith has been generally opposed to. I have to admit that it was an enlightening experience and that it may have needed to happen a long time ago. Inasmuch understanding and respect as I have gained, I am wondering if the prediction of my virtual mapping database is correct and that I will be traveling and virtualizing sometime in the future in 1968 near Berlin.

This is the first time it has paired together a year with a specific location. Under what circumstances will I leave Behram's body is yet to be seen.

Berlin Science Symposium

Behram awoke at 2:30 a.m., having an upset stomach; while he was in the restroom, I felt another type of flux and within 25 seconds I found myself closer again to my own time, with the exception this time being that it was Berlin, Germany on May 24th, 1968. I had been virtualized inside of Behram's body for 3.3 days. This time the person I virtualized into was Alberich Tanztwert, a scientific scholar at the Berlin Science Symposium. This symposium was home to advances in economics, political sciences, physics, evolutionary biology, biochemistry, chemical engineering, and so on. This time I had big shoes to fill, not only did Mr. Tanztwert hold a doctorate in physics, he also holds a Nobel Peace Prize in nuclear physics research for peaceful purposes. So far, my host appears to be feeling well and is not disrupted by my appearance; his blood pressure, pulse, and body temperature are doing fine. Dr. Tanztwert is 59 years old as of today and they are making mention of it at this symposium. He was describing for the first time, according to my virtual historical database, the usefulness of nuclear energy for peaceful purposes, such as energies that far exceed the outputs of petroleum-based fuels. To get a more clear perspective, this was happening in Germany at the onset of the waning of the Cold War between the United States and Russia. He was getting enthusiastic applause from the first half of the audience when he was talking about newly found research in cold fusion, as well as new fundamental understanding in particle physics that could help control the processes of fission and fusion. Finally, a chance for a breather was there for me. I felt at home with this host more than any of the others not simply because of his occupation, his topics of conversation, or his Nobel achievement, but because it gave me a chance to consciously complete some calculations on how to reach a mainframe computer and send the message I had prepared for eGSI. As he talked, I did notice a rise in blood pressure as one can notice in oneself when they are anxious or fearful of something. His body temperature stayed at normal levels; his pulse was fine. He was an overweight gentleman, but overall in good health. The virtual correlation factor of me and my host is 1:1.0000000000036, meaning our ancestries are less closely co-related than mine is to the co-existence factor (1:1). I attributed his rise in blood pressure not as much to my own presence as I did to external factors such as the stage lighting, the tightness of his suit, his previous meal, etc. I was able to determine that he did have access to a crude connection-less terminal and was fortunate to take advantage of the co- existence factor and a few moments of temporal unawareness to send an electronic message to Dr. Jacques Hourdeau, one that I preset to be sent within 6 days and delivered on March 6th, 2011 through sedentary tertiary mail servers. The message will be delivered solely based on TCP/IP protocols in the future. I was able to do all of this after the speech delivered at the symposium by Dr. Tanztwert, while at his hotel room in Berlin. In the message, I explained to Dr. Hourdeau who I am, or who I was and what had happened to me. I apologized. "I desperately need help", my message read. I even spent two lines on describing how I disabled mainstay #56 in order to prevent the colleagues from stopping the collider. I stressed that I was aware of what was happening to me and that I needed help in returning to my own time. I ended the message with "Please await further instruction, I am not an imposter." To a regular person, this message might seem like a practical joke; to a theoretical physicist or engineer, it may be discarded or not taken seriously. I hoped that the only reason they took it seriously was the original date of the message, May 24th, 1968. By the time Dr. Tanztwert awoke and realized he had fallen asleep while sitting at the computer terminal built into his hotel room, he laughed mildly and de-activated the terminal, after having readied himself to go to sleep for the night. I had accomplished my task without having to bribe a non-existent ISP company on a non-existing mail server. The message will probably be delivered through a spam server in the 21st century, at a speed of 0.39c. We shall see what the outcome is if Dr. Tanztwert receives the message within my residence within his body. If he tries to delete the message, I will copy it to my virtual personal messages database. It is a good thing virtual database of my time work in either direction of the thermodynamic arrow of time. I tried to sleep long after my host had started snoring in an indication that he was having no trouble sleeping after an obviously eventful day for him. I was concerned about my hosts and any potential impact I had had on them by residing in them for a mere minute, Ricardo Johanes in particular. I had a way to track how they were doing, but I chose not to for fear of a paradox that might subsequently arise. Within an hour, I drifted off into a light sleep, still wondering about the probability of invading three bodies before the fourth one had access to any sort of computer. This was the one thing that was unusual to me in this backwards time travel mission. I was almost co-dependent on my computer or any computer at this point. I also had a difficult time believing I was co- existing with a Nobel Laureate for almost eleven hours. Of course, the biggest worry I was having was the odds that my host would actually receive a message for me and discard it before I had a chance to verify that it was from Dr. Hourdeau and that he is taking me seriously. In the 1980's and 1990's, these type of server channels were meant for all e-mail communications that existed; toward the end of the first decade of the 21st century, they are almost always clogged with spam (unwanted) e-mails about all sorts of things, promising that a recipient has won the Nigerian lottery, has won prizes beyond his wildest belief, and so on. I did not want eGSI's Super Atom Smasher Chief engineer to give up on his renegade employee. I did not want to be bouncing around the bodies and consciousness of people whom existed prior to my time, in some cases, and be without a body and complete consciousness of my own for the rest of my awareness. even if I made it back, I could almost discount any possibility of ever working there again. I would be too much of a media liability for a company who has had its share of media coverage for the wrong reasons even before I applied to work there. I need to return within a yoctosecond of having departed though. The sequences and variables were saved on my flash drive. I don't want to say that I don't care how many people view the contents; what I need the flash drive for is for my own return from this adventurous void. I also know I wish to see Petra again.

Lenin Grad Beckons

I could not believe how beautiful she is and how many times I relive the tingling sensation from my first virtualization into the past from eGSI on March 6th, 2010 when I think of her voluminous hair, her confident stride, and her contagious beauty. I managed to find out not much more from Petra than where she was from that fateful day; Petra is from Leningrad. It seems that besides my ancestral virtualizations, I am virtualizing in some strange way by virtue of being around people from certain parts of the world or, in the case of Ricardo Johanes, in the relative vicinity of eGSI and my "random" accident. Of course, it is hard to say what a true "accident" is when dealing with the way that I left my own time. It was not random, but it may as well have been when I turned the collider ray onto myself. Today is May 25th, 1968 in real time; I am waking up at 8:00 a.m. in tandem with Dr. Tanztwert and his schedule is to give another talk to a prominent group of German physicists. Unfortunately for me, he is sensing more than a mere presence of allergens in the warm Berlin air that surrounds him mostly from the heat coming in through his hotel room window on the 13th floor of the Kempinski Hotel on Kurfuerstendamm Boulevard. He just took some medicine for what he perceives as a cold and it is making me ever the more drowsy even after a good night's sleep. In five minutes, I get sort of a sixth sense that he is about to receive a message on an analog route of 1.08c from Dr. Hourdeau. While he checks his connection-less messages, I see that I am right on the mark and I save the e-mail, but not before he reads it. He scratches his head once or twice not knowing the name of the sender of the e- mail. The sender knows better than not to mask the domain and ISP; it is eGSI. Not knowing the identity, Dr. Tanztwert decides to save it to his disk. I then save a copy to my virtual disk for later perusal. My host then readies himself to leave his hotel room, after having cleaned up and having packed his suitcase. He awaits the taxi, his vital signs being normal, with his blood pressure being 135/85 (his pulse normal and his blood sugar within normal limits). The taxi arrives and, while he is loading his suitcase in the trunk, I start to feel the spinning again. This time images of Super Atom Smasher's technicians manual swirl before me until I feel nothingness again. The predicted destination this time is Leningrad, Russia, while the year is 1996. The day is February 27th. The time is 10:34 a.m. For some reason, I am remembering much more and the spinning effects of the arrow of time are lasting longer. It is as though I am virtualizing into a woman. In fact, the young woman who is to be my host is just leaving the MeNATeP SPb Bank located in the city's downtown square. Her name is Volga Kominovska and from what I have gathered after my Russian language update to my virtual linguistics database, she is an 8th grade teacher. Our co-existence factor is 1:1.0000000000124. Her blood pressure is 120/80, her blood sugar is normal, her pulse rate is normal, and her body temperature is 98.9 degrees Fahrenheit. As she is walking, she notices a bit of a draft and decides to bundle herself a bit more with her fur coat. She almost notices something is amiss since she thinks she is hearing voices; she happens to be schizophrenic and has just taken some medication. I take advantage of our high correlation to lessen the impact as much as I can. She is very studious and walks with a confident stride over to the bus station, where she awaits the bus that will bring her to her work (to School Number 155, so that she can teach her biology class at 11:00 a.m.). While she waits, she readily says hello to an old friend who is waiting for the same bus as she is. I can practically hear the entire conversation that they are having, as well as much of what they talk about on the bus itself. At some point, their conversation turns to silence. Volga is a very smart lady and is taking the last few minutes of the bus ride to prepare herself for her lecture to her students. She has an IQ of over 142, as well as a strong aptitude for teaching. Additionally, in the first hour with her as my host, I have sensed that she is trying to get a permanent post at St. Petersburg State University as a university professor, all while weaving in and out of her subconsciousness and trying to find time to read my response message from eGSI. She is distracting me by peeking out of the bus window and mumbling something to herself about how poorly the children are clothed. Bless her heart, it is as if she would like to say hello to all of these children individually and ask if they are cold. She was definitely one of my happier hosts. Once again, she suspected nothing at all or very little. I heard once that Russians are very stern people, in part due to interpretations of their heritage and in part due to the climate. Perhaps it is possible to derive happiness from solely God; I really did not know her that well to know whether that might be the case. The e-mail reply read as follows: "Thank you for your e-mail correspondence, Dr. Tanztwert. I honestly did not know that you had such a sense of humor nor that you have conquered the physical limitations to time travel through electronic messaging. It has been such an honor to receive correspondence from such a prominent person in the field of physics that I wanted to personally invite you to visit our eGSI facility so that you may view the Super Atom Smasher.

Keep in mind, our research and our facility are normally not open to the public. Thanks again for the laugh." Sincerely, General engineer Monsieur Dr. Jacques Hourdeau. Well, that was disappointing, I thought. Wait a minute, I thought, there is a P. S. line. I wonder what it says, it is in finer print. "Good afternoon, people," declared professor Kominovska in Russian, "I hope you have been studying the chapters on mitochondria, cellular reproduction, meiosis, and mitosis. We are having a test today. It is your last test before your midterm. "Out of all of the gasps coming from over half the classroom, some who had apparently forgotten, there were four students who couldn't wait to take the test. Since the other Russian language update was established two minutes previously to my virtual linguistics, I decided to check the P. S. line. It read: "I am not quite sure on how to interpret this, but you guessed an incident that happened recently at one of our checkpoints within the collider installation, before it happened, which is one of the reasons for my invitation. Mr. Alen Marinkovich, a recent hire, blasted himself to smithereens by using the Super Atom Smasher collider. Unless I am experiencing a haunting the kind of which I have never seen, Marinkovich is alive, maybe alive and well in a different realm. I sincerely do not believe in hauntings. Your note also claimed that you have virtually co- existed with five other people in order to contact me and that you are "virtualizing" even now. What you are talking about is farfetched, but may have some scientific merit. I am looking forward to your visit with our facility, Dr. Tanztwert." Signed Dr. Jacques Hourdeau. By this time, about 10 minutes of the exam had already gone by and I had just finished reading the last bit of the message, primarily because I had some interference from Volga. It is saving me now that I managed to delete any proof that I had received the message as Dr. Tanztwert. She was thinking to herself feverishly about how she would not grade this test as she did the first test of the semester. Now it got me thinking about probabilities and what the odds were that Dr. Tanztwert was going to take Dr. Hourdeau up on his invitation to eGSI; of course in reality, Dr. Tanztwert is not alive by the time I virtualize for the first time into Ricardo Johanes. He would have been 101 years old. I think the P. S. line was meant for me; Dr. Hourdeau did not know how to address it, so he decided to invite the Nobel Laureate as a casual response or because he did not know what else he could do. What are the odds that I might leap back into an older Dr. Tanztwert in order to reply to the message? I did not know this for certain. Would he be able to then know that he had a "parasite?" I had a feeling I was here inside of Volga for an even more important reason; I just didn't know what it is. As of now,

I am completely relying on the virtual history database. As for Volga, her students' time is almost up; they have to turn in their exams in five minutes. Time flies when you are having fun. Of course, sometimes the exact opposite holds true when you are watching a beautiful event and you almost have the willpower to slow it down just enough that it may not matter that it will not really last any longer, it is just enough to allow you to watch that image of people running on the beach, jogging at the crack of dawn, or the image of geese flying South to Mexico, or maybe the two puppies playing with each other, acting like teenagers, or fighting over that last morsel of food. Life is about images, sounds, and other stimuli that make us feel good. Petra was my stimuli and it was beginning to take hold in me. What was even more stimulating is the fact that I was currently in her home city in Russia, waiting to use a more appropriate computer to send another message to eGSI.

Lenin Grad Blues

What is wrong with me that I cannot get Petra out of my mind, I mean, after all of the exhilarating things I have witnessed in the last cumulative three weeks, is it time to declare myself in love, or at least casually persuaded? She was supposed to be Fate in disguise, waiting to distract me long enough not to conduct my experiment. This is almost as bad as that high school crush that you simply do not talk to and that never looks back at you, only an occasional glance. I mean, I barely exchanged three words with this lady and now I cannot stop thinking about her. It may seem no more than a coincidence that I happened to be in Leningrad, the city she is from. What I needed to do now was to send another distress message to Dr. Hourdeau, to let him know that the first message was definitely not a hoax. It was a warning message and a distress call, to a theoretical physicist and to a person. God alone help me if I cannot find a way back to Meyrin; even virtual technologies as advanced as level III could not prevent a wormhole from opening up and sucking up half of the city. This might be the biggest downfall of my journey. At virtual II level, it couldn't be contained within France or Switzerland. Virtual I, the least advanced, would have opened up the closest thing anybody has seen to a real singularity in the vicinity of the earth. All three levels of virtual technologies are present in the inner workings of the Super Atom Smasher. The reason a wormhole didn't quite open for me is because the pathway was created by virtual genetics. I did not want to believe that the sole level that is present within the collider is Level III. This time, in order to send a message, a personal computer or laptop would not suffice. It would have to be a server computer or an installation mainframe that could switch to connection-less from an Internet-given TCP/IP (IP version 6). The target of the message would once again have to be Dr. Hourdeau since he was in charge of the eGSI facility. I didn't know how to approach my apparent suicide in a distress message, so I gave my initials *A.M.* This time, I am spelling out my entire last name. If he could help regulate what I am doing by tweaking the collider settings, I might be able to continue collecting information from this voyage of mine. In the very least, I will have had an adventure the likes of which I will never see again. What concerns me now is beyond science and it may be pure coincidence; the last people that saw me standing in the middle of the collider podium were Petra and the senior engineer who attempted to stop the countdown himself, but was not able to because I had programmed the log in screen to remain locked up until after the countdown. I have virtually been to France, Croatia, Germany, Bosnia, and now Russia. Could it be possible to narrow down by simple probability the country where that senior engineer is from in order to help predict the automation function of the Virtual enigma and to pinpoint where and when I might end up next? It is unlikely, but possible. All in all, these probability calculations may be completely dependent on checkpoint #56. I never thought my entire life would hinge on a single mainframe, but it may have come down to that. In the meantime, Volga has collected all of her students' tests and is ready to go home for the evening. In fact, her sole reason for coming in that day was to administer the test. She seems to be coming down with a mild flu, but was managing just fine until a few minutes ago when she started to cough and felt a fever. According to the host health database, her temperature was 99.8 degrees Fahrenheit, a bit elevated, while her blood pressure was low (118/73); her pulse rate is normal. It looked as if I was going to be leaving Russia after barely ten hours there, unless Volga spent some time recovering in bed and, with some luck, led me to a more powerful computer, preferably a server computer. I was enthused that I was able to get communication back from eGSI and that I was co-existing within a female 8th grade teacher in the 1990's. What would make this a less anxious environment is having more control over my virtualizations, as well as more control over my thoughts. I have been feeling the emotions of Ricardo, Branimir, Behram, Alberich, and now Volga, in addition to my own and it has been exhausting to try to co-exist with people with whom I normally have a high factor of co-existence. It is not that difficult to virtualize emotion, dealing with these emotions can be somewhat tricky though. It is tricky to remember to weave in and out of a host's subconscious mind and allow them to not think that they are being taken over by something like illness, madness, or an unusually bad day. In the case of Volga, her flu came at somewhat of a good time for me because she then attributed her feelings of sluggishness and cold to other factors besides anything extraneous, such as God or the Divine. By now I know that she has faith in God, but she is not the type of person who thanks God for small things on a daily basis. She feels grateful when she can get through a bad day with relatively little hassle and is the type of person that looks forward to each individual day with a smile and a reward to herself at the end of the day. I am a bit like that, with the exception that I am not as grateful during my more trying days. I don't always reward myself for the little things that I get right or the little things that I have to endure. As of now, there is no way for me to reward myself for such little things. I will be more than adequately rewarded when I am able to send a second (confirmation) message to eGSI. I will be rewarded when I know that all things are in order and that I have managed to not disrupt the natural order of things by conducting this experiment. Seeing the world is not only a reward, it is a gift. It is a gift that has been earned and continues to pay in terms of professional satisfaction. In terms of what is allowable, science always requires risks. The risk that it might rain tomorrow during an outdoor experiment is not always enough reason to cancel the activity. Nikola Tesla must have thought this when he made rays of lightening dance and tumble to the will of his coils in Colorado Springs, Colorado. every scientist has had to make a similar judgment call every now and again. Where mine somewhat differs is that it seems as though I have to make a decision for God. even one decision is a tremendous amount of responsibility and I do not remember signing up for this when I graduated from college.

Message Confirmed & Action taken

"What is it," she wondered softly to herself. "Why am I not sleeping? It is almost 2:00 a. m. I have to be up in 4 ½ hours." Volga arose from bed to prepare herself a combination of green and chamomile teas and honey to sooth her growing cough. She wondered if she was going to have to call in sick today. It would be her third sick day in three years and she wondered if she could keep her record going, even after yesterday afternoon's symptoms. She wondered if she would be well enough to grade her biology students' tests from the day before and if she should apply a different grading key than at the beginning of the year. It would only be fair to those students who are struggling in their homework and in their grades, even though it lowers the curve for the entire class. Her cough slowly diminished as she sipped on the hot tea that she had prepared herself. The steaming vapors were beginning to have a soothing effect on me as I started to drift asleep within her subconsciousness. I truly hoped it was not time to go, yet I felt that it might be that time to fly and virtualize elsewhere. After only 16 hours, I felt very comfortable with Volga already. Perhaps the probabilities constructs simply didn't allow it. I would find out soon enough if I was right and whether the virtual history database had collected as much information as I was allowed to have. My last waking thought that night was Petra. I wonder if she even knows that I am alive. I wonder if anyone at eGSI, including Dr. Hourdeau, knows that I am still living. I am starting to wonder how my "accident" had affected the morale of the crew and the very hiring process at eGSI. I think that this little stunt of mine could really put a damper on my acceptability at future positions. However, I should worry more about having a body to fit nicely into, that I could call my own in which to live in infamy. I am going to sleep now. When

I wake up, it may be that I will not be in Russia or europe. I may be back in the United States with a clearer intent on how to summon for help. At six thirty, I almost jumped right through Volga after hearing her blasting alarm. She was up bright and early and felt that she should attend work after feeling much better. It was time to deliver another lecture to her students, this time the topic was the human circulatory system. The virtual host health database indicates after close scrutiny that her vital signs are good, that her blood pressure is higher and that her body temperature is not indicative of a fever any more. After her shower, Volga got dressed into a pink bra and pink panties, as well as a navy gray dress and matching jacket.

After a touch of Obsession for Women, she took her breakfast borek and yogurt to go, while she fumbled for her apartment keys. While waiting for her bus, she quivered for a few seconds; she had forgotten her medication for schizophrenia and anxiety. As she quivered, I felt an altogether too familiar spin and I left her with a swirl. Although still terrifying, my virtualizations and de-virtualizations were getting less and less painful. I did not look to confirm where I was going next; I decided to let Destiny have a whirl at the Roulette Wheel.

Noroc in Bucharest

The spinning feeling has subsided, but the disorientation has not. I am in Bucharest, the capitol of Romania, and date is June 14th, 1998. I have virtualized into a man by the name of Alexandru Balanescu, who happens to be one of top account executives in Romania. He works for the Bucharest Stock exchange (Bursa de Valori Bucuresti). He is 41 years old. The host health database established at the time of the virtualization that Alexandru's blood pressure rose a notch (128/88), with an average pulse, and normal blood sugar. His temperature is 98.9 degrees Fahrenheit. Our factor of co- existence at the time of my jump was 1:1.00000000000031. Now what to do in gorgeous Romania? There was plenty to record in this seemingly short incursion into a country rich with history and a diverse society and the virtual historical database is already doing its job. My chief concern from a few days ago is to find a server-based computer with which to send eGSI another e- mail. This time I am using not only my last name, but I have decided on my first name as well. I also will use information that I gave out during the interview for the temporary technician's position while at Super Atom Smasher. I believe if there is a way to adjust the setting of the collider itself, it should be done. Otherwise, I needed to come home to Meyrin, the place on the border of France and Switzerland where dreams come true. I had never really thought of it as home until now, but if I am able to virtualize into my own body, I will probably stay there for as long as I am able. It is after all a gorgeous city, almost as gorgeous as Bucharest. It also seems smaller in size compared to the capital of Romania. It appears from only having been inside of my host for less than an hour that he has an office in downtown Bucharest from where he schedules his trips to entertain prospective buyers of institutional stock, an office from which he makes deliveries in person to important clientele. I think that, while the chance to get to use a server computer are somewhat modest, he is likely to have a personal desktop computer in his office, preferably with Windows 98 or Red Hat Linux. While he is driving his LS400 Series Lexus to his office, I am calculating the probability than I can send a virtual message vicariously from his body without even typing it in the event that he has something other than a Windows operating system. As he checks in at the reception desk of his office building, he is told that his wife had called three times and that she wants him to call her back as soon as possible. This alas might be my opportunity. While he calls his wife Alana from his office, I see that his desktop is already on. I had formulated the message while I was in the host's car and now it is time to see if I can send it virtually through his Windows 98. While I ascertain that his Internet connection is working and active, I turn on the message virtualization, which in turn activates the message transfer from virtual to digital, digital to analog, and digital back through analog through Netscape Messenger and sends the message going forward in time at the speed of 0.68c (Dr. Hourdeau should get the message within a few days, give or take a few minutes dealing with mail servers backed up with spam mail; otherwise he might have it within a few minutes, depending on the networking protocols on Win98). Alexandru gets off the phone with his wife and he seems upset. Of course, there is nothing I can do for him but try to ascertain if he is in any way detecting me inside of him. He is aware of nobody else in his office as he sits a minute to contemplate what he is going to do when he gets home to Alana. They are in the middle of a separation and a disagreement over days during which they care for their nine year old son Andrei. evidently, Andrei himself wishes to spend more time in rural Romania with his mother. Alexandru has been trying to explain to him that this separation between his parents may only be temporary and that he wants to spend more time with him while things are slower at work. He is being considerate of the boy, but he himself does not know if his marriage with Alana is going to last. The boy's mother wants to spend time with Andrei at the same times as his father does, and it is posing a conflict. Andrei has been through difficult times, including the 1980's, but Andrei's parents are fairly well off. In fact, Alana, who is originally from england, is living in their vacation home for the time being and it has not been as hard on the boy as it might seem to an outsider such as me. In the 1990's, there is more prosperity in this country full of culture and historical remnants of another time, as in other countries that comprise the former eastern Bloc. While Alexandru is thinking, he remembers an appointment that he has in forty five minutes with a prospective client that was asking about the possibility of purchasing a block of interest in Ambra Fashion Ltd., one million shares to be exact. He hastily finishes his lunch, washes his face, wipes it clean, and heads out of the door without shutting down his computer. He figured that he would be back later on that evening anyway. In any case, the wife has the son this evening and he would have to find something else to do besides work to keep himself occupied for a few hours. Perhaps he would call two of his male friends and go bowling tonight. It's a slight yet distinct possibility. The host health database has been monitoring his vital signs more closely during his excited conversation with his wife. His vital signs appear alright and it is time for us to go; Alexandru briefly waves goodbye to his receptionist as he heads into the contracts room to get the selected items for his client: stock agreement, a legal contract, and the certificates of stock. Immediately afterward, he heads out to the elevator and out of the building on the front side. The building itself has a nice scenic view of Bucharest, placed squarely in the middle of other modern industrial developments and landmarks of Romanian architecture. As Alexandru was driving to his location, I immediately heaved a sigh of relief that I had not chosen Dr. Tanztwert's e-mail address as a return address. Instead, I chose to try the virtual mail beacon database that could pick up e-mail messages from different servers and times and was also linked to most mail servers in my lifetime. I activated it by sending a real e- mail from Dr. Tanztwert's computer back at his hotel room in Berlin; now I could wait for the paging (beacon) signal and use a recent enough desktop, laptop, or server computer that belonged to my current host. I was still inside of Alexandru and I hoped that I would receive this e-mail while here in Romania in 1998. One of the things I mentioned to Dr. Hourdeau is to change some of the static settings in the flash drive that had to do with my customizable DNA file. If he could do this, I may have a better chance of making it back to Meyrin. While he was still on his way to his client, I intercepted by way of signal beacon a receiving e-mail from 2011 and then saved it along with its contents in the virtual history database. I would read it the next chance I get, which appeared to be now. Things are finally looking up and I am not as nervous any more than I will cause the opening of a permanent portal to Meyrin.

Super Atom Smasher on Swiss Side

Later that evening, Alexandru did make it out to see some of his college friends. They went to see a movie, and then had a few drinks while they went bowling. Alexandru consumed four beers along with a mixed drink, which is something most people who drive shouldn't do but, in his subconscious thinking, I could detect that he would know what to say if he got pulled over by the police. Given our strong co-existence factor, when he started to spin from drinking, he headed to the restroom to throw up; I started to spin as well and my spin was accompanied by some convulsions, partly his own. Before I knew it, the thermodynamic arrow of time was changing again, time was spinning in a counterclockwise direction and I started to de- virtualize into what I expected to be somewhere in Switzerland in 2005. I was off by more than five years (I guess the closer I get to my own contemporary time, the more of a margin for an egregious error). It is September 21st, 2010 and I have materialized in the form of geneticist Lars Ankenbauer in Geneva. I virtualized into him as my host at 11:37 a.m. At first, he seemed to be aware of my presence, then changed his mind, attributing it to this imagination. My host health database determined that his vital signs were fine and that he is in good health. Within a few minutes, it became clear to me who he was. He was one of the scientists who had worked on the rough draft of the Human Genome Project from Geneva, Switzerland. He had worked on sequences of 150 genes by himself, some of which are potentially genes that cause inherent conditions such as depression, thyroid disease, Alzheimer's disease, as well as dwarfism. I realized that this man had also been nominated to receive the Nobel Prize for Genetics, but had been passed up for someone else who had discovered a new treatment for a rare form of HIV/AIDS. He was currently working on re-mapping or revising genes

121, 145, 562, 565, and 584 when I arrived. I decided, rather than waiting, to read the e-mail that I had received back in Romanian space-time from Dr. Hourdeau. The e-mail was a lengthier one and at times it was written in more stifled tones of politeness rather than the same tone that was delivered the first time to Dr. Tanztwert. It took less time than I expected and I wondered if I had set the time delivery variable to the right speed, as well as mail server co-ordinates. The message was reassuring, but at the same time a stern reminder of what could have happened had I not take the steps to send a message to Monsieur Dr. Hourdeau. It read as follows: "While I wished to conclude that a previous message had come from Dr. Tanztwert, noted physicist and Nobel Laureate, I feel I had no basis to do so. I can claim this because, while I know as fact that your first message had been waiting for me in a remote mail server in 1968, it would appear that this is the work of a disgruntled computer programmer that we had employed over five years ago. It makes a reference to a deceased employee Alen Marinkovich, who left some items behind and who has been incinerated at the eGSI facility which we are to conclude happened by accident. Since the receipt of your second message and your detailed 'explanation' on how you yourself are Marinkovich, I have to give you more credence now, but I am still skeptical. Alen Marinkovich was barely employed with us for a week while this happened to him. Two staff members witnessed his incineration. We have determined the contents of the flash drive to be a long series of encrypted files for someone, in virtual format. Mr. Marinkovich, if this is you, not only was this irresponsible, this could have been the reason for the temporary shutdown of one of the biggest particle physics labs of its kind. Please continue to correspond to us. I personally believe that you did in fact survive and that you are sending randomly timed e-mail messages from places that would have nothing to do with a facility such as ours whatsoever. We are still trying to help you, as well as trying to ascertain what happened on March 6th, 2011. This last transmission is from June 14th, 1998. If we determine that this is indeed a hoax caused by bored teenagers, political activists or disgruntled former employees who are out of work and managed to penetrate our secure e-mail servers, we will prosecute to the fullest extent of the law. I do believe this is you, Alen. You do understand though, the possibilities that spring up these days when it comes to false e-mails, spam, and unsolicited mail in general. Please continue to correspond with us and we will continue to track you from where you are coming. The reason I believe you is that I have not seen these types of technologies employed in my lifetime at eGSI. I want to make things better or at least put things into perspective and to allow closure. Thank you for your patience with us." Sincerely, General engineer Mousseur Dr. Jacques Hourdeau. It is working, I thought. It has to be working; otherwise he wouldn't indicate in such a blunt fashion that he believes me. I need to send him a third transmission now; I need to somehow quell his mind and his doubts that my messages could be coming from a disgruntled computer programmer formerly employed at eGSI. If there is a chance that they could lock onto me from where and when they were at the time, I might be coming home. I knew by this time that I was turning out to be somewhat of a pestering nuisance. This e-mail was good news and I had to double up my efforts in any way that I can. What to know inside of a Nobel Prize worthy geneticist isn't necessarily beyond me, it is inside of me. I am a geneticist of a different breed, however, if word got around in the community of longstanding scientists of genetics what I had done, I would not be recognized in the least in terms of what genetics is truly supposed to stand for: to map genes for the potential of treating or curing illnesses, for potential cures that are around the corner in the form of virtual treatments or pharmaceutical drugs, or for therapies in the distant future is ethical; to map the genome for any other purpose is considered tantamount to lack of ethics, to anything other than the initial reasons for mapping the human genome in the first place, immoral and unethical. I felt I could learn something from the re-mapping of at least three of these particular genes in the human genome:

genes numbered as 121, 145, and 584. Gene #121 is the gene that is in many cases associated with depression and depressive/mood illnesses; gene #145 is the one that deals with, in tandem with other genes, and the closely related gene #584 is the one that deals with certain types of skin conditions, including the development of melanoma. By re-mapping or at least revising the characteristics and functions of these three genes, the pharmaceutical world could develop better customized treatments in individual genomes that contain the dominant genes for major depression, bipolar disorder, schizophrenia, schizoaffective, melanoma, psoriasis, and other conditions associated with these particular genes and sets of genes. At this point, I decided I would allow Ankenbauer to pursue his involved work while the host health monitoring database continued to monitor his health to see what slight changes would come out of me co-existing with someone who is less than six months away from my departure grid in the same city as the other half of eGSI's collider installation exists. Our co-existence factor is 1:1.00000000000013, which means that our correlation variance is less than 15 parts in 1,000 trillion. I simply had to stay put for the rest of my time within this man as my host and to decide quantitatively whether it is OK to even send a message from his computer if the opportunity provided itself. I believe it had to be done for final confirmation to my former employer eGSI to allow them to know the full truth of what has happened in the last few weeks since my "incineration"; I was alive and residing in the body of a Swiss geneticist who was working on revising parts of the Human Genome Project that was declared complete in 2003. The next chance I received would be the one where I evaluated why I was doing it and why I had to. In eight hours and 23 minutes it would be 8:00 p.m. in Geneva. I didn't know that I was getting my opportunity to use a computer, but when Lars stopped working in order to turn on his HP laptop I knew I had the chance to send this e-mail. I decided to take it and had just enough leverage to write it myself (I was technically still considered malware at this point), without being noticed. This was not the first time I acted independently as an enigma while in a host's body and, even though I wanted to readily attribute it to being so close to my departure space-time in my host's body, I wasn't hasty enough to do so immediately. My message read: "If this is not enough proof that you are not being taunted by any former disgruntled computer programmer, then I suppose I can think of other ways to make you see that this is Alen Marinkovich. When you hired me, you asked if my avid interest in genetics is among the reasons why I applied to your temporary technician's position. I told you it had 'something to do with it, as well as working with fine people and with state-of-the-art machinery in making 21st century science.' I truly need your help. I may be virtualizing onto the same podium from where I 'incinerated', or re- moleculizing, within a few days. If this becomes possible, I will pay for any damages caused by my actions to eGSI or any intangible media actions done to Super Atom Smasher installation itself. However, I definitely need your help because I will most likely materialize near checkpoint #56. I need you to tweak the settings on my flash drive if there is a chance at all that I safely virtualize and then materialize. I am now virtualized inside of Swiss geneticist Lars Ankenbauer and the date is September 21st, 2010. Thank you in advance for your help and understanding." I signed off as myself, then pressed send without my host even detecting that a message was sent; I made special care that viruses or other malware were not able to access his laptop due to my time on it. I then used the virtual history database to determine when I would predictably next de-virtualize and virtualize. To my astonishment, it had no other reading than 2011. This doesn't inevitably mean that I have come full circle and that my next jump will be back on the collider podium by checkpoint #56. I could not easily conclude that I am done virtualizing as a genomic enigma. I still had no way of knowing where I was going to end up aside from the year when I would re-virtualize.

Full Virtual Circle

I am afraid now as to what might happen to my current host and what might happen to me if I land on the podium opposite the collider at checkpoint #56. Would my host(s) survive intact and never know that I had been inside of them or within them, and if so, would I survive at all if I wasn't but within a certain variance beyond a yoctosecond of 12:35 p.m. on March 6th, 2011 when I re-virtualized back into myself? I was still existing inside of Lars Ankenbauer, awaiting a message that would have come to me by now. I had no way of knowing whether the beacon frequency would be on at all in order to find out that I had a message on Lars' computer. What I wanted to read more than anything was the next reply message to see if there was a way to come back from this realm. My Virtual Genomic enigma has kicked in randomly as the Virtual enigma at least three times that I am aware and it may continue to do so on my next jump. The only thing I had to base a possible return to Meyrin around is the distance of Lars Ankenbauer to eGSI, as well as the relatively close time separation from my own disappearance at Super Atom Smasher. I was nervous to face the employees and the engineers of eGSI if I actually made it. I was anxious to face Petra. In some way, the thought of seeing her again and the prospect of getting to know her and others at the installation a little better kept me going. What are they really going to think of me now if I caused the company to appear poorly in the global news media, or even in the local media? Just at the second I was thinking this, the beacon frequency activated to let me know that Lars had received a message in his e-mail inbox. Based on Lars' subconscious, he wasn't planning on going to this laptop for anything in about two hours. He seems to be a very diligent worker at what he does; in the meanwhile, I would recount the steps I had taken since the virtual history database first activated to see what information I had collected, and try to calculate or tweak the variables I needed in order to better gauge the quantum components of my landing. I will see soon enough if they are helping me the next time I land. Before I forgot I ran the host health database and it told me that Lars' blood sugar was low, but otherwise his pulse rate and blood pressure were normal upon checking. I am wondering what we are having for dinner because I am so close I am starting to feel my own hunger for the first time in nearly four weeks of travel.

Re-Virtualization At eGSi

At 5:43 p.m. on September 22nd, 2010, Lars headed for his computer. He had one gene left to research for that week and he would be ready to turn his revisions in to this employer who was having an independent group verify Lars' findings, which would then be turn directly into the Human Genome Project panel for review. If the findings were conclusive, they would be announced by the web page of this institution. Lars turned on his computer with Windows Vista in order to check his e-mail, first and foremost. In a split second, I downloaded the message I was waiting for while Lars was not paying attention. After he checked his e-mail, he left the connection running in order to download some updates for his work-related encoding software. even if you know what you are doing, it is one of the most excruciating jobs that exist. For most of us, including myself to an extent, it is still complex. Of course, I have more of a background in genetics that the average scientist. I read the message and was thrilled with part of it, slightly annoyed with the other half. The message stated that Dr. Hourdeau finally believed and could conceive of what happened on March 6th, 2011 at checkpoint #56; the part that I wasn't too pleased to hear about is that he disagreed that tweaking anything will speed up the recovery of my particles into my re- materialization at the checkpoint podium location. He was still not happy about what had happened even with the discovery that I had made. He thinks that if there is going to be a virtual "full circle" that it should happen unencumbered. He promised to leave the settings the way they were with the exception of the polarity reversal that would allow me to see the world through my own eyes for the first time since my de-moleculization. He accepted my apology graciously and was eager to see what I had accumulated while "virtualizing around." He also said he would have to verify anything that I collected independently for the sake of authenticity. He said nothing about my position being open or occupied, but mentioned that there were people at eGSI who were anxious to see me return now that they know that I am "alive". I was alive and they were anxious to see me. I am sure my parents back in the United States would have felt the same way, considering they had not seen what had happened at eGSI and had no idea of where I was. To the best of my knowledge, my parents were still in Topeka, Kansas; mulling away the time, reading the paper, watching American Idol, CNN, or whatever it takes to keep occupied and entertained these days. I almost prefer that they knew nothing about what had happened since they were going to be the last ones to find out about the would-be tragedy and the miracles it brought to me. Still, I haven't quite made it back yet and I really shouldn't be jumping the gun in the event that something goes wrong. There are no guarantees in life, as verse as we might be in handling the art called living and the artificial moves that we might make that have nothing to do with life itself. They are just detours. As I am speaking these words, I feel that my host Lars is starting to fall asleep from exhaustion and I feel a much milder spin coming over me. It is in fact so gradual that it feels as though I am on the outside of a giant space ship that is taking off. I will soon find out whether I had succeeded in resolving the conclusion to the biggest adventure or the biggest set of problems I have created for myself in a lifetime.

Are We For Getting Something?

The first thing I remember is distinguishing the shade of colors from those colors that I was able to see. It was like having infrared goggles on at first; almost immediately, I started to smell things with my own nose such as the smell of perspiration of several people standing around me. I heard voices through my own ears or at least they seemed like my own ears. I felt like flour coming together for the first time in the oven with egg and shortening to create bread, and it all happened rapidly. Within two seconds, the experience became holistic. Within a few seconds more I started seeing more shades, almost like a blind person opening her eyes and learning how to see the first time after an eyesight operation. I tried to move, but was advised against it by a familiar voice and another familiar female voice cried out: "God, it's him!! How is this possible?" The female voice was Petra Stravinova. Thirty seconds later, I was lying on the podium next to checkpoint #56, recovering and safe in my new body or so I felt. I finally summoned the courage and strength to get up from the podium, which was about the radius of a person.

When I got up off the podium, I had not virtualized into anybody else. I heard clapping and ecstatic cries coming from the gathering. I was myself again and there were at least 30 people standing around, many of whom had been working that fateful day on March 6th, 2010. I was at eGSI's Super Atom Smasher and, as fate would have it, standing right next to checkpoint #56.

Among those people that I recognized was Georges, the technician who tried to shut down the countdown. Next to him was Dr. Hourdeau, who was pleased that I was back, but immediately stated that there was something different about me. I couldn't figure out what he meant. Anyway, the woman who was standing but several feet away was crying because she thought she had seen a ghost. I went up to her and asked if she needed any help with anything else around the facility. "You don't understand, "she said, wiping a tear. "I just saw you disintegrate and re-integrate within the last hour. I heard you had a theory of how it could be done, but I am not even sure I am talking to the same person. I wish to keep crying until I know it is you." I replied, "There is only one way to tell for certain. I have forgotten where the restrooms are. Is there another mirror around here somewhere?" She pointed to the back wall. As I approached it, I feared that I was going to have a Dr. Manhattan-type glow. I didn't. In fact, I was not only in my own body, but I was in better shape that I had felt before I had left. To the staff and Dr. Hourdeau, I had only been gone two hours and thirty four minutes in terms of real time. I looked like myself, I talked like myself; if all of this was true, then who am I? As in expectation, she replied: "I think you are a man in love with cities you have really never been in, yet you have come very close to residing there." I turned around and said: "Petra, how did you know what was going on?" "Simple", she said, "apart from seeing you appear and disappear there on the podium, I heard Dr. Hourdeau talking over some routine tasks with other engineers and you got brought up. He mentioned the e-mails. I don't know how you did it, but I want to know all about it. We should have dinner sometime. By the way, you look very well, Alen." I thanked her, and then walked away shaking my head. It felt more like a month had elapsed. It was now time to thank Dr. Hourdeau for helping me land back from where I left, and to apologize once more for any damages I had caused the facility in terms of any bad press. I turned sideways at the sound of a man's voice; it was Dr. Hourdeau. "I heard about what you did and I am still puzzled. You traversed seven bodies of living people through their DNA and have lived to tell about it. I understood the e-mails that you were not, in a sense, sending me messages through Dr. Tanztwert, Mr. Balanescu, and Mr. Ankenbauer. What I don't understand is why you did this, besides the obvious renegade tendencies of particular men in their twenties and thirties? I would want for you to tell me honestly, because what has happened is scientifically significant and I wish to keep you at your position if you can keep your hands off of certain equipment. " I did this because I was trying to find myself, not incinerate myself. I had a theory and it has been partly proven by the flash drive, if it still exists around here somewhere. "In reply," Dr. Hourdeau said, "there hasn't been enough time to throw it away. Of course it is still there. I feel very relieved to have you here again so soon. You must come back to work when you feel completely well. You must tell us anything that you feel relevant to document to yourself and us." Petra, who was still standing in the corner, was waiting to hear my response. "Petra, I would like to see you on Thursday at your place, on March 11th, if you do not mind cooking spaghetti. I will bring some Chateau Bliss". She beamed. Now I have to hurry up and see whether the flash drive recorded any of my voyages or if I was just out for the count for a few hours and imagined it while in my coma-like state. Wait a minute! It is there, it is all there, including my updated virtually customizable DNA file, including my host health database files, as well as the Level 3 Virtual History Database files!! It was not all for nothing and I feel like a billion bucks!! I wanted to jump up with joy, but did not feel like looking any crazier than I had already appearing before thirty people today as I did. I was back in my own time with information from past flows of people I mostly was not related to that I needed to properly document in the present. I also needed to call my parents for I have a bad feeling they had heard of my 'disappearance' from the media. It was usually the wrong media in this day and age. The only other thing I took with me was my flash drive. I was still wearing the same technicians clothing from earlier today March 6th, 2010. It was now 1:30 p.m. I had to go back to my apartment in Meyrin. I could not hide my newly found freedom and my sense of accomplishment even if it did not feel as though I had accomplished much. I had earned recognition from some of my colleagues, who by now knew what I had done with the exception of the details. What made me happier than anything was that I continue to work at eGSI as if almost nothing had happened. I think that stipulation that I stay away from certain equipment will be short lived when the senior staff realizes that I had opened up two wormholes without triggering a singularity in the middle of the facility that could have potentially swallowed at least the facility itself. It may be a fact that I need to learn further the techniques as well as the safety procedures that are built into using this equipment, which is some of the most sensitive and equally the most powerful in the world. I had been honest with Dr. Hourdeau as far as my reason for wishing to work here. He may trust me more and it is normal that he is giving me a mild "suspension" from the collider parts inspection routine. He will have ample opportunity to see what I have seen and recorded. I have ample opportunity to get to know Petra on Thursday and to find out what this woman from Leningrad is really like. I wanted to find out just how much she knew about the cities I had visited by way of my genomic travels and if she was aware of the fact that I had been to Leningrad, at least virtually. I did not even realize how closely she had stood to the collider when it activated near checkpoint #53, only three terminals away from the fateful one that helped bring me to so many different junctions. I am seeing now that once I stopped to talk to her, her charm is still strong and her persona is that of beauty, but the defiance of fundamental forces is a little off to a person who might just yet invent the anti-positron or a full-fledged anti-gravity device. I needed to know if what I had kindled with her was in any way inventive or even imaginary. I don't think it is imaginary; in fact, I believe it is starting to be real as ever. I had always heard of the term "to control one's own destiny", but did not know until now what the person was quoted as saying. It means to take charge of you first and foremost, and to take charge of others through gradually earning their respect.

Dinner With Destiny

I called my mother the next day to see how she was doing. My parents had indeed heard something had happened and my mom burst into tears as she told me she almost ordered a Daily Mass to be paid in my memory in Meyrin. She never went through with it in the hope that I would return in one piece. She said she had been informed by a representative of eGSI. She angrily asked me why I did it. I explained that it wasn't to impress anyone or for a job promotion at a position that I had just started. It was for the scientific thrill of learning and discovering something beneficial. I also told her the truth about how it had been something I had worked on for a few years and how it has tentatively paid off. My Dad was displeased. He wanted to know how is it that my method could not have been perfected in a sort of trial run or a series of trial runs first. I told him I never knew if I would have the equipment at my disposal that was powerful enough to send me into the realm where I had been. Now I had, but since my first week there, I had crossed the line in terms of permissions of usage. Actually, I did not originally, nor does any new employee have permission to touch the collider. I had been fortunate enough to keep my job and voluntarily share any information that I had gathered by way of my virtual history database, which was a Level III virtual object. I don't believe that the only reason I am still employed is due to discovering something newly practiced in scientific sense. I just brought it to the forefront. I had not drawn out any artificial histories as had been done by certain individuals or countries in the past. I was as clean as a whistle and was probably at this point the best computer hacker there currently is in terms of how far I had gotten into the most sophisticated database—the database of human history. I had simply not recorded as much as

I could have had I been a cybernaut. If this were ever to happen, the involved parties would need a research lab of their own, a certain amount of funding to get started, and the most advanced level of virtual technologies that exist. even still, I had achieved something in my own personal sense and had validated myself and provided some validation to others. Today is Wednesday, March 10th, 2011. I am going to meet Petra tomorrow and I am currently shopping for a type of Chateau Bliss that would warm both of our hearts and allow us to talk for a long time and simply get to know each other. I jokingly thought to suggest this to her, but it was bad timing and I had just returned from my last virtualization: I thought to suggest borscht, but I decided not to. I wonder if she is a better cook that I am. either way, I am choosing a Chateau Bliss from 1988. This will be appropriate for the evening that I believe we have planned. I don't have a backup plan for the eventuality that something I plan on happening does not happen. It really doesn't matter. After this outing, I will go home to fix some apple pie for our dessert, but not before purchasing a dozen white roses at the Florist Shop at the corner of Rue Lect & Rue Du Cardinal Journet. She needed to know she will always be somebody special to me. I am not there to prove what is immutable, I am here to prove what cannot be changed can be the very thing that saves humanity when push comes to shove. I am anxious to learn what her thoughts on string theories are, as well as what state of the universe does she accept, the traditional Big Bang theory, Inflationary, or some other version of the Multiverse. Not that I am a penny pincher, but I have not met an extremely well-funded physicist since my college days when government funding was more bountiful. If I ever needed funding for any project I am allowed to do separately from my traditional job, which eGSI has not become thus far, I wonder if she had any connections and would she ever be willing to have a work- related relationship outside of eGSI. There is one way to find out and I have a strong intuitive feeling I will find out much more in the following days.

Getting to know Petra

What is it about a first date? When you wake up in the morning, you feel that you will have all of the energy and all of the cunning to do anything you have to and still have reserves left for the lovely evening ahead. I was drained by 1:00 p.m. on Thursday, but I came back from my lunch break and did some routine procedures as I had taught myself from my eGSI technician's manual. I winked at Petra afterwards and told her that I would be there after 6:45 p.m. and that I just needed to get directions to her house. She provided those directions. I kissed her softly on the cheek, saying that I would see her mostly likely at 7:00 sharp. She smiled and said she would be ready. I continued about my third routine check of 8 checkpoints that needed to be reconfigured since I had been back. There was a lot of work to catch up on since my departure and return. Since the limited airing on CNN Science News about the incident that for certain had left me in the form of dust, there had not been any leaks as to the intricacies of my life or death, or that I had since re-materialized back at the same mainframe from which it was thought that I had committed suicide. In fact, from what I knew, nothing was to be released until Dr. Hourdeau and I had had a chance to talk about the collected data that I had virtually record during my jumps. I was given input and agreed with the senior staff that my return "from the dead" would not be announced until there were tangible specifics as to how it happened. As closing hour drew near, I felt as tired as if I would have had I worked ten hours at a construction site. I needed to get some coffee. Something was fatiguing me even more than what I could realize and it all happened since I've been back to work. After two latte's, I felt better, but it felt almost as though I have been de- materializing in a sense. even after having studied kaonic decay as a normal process through which dead matter is recycled throughout the human body, I had the funniest feeling something else was eating away at me. At first it occurred to me that it could be my conscience because I felt morally guilty that I had "resided" in their bodies and souls, even though I had taken the trouble to help maintain their vital signs. I still had the records of my former hosts' vital records recorded in digital format on my flash drive under the directory Host Health Database/ Vital Signs. There was nobody or nothing I could refer to for symptomologies related to past time travel, so I decided to see if a quiet evening at Petra's would do the trick. After verifying the last routine, I grabbed my jacket and clocked out, leaving the clock card sticking out by an inch for the next morning. I knew there was a distinct possibility that she may not wish to see me again with the exception of work. I felt I had to impress her tonight by doing something enlightening as only I can do. Still, I simply had no tricks up my sleeve that would seem to work for the occasion. As I was getting dressed I remembered the flowers that I had put in the vase with water last night. I went through to the kitchen to where they were as I was putting on my shirt. There they were glistening like the lips of Petra herself. In fifteen more minutes I checked my apartment and it looked tidy enough to leave to itself. I double-checked my tie, grabbed the white roses, the wine, and the homemade apple pie that I had made yesterday and bolted for the door. It was already 6:35. I knew it would take at least thirty minutes if I was lucky to get to her house based on the directions I was given. My hybrid car was no 400LS Series Mercedes, the type Alexandru had in Bucharest 13 years ago. I knew I would be a bit late, but I decided against calling her. I would be there soon enough.

Dinner is Served

It was 7:04 p.m. I rang the buzzer. Within a few seconds, she popped her head from around the curtain, smiling. She let me in after a warm welcome kiss. I brought in the apple pie and gave her the white roses. I asked her how she was and if she thought that this might interfere with our working relationship. I already loved her, but I didn't want this to be the reason either one of us quit or, more likely, got terminated from work. She said she thought that we could work it out somehow. She cracked up all of a sudden and said that she had never dated a time traveler. I said, "That makes two of us. Would you like to ever accompany me on one of my trips if we ever get the technique of travel perfected?" She smiled. I didn't realize how fascinating she really was and, on the flip side, how fascinating I was to her. When I told her how much I had thought about her during my trips throughout peoples' bodies, she almost cried. She shed a tear when I told her that I had been within a woman named Volga in Leningrad. I had crystal clear pictures of cities I had never truly been to, particularly of Leningrad. We ate silently for about 10 minutes before I broke down and told her how much strain I was under that day when she was stumbling around the facility, before I blasted myself with the timed collider. I told her I haven't really felt the same about many things since my virtualizations had occurred, but I knew that I loved her and I was sorry if she thought that I was taking things a bit too swiftly. She was waiting in stillness when another tear came down her eye; she spoke in Russian, "Ja tebja ljubljo. I wasn't bargaining for love at this job, but I am truly blessed that I have found you. I feel safe when you are here and happy when you are near." I told her I hadn't been certain that my stunt at eGSI was going to work even though the calculations I had made seemed to point in that direction. At the time, it was simply an imperative. I was implying if she minded dating a risk prone individual. I described seeing certain buildings and sights from Volga's perspective and she laughed heartily. I described different things in great detail and it would not have mattered, with certain exceptions, when I thought I had just gone too far in "accidentally violating the host's rights", if there is such a thing at this point. After about an hour, I remembered the wine and she brought out two glasses from which to drink. I found myself pouring her a glass of wine, trying to remind her that we have to be at work in the morning and that I was just reminding her. She agreed and took the wine glass from me. I poured myself some wine and we toasted. We toasted to romance and work friendship. After we downed the wine, I reached over and French-kissed her once. She told me to keep going. Finally, we were in bed together and we made love in a way that truly complemented the evening. I was happy she was here with me. We continued to kiss until I decided it was time for me to go if I was to be well rested. I suggested the same for her. She laughed and wished me a good night. "Please drive safely because I want to see you tomorrow," she stated on her way back in. "Oh, you will." As I drove off, I knew I had pursued things fairly swiftly and that we did not need to sleep with each other this evening. My chief concern was our work life. Surely it can be worked around, but whatever happens can now be blamed on one of us, particularly me, because of my disappearance act/re- appearance act. I knew what I wanted and she was whom I wanted. Right now, the time frame that counted was not so much the past or the future. It was the present. I have a strong feeling that she is the right person. I am ready for the tribulations as well as the happiness.

The Encryption to her Heart

I got to work three minutes early, clocked in and went about my early morning routine of checking the first fifteen checkpoints that were marked in the technician's manual. I had a feeling today was going to be a tumultuous day, in part because of Petra, and in part because I suspected that the press might have somehow gotten information that I was still alive. So far, Petra had not come in yet and I had a bad feeling that she might not. She could have called in sick. In fact, my best guess is that she was feeling uncomfortable about working this type of job with a love interest right around the corner almost at all times. It is never an easy proposition, the gossip from co-workers adding to the inner turmoil. I truly enjoyed myself last night and was happy that I went over there last night. She was cultured and had much class. What I saw deep down in her was a girl who knew what direction she wanted to go in, as well as a young determined woman who had overcome trials and tribulations in life to get to where she is today. "I heard that," a female voice behind me stated. I turned around to see Petra standing there. She was grinning. Upon verifying that nobody else was watching we shared a kiss. I could tell that this relationship was going to be a flamer. I reminded her about what we talked about and that we should keep things professional, at least until we saw that it was OK with eGSI's management. She agreed and asked if I wanted to come over again in order to help her re- arrange her apartment. I quipped that she never got tired of re-arranging things, including at the particle level, and told her I would be there about 6:00 p.m. She grinned and whispered that she loves me before walking away. This was going to be difficult, but I am going to have to find out what is permissible before I could even kiss her at work anymore. I had finally finished checking checkpoints #141 and

#142, when someone called for me from some distance away. It was Dr. Hourdeau himself, who had wanted to talk to me more since my seemingly hour and a half long departure just a few days ago. “Alen, he said, almost out of breath, “I have to talk to you. What you discovered was revolutionary. I understand the ethical implications as a physicist, but I am not a geneticist who could write a dissertation about the immorality of certain things hidden within your methodologies. I also know that they are in their preliminary stages. However, I am having european news agencies calling left and right to find out how you came “back from the dead”, as well as a CNN science reporter sending e-mails on a weekly basis. I have to tell them something, and even though we agreed not to talk about this to the media until we have had a chance to review your data, I have to give them something tentative in order to keep them away for a few more days. We need to do this. Could you stay later today? I have asked Ms. Stravinova and Georges Pouchet to stay late with us to discuss what our next move is. We are definitely not accustomed to this much excitement at this installation. “I would love to,” I replied, “and I think I would like Ms. Stravinova and Mr. Pouchet to stay as well, yet I cannot speak for them.” “They have already agreed, Alen,” replied Dr. Hourdeau. “We have to stay for a few extra hours to analyze this virtual data that you have collected while ‘traveling’. Don’t worry. We will resolve this and this is something anybody who is eying a serious career here needs to understand. We are here primarily to conduct realistic real- time tests on environments that resemble singularities and to test the underlying fundamentals, constants and variables of the Big Bang, its variations in cosmological terms, the Inflationary theory, as well as other cosmological research. We normally wouldn’t have much time to devote to an individual’s customized states of quantum flux, but it happened here. We have to research this, and if this is something that we can technically report to the Science Journals, we certainly will.” By now, Petra and Georges were already nearby and talking about something similar that was going on, namely, the press that kept calling the facility. They approached and joined in the conversation. “So much for re-arranging my apartment, hey stud?” she quipped. I told her we could do that as soon as we weren’t needed here. I also gave her a long look because I had no idea on how much time was going to be spent nor how much press this topic was going to attract. She laughed and pretended to whisper to herself. I am an unusually private person most of the time. She understood. Georges looked over and remarked how he was so convinced that I was dead that he started to place a memorial reef and flowers to indicate where I had de-moleculized. I apologized to him that he had to witness what he did and that it must have seemed like none other than an attempted suicide. He said he had a funny feeling I was either making a statement or experimenting with something, although in his mind he thought that something might have been an illegal drug. It was a done deal then. The four of us, in addition to two other people I don’t really know, would meet after 5:00 p.m. in the conference room. We probably would not stay longer than 8:00 p.m., yet we would stay as long as it took to quantify and provide qualitative analysis and conclusions of all of this data. We would spend the first hour testing the virtual particles in the messages themselves that I had sent and the one that I sent from Berlin as Dr. Tanztwert was indeed 43 years old; the other two were respectively 13 & 15 years old in terms of relative time, and the tachyon scan confirmed it. The other hour was spent what to tell the press; even though I had told my side of the story as it being more or less intentional, I thought we should tell the press that it was something of an accident with an independent theory that I had put forth when I first applied to this job. We all finally agreed to say that it was a job accident and to tell a partial truth, that I was pulled away at the last minute and that the involved parties were embarrassed to tell the “truth” as it had actually happened. I had been suspended for three week, but my working relationship allowed for me to stay with the company with a pay cut. Petra suggested an inspection of our cameras, wondering if these devices could ever be confiscated to determine the truth if it ever became important enough to know. Dr. Hourdeau told her that he would worry about that if the occasion ever arose. As I have said before, there has been for some time a growing movement to regulate the activities of laboratories and installations such as Super Atom Smasher for the safety that they pose the global environment that they are in. If this ever fully came out, we were in trouble. Dr. Hourdeau himself finally suggested that we should tell the press the truth, stating that I am a trainee who was touching a button or a series of switches that I shouldn't have touching and that I de- materialized and materialized within two hours of time, which was the visible truth. What he suggested was that we should not talk about the information obtained during that time. I knew I now needed to keep my silence unless I truly did not care about my job. It definitely put a damper on how much of a priority Virtual Genomic Time Travel would be on the list of people working at eGSI. This may also affect my long-term tenure with eGSI. However, there is no unwritten law that says I have to quit my position at eGSI for this reason. I can continue to make a living and, at some point, genetics can enter the realm of priorities as protocols can allow. If I were to attempt replicating the use of the collider to propel myself into the past, the chances of returning and making full circle virtually might be slim. I doubt anybody would come to my rescue this time. My absence in terms of mass and energy would not create a singularity. Perhaps there is an encryption to Petra's heart in the event that I ever lose her. I am not really a romantic; I am as pragmatic as is required to achieve an end result. It would have to be written in another programming language that has not been invented yet, in some universal language code. Hopefully, even if there is such a thing as an encryption to love, it is never discovered. It would take the prowess and conquest out of romance. It would make love such a bland item in the grand scheme of things. The truth is that there are some things that are best pursued alone, while others are more of an active social phenomenon. Discoveries that benefit us all are those that are tied in importance between discovery of self and discovery of humanity toward others.

Encryptions from the Future

How was I going to continue my research now? After having been told that my work is a low priority due to recent events at eGSI, I had to find new ways to continue doing what was one of the reasons that I applied to my current employer in the first order. I did not want to leave this job: aside from the beautiful healthcare package and the retirement benefits, it has everything I need, yet much of it is no longer accessible to me because of what I had done. I needed to find a partner that was willing to work with me in building a cybernetic being based upon my own genetic code, my own customizable virtual DNA file. There is no such thing as an all-encompassing genetic code that one starts from, a universally encrypting language code. I still did not know how I was going to get out of that big media splash that I truly caused somewhat intentionally. It was to engulf me like a giant 100-foot surfing wave. For a scientist to do research and work in this particular field, it is a great distraction to have to worry about fame in any sense that can occasionally occur during times of intense discovery. In addition, infamy was not my only concern. My health was starting to become a concern since my bouts with fatigue and other issues prompted me to see a physician on March 27th, 2011. I got a clean bill of health, which made me wonder if beyond some type of depression, my virtualizations had caused these unusually strange feelings. I did not wish to worry about them if a board certified physician had already told me that there is nothing to worry about. As far as having a project partner was concerned, Georges himself had practical experience in cybernetics; although he had never been certified by any credible board or college, he had ten years of experience in building bionic arms, legs, as well as an internship from the late 1990's during which his specialization was to help people with muscular dystrophy by way of implementing new bionic limbs in their everyday living. He was a whiz when it came down to building cybernetic organisms in his basement in Meyrin. He was an engineer. If I wished to work with him, I wanted to make sure that he wouldn't be hesitant because of what he saw last week. I wanted to make sure that he was comfortable with me. I had been around cybernetics installations, but had never quite tried to design or build anything that looked like a cybernaut. I approached him on the 14th after lunch and made a proposition. I told him the essence of what I had done (he surmised as much); I asked if he would help design a cybernaut for that purpose, something that had predetermined, customized DNA in virtual format at level III. He told me, in all honesty, that he would have to think about it; one of the main reasons being because of what it was being built for. I knew the answer was probably going to be a less than resounding *yes* and I then proceeded to tell Petra about what I had just spoken to him about, to see if she wanted to contribute anything. She wasn't in a great mood, but a kiss cheered her up. Upon hearing what I had to say about cybernetics, she shrugged. Petra was more of a lab physicist/chemist. She knew what she could do and rarely dabbled into anything else that didn't quite conform to her specialty. According what she knew about cybernetics, there were very few intermediaries that could do specifically what I wanted them to do. She knew the reason why the Virtual Genomic enigma had to be part cybernetic. She said she could possibly help with the nervous system and the cybernaut's circulatory functions. She had otherwise never done anything like this before. She then said that it was a pity that one could not build love and hate right into a cybernaut; since the world itself would treat it as human inasmuch it would treat it like a machine. It had one purpose, the purpose I was building it for—for the recording of past time flows and to map out human history like a grid, much like one day the scientific community may map out our Solar system and the surrounding galaxies in a comprehensive way. The human history verification bot would be one name for this invention. The changes in the arrow of time would not affect it. It would gather and collect much past the date when any of the data collected would be used to save humanity from itself and other cataclysmic events, from various apocalypses, or from anything within the same category of events that may arise. It would ensure the survival of humanity past any future times of challenge, such as pandemics, epidemics, droughts, floods, weather anomalies, and global warfare. When virtual technologies evolve into levels IV and V, it will be immune to all causality, which is a terrifying thought indeed. That is where the Unified Global Initiative came into play, an organization of historic proportions that is yet to be founded. Soon there might be a reason to found this organization, the reason being world peace and other humanitarian purposes. The reasons would be egalitarian and meritocratic in nature. Why wouldn't a person work if his historical fate is tied to the ultimate fate of himself and other human beings? It is for the nature around us and for the nature of who we really are. We are nature and this is the evolutionary principle that we are waiting to discover. Virtual Genomic Time Travel is an egalitarian enterprise in that it can benefit many people in many different ways. It is egalitarian because there are finally people there who can bring benevolence to many millions across the world, benevolence and closure. There are people that can quell fear, injustice, suffering, and torture in those places in the world and in those walks of life where these elements have to be headed involuntarily. I needed Petra and Georges in order to help me fulfill my dream and they can potentially be involved with the formal aspects of Unified Global Initiative as much as I am. In fact, they are the key to allowing project Cybernetic Virtual Genomic enigma Travel to continue into the next several years. On April 15th, 2011, the three of us are set to found the UGI (Unified Global Initiative) as a scientific initiative for preserving and telling the history of various parts of the world in an objective way, in a way no human being could ever possibly do so. We knew that at this point in history that history itself would be difficult to preserve going forward and that the accuracies of historical lessons would resonate less and less with the youth of the future. We were preserving current and future history in any way we could that was benevolent, meritocratic, and egalitarian. History needs reconciliation that can only be provided by knowing this history. A history that can benefit humankind need not only be holistic, it needs to be comprehensive and complete.

Whispers through A Mystery Canyon

I went to sleep in the evening around 11:00 p.m. I had kissed Petra and wished her a good evening half an hour ago. I was even wearier than I thought than I had been at work today. I turned out the lights and rolled into bed. Within 5 minutes, I was asleep. Or so I thought. I felt as though I was back in Ricardo Johanes body and that he had died, and that I still couldn't get out. I was screaming, yet air was not moving toward Ricardo's lips like I wanted it to in order to be heard by someone at the emergency room where he was being pronounced dead. He had beads of sweat trickling down his forehead. In another instant, I was at a beautiful canyon with lush grass, trees, vines, birds, animals, and I was relaxing. All of a sudden, I heard whispers. The whispers were getting louder. The mystery canyon started to resemble a conundrum in a sense that the whispers were getting louder with every change in scenery. I didn't know if I was myself or if I looked like someone else. I couldn't see much around me but a trudged couple of paths where I had been left to die. I was bleeding and the only sounds that were getting louder were the whispers. The whispers were coming through a mystery canyon I could not even categorize or classify. I could only start to describe it. The sounds were unintelligible and soft, but they seemed to create a wave of sounds emanating from around my inner sphere. It was if they were looking for something inside of my psyche that simply was not there. It was as though a being was trying to unlock me with a sound encryption and everything she was trying didn't work. These were not there through peaceful means and it was as if the sound waves were trying to warn me of something and hurt me at the same time. I started to decipher the sounds as the voices of Ricardo, Ivo, Behram, Alberich, Volga, Alexandru, and Lars mixing with each other. It was as if they all had an individual message and some had a mixed message to deliver to me. I listened, but no matter how intently I listened, I could not make out the meaning or intent of the mixed messages. I could start to hear songs coming together, sounds drawn apart as waves, melodies jingling as a collective, notes ringing out as individuals spelling out phrases at a varsity football game, along with beats and mixtures of beats trying to encrypt what is not always hidden. In fact, the door is usually always open for the right person. It is usually open for Petra, but she is not there to gather its riches. All of a sudden, with a loud gasp, I awoke to realize that it had been a nightmare. I realized that I could not ignore the dream. I realized that there had been some anxiety as well as psychological fear built up in me from these voyages and there were physiological as well as psychological. They were starting to come out and I was tapping into fear, anxiety, and even depression that I had that I thought I had rid myself of before I got hired at eGSI. As in many things of a natural or a social nature, psychological phenomena tend to equalize themselves when the balance on one side or the other is overwhelming. Dreams are an indicator of things that can only be sorted out or smoothed. As much time as one can require when it comes to peace, that much more is sometimes required to fill the void that required adventure to fill it. As times goes on, certain compartments that are filled during compartmentalization are emptied and filled anew as part of a life and health cycle. With time travel, this cycle can be stalled or even stopped until the basic needs of the Virtual Genomic Time Traveler are met in order to complete the next cycle. I've been gradually recovering from these nightmares and even the doctor that I saw the other day said that I would be fine and that I am probably a bit overworked from starting a new position in a demanding field. He was not joking in any way. I knew the mysterious whispers through the ever-changing canyon are not voices that wish to reveal the future to me, only the past in the context of the present. If these voices could speak freely, they would talk of the betrayal that my conscience revealed to them that I was there inside with them and relatively silent like an insidious disease. My presence was certainly foreign and the subconscious of my hosts was aware of the presence that was in them at a given time in space. The dream weave itself is one eternal dream that is filled with success and perhaps pain in getting sometimes excruciating efforts overcome and joyous goals reached in times of tragedy past. Perhaps these whispers come from a worm hole that opened up nearby within an ancient canyon and have not found their true audience.

Countdown to Cybernetic enigma

I clocked in at 7:59 this morning on March 20th, 2011 at eGSI. Petra greeted me with a smile and some coffee, along with some scientific news about W & Z bosons. By now, a few other colleagues had begun to notice the attention she was giving me and concluded that we were an item. They also noticed that I was feeling more cheerful and thought, for the most part, that I was being professional about our relationship, as well as my relationship with her. All with the exception of a physicist named Pierre, my job at eGSI was coming along very well. I did, in fact, suggest something to Mr. Pierre Girard when I was first employed at eGSI, before my incident with the collider ray. It had to do with the security of the collider that was related to leaving one of the mainstays unsecured so that anyone could get in. He now appeared more distant from me and had apparently decided to keep our relationship that way. In relation to the news that Petra was telling me about this morning over coffee, it looked like last week's invention regarding W & Z bosons could have something to do with Petra being a bit more involved in the cybernetic development of the next stage of my project. She is starting to get excited about the prospects and has promised that, if there is a will, there will be a way to become integrated with the cybernaut as much as it is scientifically and ethically possible. She wanted to suggest the combination of the best parts of our DNA in order to build a near perfect Virtual Genomic Cybernetic Time Traveler. I shuddered at the thought not because I didn't think her DNA was not adequate enough; in fact, it was superior to mine in many instances.

What I was afraid of were the would-be repercussions to her if I did this and to our relationship. Not many people could tell me that I didn't have the foresight or excellent planning abilities; sometimes, though, I did not have the best rationale or reasoning in the world for wanting to plan certain things too far ahead. The implications of what she was telling me were that one could take a genetic sample of tissue, manipulate the bosons at a quantum level, and have an altered set of genetic tissue available and ready for manipulation. She wants to be inside of the cybernaut as much as I do. I told her I would have to think about it. She knows she would probably get her way anyway, but what bothers me is that her DNA has never been exposed fully to Virtual Genomic enigma conditions. She will be the one working on implanting the circulatory system and part of the nervous system inside of the cybernetic organism. I plan to be the virtual geneticist who works on the customized file for the new artificial organism. Georges will be the mind behind the bionics of the cybernaut and has already said he does not want to provide any sample of his DNA for this organism. He has seen a sample of what "raw genomic travel" can do for a living breathing human being and, even though I had not gone very far for very long, what alterations it brings. He has seen what my de-moleculization did to my performance at work for a few days after that eventful afternoon. My goal is to one day be able to touch members of ancient civilizations that have helped form what we have here today in this world, the Greeks, Sumerians, Confucians, Romans, Byzantines, Ottomans, Native Indian tribes, and so on, to record what they were thinking, saying, how they were living, and how they progressed in time relative to our time, the 21st century. I have notions of each of these eras in our past collective histories, but there are very vague. I am in talks with Georges to start building a cybernaut in his basement and I have started to give him the first of the 10% installments from the next six months of my salary. I am still a technician who is doing rather well at eGSI Super Atom Smasher and keeping up with the rounds and the security of part of the largest particle physics laboratory in the world.

Justification Required and Found

It was April 2nd, 2011 and, after a long day's work, I was at home watching the local news. I decided to watch some current international news. It appears that Iran's nuclear program has continued to develop beyond the expectations of the United Nations, eU, as well as the United States and Russia. North Korea's leader Kim Jong Il is still in power. The world has been tangibly devastated due to the global recession that started in 2008. It appears that certain countries, the United States included, had been trying to strong arm other countries in the world into boycotting products from Iran & North Korea, as well as Venezuela. There were talks among other countries to visit Iran, and separately countries like North Korea, to try to assuage the resulting tension that is a direct result of these actions. even though the majority of stockpiles of post-Cold war era nuclear weapons have been destroyed, there was still tension that reminded people, old enough to remember in many countries, just how failed the policy of nuclear proliferation was in the 1960's and 1970's. Conflicts are still possible. As it turns out, the old logic hasn't completely faded. The likelihood of conflicts still rises when it comes to inequalities in trade as well as recessive times for the global economy.

Western countries are becoming more and more concerned about former third world countries. How could one even start to quell such conflicts that are based on centuries of complex relations, and overall political differences? It is only possible to go back and to record what we do not know today for sure, only to obtain it. What we know can hurt us; but it also can make us wealthier experientially and more savvy in dealing with potential global conflicts in the present. It can make us for capable of multitasking in the event of something "astronomical" that we might not quite know how to deal with.

News of Asteroid nt9

On April 4th, 2011, we received some general news from the Hubble Telescope the direct consequences of which were headed in the direction of planet earth. The telescope had picked up readings of a gigantic-sized asteroid that was several solar lengths away that was on an indirect tangent toward us, but once the trigonometric factor was calculated, it is likely that impact will occur in 2013 sometime in the middle of the year. It was an asteroid slightly larger than the size of the one considered to have consumed the dinosaurs 65 million years ago. Historically, there was no precedence set for dealing with this massive threat. We had less than two years to react to this change in the present grid. What were we going to do? I walked down the hallway and immediately ran into Georges, who had just gotten off the phone with someone. They had been talking about the same thing. Petra approached us five minutes later. I proposed that we double up on our efforts to build the first time real-time based genomic cybernetic enigma, even if it means pitching in more money from our paychecks. Petra had not been thus far putting in any money; she proposed between 18-20% of her income toward the cybernaut's development and launch. Georges looked at us both as though we were crazy and suggested he could add 14%-18% of his monthly pay to the project. We knew what was going on and that we would not have this project ready until next year. The deadline was set for January 2013. That would give us approximately twenty months to prepare for impact from NT9. Someone had to act and this also meant that we would not have a moment's worth of time to spare from eGSI Super Atom Smasher itself.

Many times, these predictions had been wrong. I for one did not want to see the prediction turn out to be correct. There were so many things I wanted to do; I wanted to see the Inflationary cosmological theory tested here at eGSI. I wanted to go out to a special place and propose to Petra. It may not be the time, but neither of us is getting any younger and, if I am going to be working with her side by side for so many hours, for some strange reason I would rather work with her as my wife than as just a colleague I have a strong romantic interest in. The question I did not have answered is how exactly did she feel about it. Georges himself had a pretty good idea of what was going on, but it did not seem to faze him. All three of us agreed on the idea of the Unified Global Initiative and were pursuing the founding of it by February of 2012 to take control of the first virtual time traveling cybernaut, the first mapper of the local and globalized space-time continuum. I knew all three of us have good goal mapping skills. We are proficient multitaskers. And yes, we are all geniuses within our own specializations that could very well make this project not only feasible, but also plausible to finish next January, in 2012. Petra would still be applying biochemical techniques of fusion to construct a circulatory and nervous system, Georges was still handling bionics, while I was handling the quantum mechanics and the virtual genetics side of things. The roles were still the same and there was plenty of room for supplementing our individual roles. It was coming. Change was coming in the form of a potentially loud wake up call. We had determined four general phases for the construction and enabling of a cybernaut: the design phase, individual sub-phase completion, integration phase, & online and completion phase. We would be having a complete design of all of the crucial parts by May 15th, 2011. Sub-phase completion would last until August 25th.

Integration phase should last until December 10th, 2011, while the online and completion phase is expected to last until January 15th, 2012. If this is going to go as planned, there was something that I needed to do that can wait no longer.

A proposal of A different type

Now that we have the phase completion squared away, there was something I needed to do that could no longer wait. It had to do with Petra. I loved her dearly and a hypothetical rejection of me by her would break me romantically and emotionally. The professional would have to go on with or without love. either way, I had to find something out and there was only one way to know for certain. I invited her over to my place for a lobster dinner and wine after which we had dessert. I presented her with a small gift box that was wrapped and marked "Open at your own risk." She looked stunned and took the box, separated the note from the box, and opened it. Her eyes looked even more stunned than before when she saw the engagement ring inside. She started crying. At that point, I got down on one knee and gazed into her beautiful blue Russian eyes. "I love you and have loved you since the day I met you. I want to spend the rest of my life with you. Will you marry me?" She nodded and said "Da" after she blushed and grabbed me. She hugged me and kissed me powerfully. "I fell in love with your sense of adventure and your willingness to take risks and to take charge of any situation. I have fallen for you for the man that you are. Ya lublu tebja." We kissed on my couch for a while, then got undressed and made love for the rest of the evening. She was happy and I knew her moods enough to simply hold her and stroke her hair. I knew this was a lot for her; nevertheless, I knew how she felt about me. She was afraid of the toll that our working relationship would take on our private life. My first choice in life would not have been to work at the same company with even a love interest, let alone a future spouse. I was glad Georges was going to be working with us on the cybernaut. He was one of the first to find out the next morning and he congratulated both of us. We both assured him that we did not have to be working as much side by side until the second to last phase of virtual cybernaut integration phase. I think we will be fine. As for Petra and I, this is going to take some getting used to. As for another time in the next two years, we might be working feverishly side by side of each other to help stop the threat to life on the planet. If we can avert this fate, there will be much time for privacy and private moments. The cybernaut now must have a name, not like Alpha-1, or Omega-4, or Zeta-13. It must have a personable name, something we could all agree on. Petra suggested Gustav, while Georges suggested Ricardo. I thought I liked a name like Ricardo or Gustav, but I wanted it to be more culture-neutral. I have thought about how to phrase this without sounding silly, but I have a name that may take some getting used to if it is selected: Gamma-Gustav. After I suggested it, it seemed funny to Petra and not so funny to Georges. They are my colleagues, my sources of input into this cybernetic project, the project that may be suited to save the world from ourselves and beyond. I don't think that name will work after all. We have to find something unifying for the sake of our efforts and the sake of the institution that inevitably has some influence in its construction. Two weeks in the making, we have unanimously decided on a name TANG-0000. Dr. Hourdeau does not know about our side project and will not find out if I have anything to do with it. He would consider this project something that is wasteful and will take away from our individual learning curves, our motivational energies and our dedicated efforts to Super Atom Smasher. He will know the development of anything extracurricular that I engage in on an as-needed basis. What he does not know could hurt him, but doesn't necessarily have to. The beginning is here, the start of TANG-0000. Much of our research has been based on solid academic research and practical training at eGSI, with personal opining and group brainstorming taking up a solid, yet a significantly smaller part of the process. We needed materials, genetic samples, alloy parts for the limbs and peripheral parts of our cybernaut, as well as hours of dedicated work, along with plenty of coffee. We definitely did not need decaffeinated coffee. Our group was going to be one of probably hundreds, some bigger and others smaller, who was going to attempt to save the world from an ensuing apocalypse the likes of whom anyone has even seen. In the end, some of these alternative groups of scientists may have to band with us, or we may need to band to them to cover all loose ends in securing a future for ourselves and our children.

The Cybernetic Design Phase

On April 6th, we are feverishly bringing together designs for the cybernetic time traveler that we would use in bringing the first (design) phase to life in Georges' basement. We would have to spend as much time at his house in order to meet our own designated deadline for phase Two to begin. It was also very encouraging that Georges, who lived with his ailing mother in Meyrin is allowing the three of us to meet and to work on our respective tasks there at his house with his mother there. She was not very curious as to what we were doing and was very pleasant when we finally met her. She did not want to let go of Petra's hand until she realized that she was not a love interest of Georges. She was very cordial to me. When we compared designs, Georges realized that some of the designs that he had brought home were from eGSI's left wing. He had us promise not to bring up these particular designs to anybody else who worked at eGSI Super Atom Smasher installation, especially Dr. Hourdeau, to whom they had to be returned if he ever asked for them. He said he would tell him that he accidentally brought them home one night and kept forgetting them at his house. The cybernaut's body shape would be that of an anatomically correct humanoid, with the exception that TANG-0000 would have a bronze-colored dermis. He will be designed with a set of virtual organic traits, circulatory, muscular, digestive, neural, and epidermic, as well as those that are able to mimic human tissue, organs, nerves, and limbs. The body will be based entirely on virtual plasma. Base silicates will be used in the production of TANG-0000's circulatory system, his brain, as well as his neural membranes. Titanium and platinum are to be used in compounds conducive to high temperature, as well as necessary to pick up cosmic background frequencies for the missions that he will be designed for. It is the plasma that is to keep the organic from the virtual plasmodic. The proper mixture of the three: organic, virtual, and plasmodic, will enable TANG-0000 to travel through time in a virtually mapped space-time grid, the same grid that will enable the immersion of future virtualized material into the Book of History, Nature's Diary. It will be TANG-0000 and he will have more to report than I have had to during my recent voyages through the genomic continuum.

The Virtualized Historical Grid

The virtualized historical grid is the only other mapping of the underlying structure of history besides the one that is provided by Nature itself (in the case of Nature, there are not nearly as many landmarks to enable a traveler to know where she is and where to go). In many cases, the virtual grid coincides with the nature of space-time. The goal of the completed grid is for there to be a 100% coincidence, which unfortunately, there never could be. The grid at its final completion is built into Nature and the space-time fabric. It would allow TANG-0000 to eventually travel relatively from January 18th, 2012 to August 27th, 1691, or from August 27th, 1691 to March 28th, 1368 with minor statistical deviations from the actual event. This grid is the time traveler's interstate system. Once there, you could only pay for your item and leave; there is no loitering at the rest stop because a paradox is always possible and then you have to pay for much more than just a toll. What about going back to the times that precede information that any virtual history database (or any other database) might have recorded? Is it enough to try to gradually map in a direction, in reverse, until we have enough knowledge to go into the next phase of history? It may not be, but we have no other choices. Is it even enough that we might never know certain things for certain because of particular cataclysmic events that happened at some point that disrupted the cosmic background radiation enough to where we might not know what part of the Mesozoic we are in? I dread to think as though there are not enough chances to find out everything in an absolute sense, or to think that there are no more lives, as in a virtual game simulation. There are of course some events that are so well hidden that they need to be unmasked several times before they are truly revealed, all for the power of long distance learning. And for there to be multiple dimensions to history you need to add the virtual dimension, along with other dimensions such as intangible imagination itself. There is probably nothing equally important and intangible to the virtualized historical grid as imagination. The grid is as complex in design as high speed trains found globally from the 1960's, such as Shinkansen trains in Japan. It does not in any way diminish the need for the human element, for togetherness. The grid is our guide, but love is our guiding principle, a love of the necessity to know and a love of the science that is who we are and who we can be. Is it enough that we are doing it for everybody that it can benefit today from the day of its inception, in a way that it gives hope? It is not enough that it is a product of egalitarianism, a product of merits that belong to every one of us, from the work of me, Petra, and Georges, to the work of the salmon fishermen somewhere near the North Pole? I never quite posed the question to Petra and Georges that way. So far I have assumed they know where I am coming from and why I am positing myself a certain way. Asteroid NT9 gives us all the reason to change gears and kick into action.

Pre - Homo Sapiens Time Travel

How would humankind ever summon the ingenuity and prerequisites necessary to travel back to an era before Homo Sapiens ever walked the earth and started the first hunters and gatherers society? Is this more of a congruent, comprehensive mapping process, or is it something more metaphysical that would require that we first transcend ourselves? What would be there to transcend if we are no longer, in a sense of feeling and perceiving, human? We could no longer at that point rely on the Virtual Genomic enigma, we would rely solely on cosmic radiation and other variables to map points in space that belonged not to us. We would need the use of cybernauts that only have certain types of alloys in their compositions. We could rely on the totality of mapped history to help us improve and continue the mapping of the process that is the amniotic evolutionary past that led up to the dinosaurs, peoples, wars, gardens, interstate roads, and so on. If you think this might be going in the realm of the absurdly impossible, then keep in mind that we have the bones and numerous fossil samples to prove what we are putting on the line. It is not just a series of scientific reputations, it is a continuity of experience and evidences that we are not only based on, but our concept of progress is also based upon. It is possible to remove oneself from certain realms of thinking and safely open certain types of Pandora Boxes that offer us solutions to questions that have boggled the mind for centuries.

Phase two – individual phases of the Cybernaut

With virtual plasmodic being created by Petra Stravinova, and bionic limbs and movement to be created by Georges Pouchet, I had to focus on the rough draft of the universal genetic code in terms of my specialization in quantum relativity. I was not focusing on my virtual DNA file at this point. I was focusing on gene splicing that would involve DNA sequences from Petra and Georges, as well as my own. I was creating a recombinant file in virtual mode that contained proportionate ratios of our individual DNA sequences in such a way as to reduce security risks and allow the cybernaut to travel in directions none of the three of us could ever take as separate Virtual Genomic enigmas. Georges had changed his mind from before about using his DNA and was allowing the proportion of his DNA to the overall sample to be a smaller one, more or less 10%. The cybernaut would have the best of all three worlds, with the limitations of no more than one at any given time. With Georges sub-phase to be the first of this second phase, Petra and I focused our attentions to our individual tasks in order to have all three sub-phases ready for the commencement of the second phase. Petra shared an office space at eGSI with another engineer who had a biochemistry lab in her office. Measuring the proportions of 1.02589P of combined nucleotidic DNA in a mixture of 50% virtual plasma, 25% ionized matter, 20% mixed alloys, and 5% anti- matter, Petra was able to carefully craft together the necessary "soup- like" ingredients of the virtual plasmodic liquid that was necessary to create the organic and "non-organic" portions of the cybernaut's internal organs.

She is working diligently to bring about the transformation from this early crude stage of the cybernaut's awareness to the moment when he stands strong, ready not only to record, but to protect the data that he gathers along his way through the initial grid that I had almost accidentally discovered. I have to give her full credit to her for her effort as well as Georges for his part in this. Mr. Pouchet in constructing the bionic arms and limbs is taking extra precaution for the metals and alloys that go into those limbs from not being detectable by any other known environment. The alloys have to be just the right mix of nickel, steel, and titanium. The alloys have precisely the correct conductivity index for the electrical impulses to give it life, to give it mobility, intelligence, an integral safety net, as well as all of the epidermic feeling that metal alloys have to offer in the sense of bionics and biometrics. The ratio of the customizable DNA virtual file would have to change from 50:25:25 to 33.33:33.33:33.34 to 50:40:10 to something that indicates a mutating recombinant DNA file in virtual format. In addition, there were a few scientists whose inputs we gathered and consulted with on several occasions. even though all aspects of bionics, biometrics, and cybernetics are not entirely our specializations, those scientists sheer existence was focused around those occupations and were willing to tell us, in some particular cases, their opinions when something precisely wouldn't work. One of them, Shevo Oneid, told us that he didn't think the alloys composition in the limbs was the type necessary for the quantum mechanics or the type of work involving space-time travel. Upon hearing of this, Georges tried further compositions that he had not mixed before and discovered that Dr. Oneid had been right on target. The August 25th deadline was coming up. Petra has planned, devised, and created organs such as a di-lithium heart chamber that has twice as many chambers as regular heart. The cybernaut is also anatomically correct. The di-lithium charger could be made into a virtual one in order to power the heart of this being. I was almost on target with my sub-phase of phase II and, in addition to completing my personal and professional journals, had found the sequences of fixed and recombinant DNA in virtual format that would work within the complex of TANG-0000. This effort was going to be remembered in history as one of the fastest in building a unique cybernetic traveler and as one that would save the world as we know it.

Integration Phase

We have now reached the phase where all of our work needs to be integrated together to create a rough draft of TANG-0000. We briefed each other on our individual progress levels and found that we were just about there. The date is December 11st, 2011. Petra has regulated the functioning of the di-lithium heart and integrated the functioning of the future organs of TANG-000.

When I look at her, I see someone whom I want to be the mother of my children. She is lovely and brilliant. I am proud to have her on this team as part of an initiative to save the earth from impending doom. Georges is coming along himself. He has found the perfect alloy composition and has been tinkering with the limbs of TANG-0000 for the last 3 weeks in order to perfect the movement of the limbs. All nervous system co-ordinates are functioning properly and movement is uniform, steady and strong. My part has been in some ways trickier, although not unmanageable. It is now time to integrate the combined DNA into this cybernetic traveler and allow it two weeks to become TANG-0000, the cybernetic Virtual Genomic enigma. The day is December 15th. We are all a day early in our estimations and have found a way to combine the outputs of our labors and to commence phase III of our project. The organs and circulatory systems are in place. The heart is ticking and the power crystal is charged. The DNA samples have re- established themselves into lasting sequences that will recombine into something random and necessary in order for virtualizations to take place.

These initial travels will establish the virtual historical grid that is necessary for ample auxiliary information to be collected. There are no promises that neither I nor my colleagues can make at this point, particularly since most people do not know what we are doing with our spare time. It has been very trying and exhausting at times, but it is worth every second of it to me. Petra understands my passion for this endeavor and for trying to be the Good Samaritan that my parents have frequently told me does not pay the mortgage or otherwise help in my daily life. I have understood their points well growing up and have not rejected them. Once in a while, I completely concede to this notion of helping others indefinitely. At this point in our history, I have to keep a keen eye on the world around me and the world from beyond and take what my parents have to say with a grain of salt. I've had to try and I am making the most honest and prudent attempt I have ever made in order to help save the world from the tomorrow that never arrives. It has to arrive because we will not be there to greet the next day if it doesn't. It is not as if, on a few occasions, I haven't considered the work of the past several months as endless hours to no avail since I often consider the conclusion that TANG-0000 will save the world a very risky proposal. I am not denigrating the hard and dedicated efforts of Petra, Georges, and others. We saw the opportunity to help and we are taking control of this situation in which many lives could be extinguished and many more could be stuck in bunkers around the world for a very long time. We are taking a chance to change the world, or to "retain the change" from our spot in the space-time grid, from the spot in history where we stand. In a sense, we have a train to "catch". On today's date, December 24th, 2011, we have created perfection as it was supposed to emerge from our efforts as believers and as good Samaritans. As scientists, we do not have a fiduciary duty to humanity. We have the right to attempt what has never quite been attempted before for a humanitarian and self- preserving cause. It does not have to be the end; in fact, this could very well be the countdown to a "new beginning", the beginning of something so progressive that it nurtures that which is good and came before it. The world needs continuity, as well as positivism in lessons from the past. Human progress need not be a bloody spot on the existence of Homo Sapiens. evolution still continues in the eyes of history and it continues in a way that leftover remnants have to either be taken along with it, or discarded as something that does not belong in its relative time. History has seemingly been unmerciful, but it did not have to be that way. History has been discharging, but it did not have to be that way. When progress takes a detour in such a direction for a long time in relative human progress, decades or centuries, it does not have to be ever-accumulating or progress for the good of humanity.

In fact, as has happened before, this progress is tainted. Progress is tainted by not mere disagreement or conflict, but by conflict that is not unresolvable at the time. The parties simply cannot reconcile their differences in a way that would be amenable to each other. It is all part of a hard struck progress that Georges, Petra, and I, as well as many others, have been so determined to unravel in a history that cares so dearly about its brothers and sisters, yet neglects the children underneath; the history that could one day be the unraveling of our own existence because of gross negligence and the unwillingness to compromise what should be, where it should be, and how should it be first. Now comes the final phase of the finalized project of creating the virtual time traveling cybernaut TANG-0000.

Online and Completion Phase

This concludes our project of designing, constructing, testing and evaluating TANG-0000, which has been approved on January 14th, 2012. I have made the final splicing tests and have determined that, based on my peers' recommendations, that the total design and construction is a complete success. Our cybernaut is ready for its trial run. He is anatomically correct, talking as a teenager, as strong as a young man in his prime, but is as mature as seasoned politician. He is looking forward to standing on the podium that was assigned to Petra, in this case, his surrogate mother when she met one of his surrogate fathers, myself. He is glad that he has two fathers in that it has its advantages. Convincing the leadership of eGSI to employ the main ray of Super Atom Smasher with respect to TANG-0000 will definitely be a formidable task in itself considering that I had to sneak onto mainstay checkpoint #56 in order to pulverize myself, in order to virtualize into the space-time continuum. I have a feeling that Dr. Hourdeau will not be receptive, but can nevertheless be convinced. I was able to convince him by sending messages from our past that I was still alive and that he wasn't the victim of a prank. I have decided to approach him alone and to request use of the collider for a certain day, perhaps January 20th, 2012. If my bargaining skills are up to the task and I am successful, we will have a method of tracking TANG-0000 in a way that is commendable to the amount of hours as well as final value that we have respectively put into this project, between mostly the three of us. After having reluctantly given the permission, I told Dr. Hourdeau that he would not regret this decision. On the morning of January 21th, we were approved for three and a half hours on the collider installation #62, which wasn't the original mainstay checkpoint that I virtualized from, but what could I expect? Petra, Georges, and I made the mainframe inaccessible for ten minutes during the countdown before the cybernetic virtualization after all the checkpoints within two mainframes away in either direction had been disabled and temporarily locked. We held hands with Georges as we watched the countdown to either the de-materialization of our efforts or the beginning of a new era in scientific research. We knew that there were other ways of dealing with the threat of an apocalypse in the middle of next year. It was not about drinking and celebrating the life and livelihoods that we already have had. It was to find a way to retain it, the love, the friendships, the limited control over our own destinies that we and the rest of humankind had had up until now. The countdown arrived at 4:43:58 at 7:35 p.m. A bright light shown in the direction of our project from a camera crew, belonging to a news agency that did not seem to belong anywhere in our installation. Dr. Hourdeau came in around them and apologized, saying that they had gotten wind of what was going on and could not be stopped by him alone. The countdown was at 4:01:02. One of the reporters came up to me and asked if I was Mr. Marinkovich. I nodded. He asked if I had any comment on the incident of March 6th of last year. I told him I had attempted to conduct an experiment that did not work out and had been sent home on suspension, but with pay. The reporter himself nodded, but did not quite believe me. I explained what we were doing and that we were not necessarily pursuing the Holy Grail of Physics. We wanted to see if we could send a cybernetic installation of our own into a tangible previous space-time and to track it. I explained that it was a side project with the permission of eGSI. He wished the three of us luck and asked if they could tape a segment for their evening news. I looked to Dr. Hourdeau, who nodded but had to ask that they limit it to thirty seconds or less. By this time, I told them to cover their eyes with any sunglasses or other protection available. There is less than 30 seconds left on the countdown clock. I also advised them to stay within 20 feet of the event.

We are now at T minus 9 seconds, 8,7,6,5,4,3,2, one, 0.5, 0.4, 0.3, 0.2, 0.1; we have virtualization and de-moleculization! In a split-second, for as long as the ten or more minutes that TANG-0000 stood on the platform, he was gone. He had vanished in the same way as I had, which I will be carefully noting in my journal. everything that went into him was recorded in that journal, as well as my personal journal. everything that occurred from the last 30 seconds of the countdown, including the de-virtualization itself, was recorded on live podcast, live camera feed and shown on the local Parisian news the following evening. What we had accomplished was not immediately known. TANG-0000 was equipped with much more than just the things I had available to me when I was jumping: he has a virtual host health database, a zero-based (real) history virtual database, chronological World Wide Web access in level IV format, virtual sampling and collections database, real-time cosmic radiation based e-mailing, as well as an urgent alert database. We are already synchronizing with him in relative space-time and from within the Virtual Bubble. We have put too much work into him to allow him to fail in this fact gathering mission, the mission that may help avert the path of NT9. We have synchronized at a level of 35.56% as I am writing this passage and we are to be in constant touch with beacon frequency wireless signaling. He is more resistant to the reversal of the thermodynamic arrow of time than I ever was; of course, I did not have a choice. We will be constantly monitoring the creation that we have brought into this world not as a protector, but as a being that could highlight the errors of history.

Tracking Tan G-0000

The first transmission from TANG-0000 came at 12:01 a.m. on January 22nd, 2012 while Petra and I were in bed holding each other. She kissed me and arose to see what it was. She shrieked when she realized that it was our guy. We had been synchronized at 100% for over an hour now (from 10:35 p.m. on). The information that we had was promising. TANG- 0000 has landed in Budapest and virtualized in at 8:01 a.m. on June 11th, 1981 in the middle of the Hungarian Symposium on Thermal Analysis that was held in Hungary. It appeared that he was only going to be there for a matter of minutes in real time, but he was collecting everything that we needed from that particular symposium in the virtual sampling and collections database for future use. He was mildly excited since we had programmed him with knowledge of contemporary sciences, but he was not even mildly amused when he first had to co-exist with one of the scientists there at the symposium. Their co- existence factor was 1:1.0000000000019; the man apparently started to perspire and become anxious enough to leave for about 10 minutes. Luckily, due to the recombinant DNA sequences mixing, he was able to adjust the setting to a more comfortable level for the scientist to return. The scientist's name is Ambrus Keresztes and his vital signs are normal now, according to our readings from 2012: his blood pressure is normal, blood sugar slightly elevated, his pulse rate is normal, while his temperature is 99.1 degrees Fahrenheit. Within a few minutes, history flowed as it always has and TANG-0000 had left the body of the scientist in a different direction, to the Belgian city of Mechelen, where he has virtualized into a young barkeeper by the name of Adelgonde Schulz on February 16th, 1983, who is scrubbing her counters in preparation for the busy day ahead of her. Ms. Schulz has suddenly received a jolt of energy, a second wind per say, and has decided to sweep the bar's flooring one last time. She is also murmuring to herself that she has to check the functionality of the alarm system that her boss has purchased rather recently. It is raining in this city and at the time of his virtualization, TANG-0000 has discovered some of his human characteristics and traits. He is part metallic, but is still vulnerable. His vulnerability stems from his humanity and the depressive sighs of Adelgonde are what bring out this mortality at this very time. What he does know is that his predetermined life, his cybernetic parts, has longevity of 300 years. He is not a product even if he is an invention. He is not meant to feel this way. His human side is well aware of the cataclysmic proportions of the asteroid that humanity is expecting the year following his manufacture. He is human in a sense and has an understanding of himself and others. He has few other socializing skills. He does not challenge this mission in the least and his assessment of his probability of failure is that it is statistically slim. He feels almost human while residing inside of a woman who is experiencing a case of the blues on Ash Wednesday, thinking of her former boyfriend who is Catholic. She is very beautiful and has been left alone on this lonely evening to opine after she broke up with him last Thursday. TANG-0000 can relate only because he has some superficial concept of what love is. We can almost relate to this person even from when and where we are in this. Petra is so anxious about this experiment that she has finally picked up a cigarette after having not smoked in almost eight months. I caressed her to assure her that everything is alright and continue to analyze the data that has come in from the scientist by the name of Keresztes. The symposium on Thermal Analysis yielded much information that we desperately need in order to compile a comprehensive database of past knowledge and references that would serve a significant purpose in identifying ways to evade or destroy the asteroid. It has made it very difficult for me to sleep for the past few weeks since I have known about this asteroid threat and have taken it upon myself to do everything in my individually limited posture to stop the threat from materializing. I ask Petra if she is OK and she looks stunned. "Of course I am happy Alen. I just want for him to succeed. I am his surrogate mother in a sense and I have never been a biological mother. I wonder if we had any plans for the real thing." I was a bit taken aback. "There is nothing I would want more in this entire world than to be a father with the exception of seeing that this child of ours has a place to grow up in. Currently, our world is in danger and we must do what we can to make it relatively safer. I would love nothing more than to have a child, but now might not be the time." She smiled and agreed. We crawled in bed and slept for a few more hours until 6:30 a.m. when it was time to get up and face the realities of the world again. The main reality had to do with both of us having professional careers and both of us being in love with one another and being engaged to be married. The disparity was getting to be easier to handle because our work environment was more lenient than any workplace I had ever known toward couples. We were not being mocked for our efforts with TANG-0000 in mapping the virtual historical grid because some of our co-workers such Pamela and Jon, who are Americans, had similar ideas but never followed through on procuring the necessary materials and space at the laboratories of eGSI. They have found perfection, though, in their daily routines and are some of the most efficacious people with whom I have worked. A mere fifteen minutes later we received another message that he had jumped again, this time into a Roman Catholic bishop in Trieste, Italy on November 4th, 1975 as he was delivering an evening Mass to the local residents of the south District of this city. As we tracked we discovered that the timed virtualization was to last only three minutes, which was just before the breaking of the eucharist was to take place. He de- virtualized. The bishop appeared incrementally stunned, yet recovered in time for the very act of Communion itself. The Mass went on as usual all while TANG-0000 shifted into a young woman from Madrid,

Spain by the name of Felicia Ortiz on the day of September 12th, 1979 in the middle of the midafternoon Siesta between 3:05 p.m. and 3:07 p.m. Her temperature was 98.7 degrees Fahrenheit, her blood pressure 120/80, her pulse rate normal, with a normal rate of blood sugar. She was vivacious, pretty and spunky, with dark hair, a gorgeous face and a glossy smile that brought happiness to the world. She was also hosting TANG-0000 for the next day or so. She was a political science major at Madrid Universidad. He was definitely becoming more of a product of Petra's, more so than that of my own or Georges. If he had sexuality, it was becoming clearer by the moment that he was bisexual. It was also becoming clear that he was also heterosexual when hosted by a generic alpha male. What was to become of the newly found information was still somewhat of a mystery in terms of quantum physics, biochemistry, or genetics, but I believe the tangents upon which TANG actually moved were those that were close enough in relative terms to propel him to a certain point in human history where information could be verified, and then obtained and verified, if necessary. As we track TANG, we perceive the graceful thermal images of Felicia as she moves through the market, while he is attempting to try certain foods in exerting his will over her in a metaphysical manner.

Quantum Virtualization into Portugal

After having spent one day and a half in Spain, TANG-0000 de-virtualized out of Felicia and re-virtualized into a sheep herder named Rafael who in his time lives near Lisbon in the year 1891, on August 17th, at high noon. Our tracking indicated that TANG-0000 was completely at peace for a few seconds in this environment with the exception that he did not worry much for the first few minutes about gathering anything scientific or epistemological. His updated virtual history database accomplished this task for him. He has found his humanity but he is still finding his reason to protect humanity with himself included with the zest that I have. He is still an invention of mine, as well as that of Petra and Georges. He is happy for now. I now know that these types of virtualizations have served in my case not to lose focus of things that are of the utmost importance in life while enjoying my travels in space-time. I did not have his attention span because I am definitely not cybernetic. We are not allowed to send any stimulating messages or e-mails to TANG-0000 unless we see it fit because of the negative influences and potential paradoxes that we might cause and bring along with them. He is taking samples of the warm Portuguese air, the level of dry spells, the humidity, the ionization readings, as well as other meteorological conditions that are later to be updated to the global virtual sampling and collections database. In the meantime, he tends to the sheep as Rafael and wishes that the weather would remain as beautiful as it has been for the past eight weeks. His wife is at home cooking supper and tending to his five children (Pedro, Fernando, Isabella, Maria, & Mateo); she is cooking tripe and vegetables with carrots, cauliflower, and rice. This information was obtainable to us through reading the mind of TANG-0000, as well as through his actions as Rafael.

He is absorbing the literature on Portuguese culture from the 21st century and making the comparison between this data and the immediate readings from Lisbon. His readings in this time are weaker now because, after supper, Rafael and his wife are telling their children tales of monsters and tales of ghosts from the past and about God himself, as well as Portuguese legends of old. Rafael tells his older son about the young herdsmen who once killed a two-headed monster in Scotland and was never heard from before. Years later, his ghost still wanders the village from where he left and was never seen again until 1848. The vital sign readings coming from Rafael are normal; he is very tired because of having herded his sheep today and is starting to fall asleep in his chair. He has a relatively long day tomorrow and wishes to be well rested and not inundated with sleepiness that results from tending to his other flock. He loves his wife Isabella very much and he loves his children more than anything. These are feelings that TANG-0000 cannot relate to even on a superficial level so he comforts himself with the readings of the ages of a few trees from around his home, as well as carbon dating the soil around the house of Rafael. He then analyzes and confirms his analysis of the native birds in the updated virtual version of encyclopedia Britannica, with respect that a few of these species of birds are native to england, and not Portugal. As he pats the children on the heads to tell them how much he loves them, TANG tells them individually that tomorrow will always be a better day if they are having a rough day today. He also tells them that he has named all of the sheep and that his favorite sheep have the same names as Pedro & Fernando and that he loves them the best because they remind him so much of his sons. Mateo is a beautiful young boy who was found roaming the village side a few years ago until Rafael and Isabella decided to adopt him.

He fits in very nicely into Rafael's family, but he still speaks a type of Slavic language from a country that has yet to be recognized by europe itself as today's Slovenia. He is a silent, but a sturdy boy who helps his step dad with various chores around the sheep. He rarely cries and occasionally says the word "Jahnacie", but he is not like his step-brothers. He is more aggressive than they are in part because he has to be. He acts lovingly with his step- mother and loving with his step-brothers, showing an artistic side of himself whenever he is around his step-dad. The girls, Isabella & Maria, love their step-brother and frequently try to get him to play with dolls. He has one time and TANG-0000 found him. TANG-0000 is getting ready to depart because of a threat from an internal paradox that has arisen from our cybernaut having feelings like a father for the first time. He is de-virtualizing slowly, almost regretting having to leave. He is happy at the apparent experience that he has gained with children of another time and, generally speaking, living with children. He marks it down in his personal log. He has vanished and, while his particles virtually stream in another direction, a part of him is sorry that he cannot be human in the full sense to be able to experience more from life in the coming year.

A Linguistic Virtualization

It is July 24th, 1884. The day is Thursday and the time is 9:45 in the evening in the city of Titel in the province of Vojvodina. This province is actually a part of the existing Austro-Hungarian empire (part of the Republic of Serbia until more recently in today's time). TANG-0000 has virtualized into the body of Mileva Marich's older brother Jovan. His vital signs remain stable in that his blood sugar, body temperature, blood pressure, and pulse are normal during the transition between Rafael and Jovan. He is having a lovely time with his brother while they are drinking with their father, while Mileva Marich (who becomes Albert einstein's first wife on January 6th, 1903), is busy playing with her dolls and reading a medical textbook which she picked up after her father had left the room. TANG-0000 is telling his "sister" not to read books that are not meant for anyone but adults. She does not wish to listen to him, but she caves in and hands the book over. She is overwhelmed by something she has read aloud by about anesthesiology and is considering studying medicine when she is old enough to go to college. She knows according to what she is telling her brother Jovan through TANG-0000 that this is something she wishes to pursue and wants to finish because it will make her parents blush with pride. She leaves her brother there and walks out of the room in part because she is angry and in part because she feels it is a moot point to further discuss to have an intellectual conversation with him at this point. TANG-0000 attempts to understand the interaction, but senses that his host Jovan is experiencing some mild convulsions due to the event, although his blood pressure and pulse readings are normal. Within a few seconds, TANG-0000 de-virtualizes from a young man whose sister becomes the first wife of the famous scientist who gave us special relativity and general relativity to another human being that gave us something a bit more chilling. TANG-0000 has to go so as not to cause a linguistics paradox while inside of Mileva's brother the kind that Cyril & Methodius had not seen since the linguistic and cultural break up of Serbians and Croatians, centuries ago, in the Balkans.

Virtualized Cold Fusion

Next, TANG-0000 virtualizes into Ukrainian scientist Anatoly Zemenko on February 25th, 2009 in the city of Kiev. His temperature is evenly 99.0 degrees Fahrenheit. His pulse and his blood sugar are normal. His blood pressure reading is 124/82. He is not overweight and is in good health. Dr. Zemenko is a scientist that deals with the decade old technique of cold fusion. He is not aware of TANG-0000, but he is aware of the chill coming in through the air conditioning unit from the outside hallway and he gets up to turn it down a notch. Cold fusion was almost rejected as a failed technique in the late 1980's. Cold fusion itself refers to the nuclear fusion of atoms at conditions close to room temperature, in contrast to the conditions of well understood fusion reactions such as those inside stars and high energy experiments. Cold fusion experimenters reported finding small amounts of nuclear reaction byproducts, including neutrons and tritium. Interest in the field was dramatically increased by Martin Fleishmann. Dr. Zemenko is a leader in this field and TANG-0000 could not have come at a better moment. TANG has turned his virtual collections and sampling database on its most sensitive settings and is recording the nuances between Dr. Zemenko's overall mood and his stability relative to his own thoughts and attitudes toward what he is doing at the moment with regards to a scientific paper that he is writing about the topic of cold fusion variability in amounts of byproducts with regards to incremental changes in room temperature. His paper consists of applied virtuality to the concept of incremental increases in cold fusion to produce the same amount of nuclear byproducts. The historical accuracy or the virtual historicity database has come on to indicate that there are certain inconsistencies with one of the last virtualizations, namely Rafael, one of them being the species of birds that were discovered by TANG-0000 while in Portugal, namely, one type of bird was of Portuguese origins after all. There is also inconclusive evidence after other temporal analysis has been conducted that the soil samples from around Rafael's house are that much different from Spain or France. everything else he has gathered, mostly from Jovan Marich, has been conclusively and historically accurate. Petra has been tracking for the past two days on and off as I am warding off a spell of depression, the kind which I have only had to ward off once before in my life when I was choosing my career path. She is patiently marking down the variations and changes and has called me only once to ask for my opinion on a particular issue regarding the synchronization process. While Dr. Zemenko is working on a particular detail, TANG-0000 has detected a slight health concern that justifies the activation of the virtual host health database. It comes to the attention of TANG that the doctor has the very beginnings of a small tumor in his left lung, in other words, the beginnings of lung cancer unless removed. TANG- 0000 is depressed because there was no logical way to remove it without causing a paradox or even to warn him of his health issue. He is a quiet person; at least I know his inventors think of him as a person and, in some combinations of his virtual DNA splice ratio, developmentally emotional and devotionally instrumental. This has much more to do, however, with the lack of nurture that we could not have given him in a matter of days through simply programming his neurological database with information on human nurture, by not raising him like a boy in a matter of several days of social engineering. He has emotions that are present and equivalent to the level of a twenty one year old man, the strength on a grown man (with a value added metallic power), with the composite IQ of 200 (proportionately from his surrogate fathers and a surrogate mother).

He had virtualization issues at times with the added ionization within his titanium parts. From all aspects, he was much more verse at this than I ever was. He has a personality and almost possesses a soul. He is my surrogate son. even if my future wife and I never have children, we will always have TANG-0000, and TANG will always have Georges Pouchet. He is now virtualized inside of the mind of an authority on cold fusion and has discovered past information (even from just a few years ago) about the host's health. He is truly depressed in a way that only I can track. TANG-0000 can't even inform the scientist of his future traumas. He starts to cry and Dr. Zemenko starts to wonder for a second on why he is shuddering, upon which he puts on a sweater on top of his thick cotton shirt. After he verifies for a split second that his virtual history database has covered all angles and practically transcribed the gist of what he is working on, he checks his host's health once more before he readies to de-virtualize again.

A Marriage in Space-time

Petra kissed me this morning and asked me an important question. She has been living with me for two weeks now after we made the joint decision that it would be more cost effective for us to live together after the personal funding we had put into TANG-0000 drained our savings. We will never regret it, no matter what happens. The question was where we wanted our wedding ceremony to be held. We never planned on staying engaged for a long time, but even though we don't regret the existence of TANG-0000, we have to be realistic with what we can afford from our two salaries. I told her we might have to stick to an itinerary in Italy or Germany, or even Switzerland since neither one of us had seen as much of Switzerland as we would have liked. I asked her about going to Russia. She told me that it sounds attractive, but she has never wanted to be in her native country for her honeymoon as a personal preference. What I wanted wasn't necessarily what she wanted, but I had long since realized that marriage can be a compromise. I wanted our honeymoon decision not to result from a compromise between a few locations that neither of us had our entire hearts invested into. I wanted this to be the best night of our lives. I couldn't wait to be one with her in the bond of matrimony. After we checked the daily news, I turned the browser onto the Scientific Journal's website in order to try to find new information about NT9; so far this week, there isn't anything new to ponder over in my anxious awaiting of news from TANG-0000's new virtualization. When there is some news, I usually have to sit down to run the variables of synergistic progress creation based on multiple virtualizations at the same time. I am not necessarily thinking of doing this again, but Petra has already said that she would gladly volunteer to manage two synchronizations, even though she might not be as glad to see me do this before our upcoming honeymoon. I have not made the decision because of my previous experience that could result in a network of virtualized genomic travelers. In fact, the timing could not be worse, for I am in line for a promotion at my job at the eGSI installation. I definitely have to check the sync between TANG-0000 and us every night (on our own cost) in order to verify that the process is going smoothly and veritably without safety issues. Safety issues are a huge concern at my place of employment. The fact that I have not lost my employment contract at the installation over my stunt last year does not concern me as much as my own negotiating power with the next promotion that might come along if I opt to request another "favor" from Dr. Hourdeau. When I started this project, I truly did not realize the financing and decision-making processes involved when it comes to subtracting a thousand here, but adding several thousand over there. It would not be advisable for me, or Petra, or Georges for that matter, to assume another thousand in debt even if it means saving the world from something more unpredictable or even otherwise unstoppable. It is probably best that I stay on this side of my parents' virtual ancestry line. It is best if I improve the network security of our project not only because I enjoy being the networking type, but because I am a natural technician. I told Petra later at work what I had been thinking of and she giggled. She said I was crazier than my mother and that she couldn't wait to meet her. She also said that she might want children one day to show them what their mother and father have built for them and the world. She would want to raise them as egalitarians. She always knew how to think of a higher cause and to make the case for it silently and vocally when she needed to. I truly love her and can barely wait to make her my wife. I grow with her daily and the funny thing is that we actually do have separate work lives for the most part and we each have a few friends that are intimately only ours. Life is not a fantasy however and we have to make practical choices and hard decisions. By the end of the next workday, we have decided that we will wait until New Year's eve to wed at the Sea View Wedding Chapel in Cote d' Azur in Southern France (it will cost a pretty penny). We will make it official at work next week and contact our friends via mass e-mailing the same day. I have already let my parents, who are now in Braddock, PA; know the date, location, and other itinerary. I am trying not to think much of the asteroid NT9, but it has crept up in my thoughts in the last few days. I do not wish for this wedding bliss or our coming years to be replete with thoughts of doom or apocalypse. When I asked Georges to be my best man and he replied positively, we couldn't help but to talk about work and other topics for a while. He too is afraid of the asteroid topic itself, let alone scrutinizing the possibilities of where NT9 might land. It is a time for fear, but I am not afraid. I have love, empathy, and companionship. I have a purpose in this world, however rebellious or even juvenile it may sound to some who still look for themselves. I am making myself part of the solution to help in redeeming humankind of its iniquitous errors for, if we go to war during this time, I want to be one of those to point out that war is wrong and that we do have a common enemy.

Historicity & Social Inequities

Would it work for the sake of argument that we rely on data that is hard to verify within a certain time period as having happened when we are already taking a risk of losing resources in the fight against a giant asteroid and working to stop terrorism at the same time? Would it be better if we had an alternative even if it made less sense but was more popular? I would be the first to listen and contend that TANG-0000 could be a maritime experiment meant to provide benevolent solutions and longer lasting solutions to problems that happen to intrude on global democracy. He is an ongoing experiment and will provide meaningful information as a scientific resource and a breakthrough, but the data would be hard to verify by a second person, a third person, or even an entire crew of physicists. Would it be best in the case of a global emergency to save as many people as possible in bunkers or in shelters in various geographic locations, or to choose a method that may save anyone from things that could not otherwise be stopped? I prefer my solution yet I know it has never been tested as 100% fully reliable. I could be doing other things with my time, art for instance. Historically, there is no branching of alternative paths that could produce a totally different earth or space-time from which there may only exist about 4 billion people or less on earth since the 1980's, five billion people since the 1990's after various regimes, as opposed to 6, 692,030,277 or more people since 2008. There are only chapters or excerpts from the past that are meaningful if there is an information component that could be used in some valuable way. In a continuous sense, all of it is of utmost significance and has to be taken as continuously relevant. Does history take human development seriously or is it a step-brother whose progress somehow got entangled with the seed of history as it was sown so many moons ago? Is it possible to create an identical virtual earth, as well as to virtualize the asteroid in such a manner so as to allow the asteroid to pass through our earth, the virtual earth, as if nothing cataclysmic happened? It could be possible and descriptive in a sense that we may never know what it will take to start that fire. Petra asked me once if I had a way to update myself (in the event that I ever virtually traveled again) or TANG-0000 to events that had happened in the present upon returning from past flows. I told her that I really did not since I had designed Virtual Genomic Time Travel as a self- updating process and that genetic equalization would bring about a self- update that would bring the traveler back to everything that is happening currently without any questions or confusion from the traveler himself. She is worried about TANG-0000, particularly since he has no outlet for this relatively new thing we call emotions. I told her that although he is of our DNA even though he was never meant to have the emotions for any other reason than to make judgment calls and, if he survived, that I would help him understand the need later for what he is doing now. He is currently on what could be the single most important mission of his life. There is a discrepancy and I will address it with him later. Currently, I would be out there, traveling virtually myself, if not for what it would do to Georges and Petra and the strain that it may cause on either of them at work or in their personal lives. I did not want to impose the responsibility for TANG-0000 on either of them, especially her. Petra knows I would never "suffocate" her with distance love or not let her have a personal life as a result of our marriage. She knows I am not the type to burden someone with a situation or a problem while I can still handle it myself in a given way. That way has to involve success in not deviating from a failure threshold, or not crossing the boundary of what my values tell me what is moral and what is immoral. She knows who I am not and who I am to her. TANG-0000 as a cybernetic being is as virtual as I was when I traveled through the past history in the form of a virtual enigma in the sense that

I would never truly be able to know those people once I had de- virtualized from their bodies. He knows that he is fulfilling a mission from which the world can survive and that he has and will have a purpose closer to his calling, but will never have the full independence because he has not only one creator, but co-creators in a sense that he was built. Petra, Georges and I own our respective DNA's in that we have patented our own before he was built; it was something that had to be done. We have co-ownership of him and, since we could never patent our own respective DNA sequences within him, we could never patent him either because of a moral choice and necessity, not because we do not have rights to him. He can never be patented in this case because the DNA itself cannot be patented within TANG as a life force, without the will of the DNA donors or without the will of an entity that is not considered human. He is a virtual and a cybernetic being yet human in many ways that are amenable to description. The information he gathers is what this world's safety is partly based upon; the secondary yet more important purpose is to know how to use any valuable information as data in necessary times. How we use this information determines the continuing course of human history as it occurs within this world and even this solar system. We may not agree on how to proceed, but this trait of humans has occurred in previous bouts between humankind and historicity. Historicity has won over the human emotional component that often fails to conceal certain details of its truth—the truth that we are digging for and searching for at this very hour. It is the truth that will liberate us and give us the capability to be networked with a brighter future.

The Solidification of Human Knowledge

Human knowledge since recorded times has always been diverse and widely spread among certain peoples, based often on iniquities and entire nations making sure that certain truths hold true to the most fundamental level. From these times on, there has been a certain progression that has allowed knowledge to become more universal and widespread to many different nations, or to arise independently, albeit not excluding certain nations who lack infrastructure, databases, workforces, and investments to make into the preceding three. Through Virtual Genomic Travel, this information can be collected, analyzed, and utilized in such a sense that it adds to the barriers that are set up to defend humankind from the types of disasters that it cannot only create itself, but come from elsewhere. We need to be who we are because of the fundamental meaning of existence. If life is not progression, then the obvious alternative is not destruction for the sake of starting over again. Humanity has historically started over so many times it seems like it is a corrupted copy of a software program that was never tested. I cannot find the next stumbling block if I allow myself be submitted to Virtual Genomic enigma Travel in order to provide a helping hand to TANG-0000. There may need to be more models of TANG made if we really wish to speed up the process of collecting, analyzing, and utilizing the vast oceans of information that are embedded into the pages of what I have dubbed Nature's Diary. For now, TANG-0000 is one of a kind. We have barely over a year remaining until the asteroid arrives and lands in a probable number of places that we simply do not have the technology to yet predict. As our fates our sealed, I have a sense of pride in what I have done and what I am tempted to do even more so with every passing day. I will not do it for Petra alone. I do not wish to unleash a chain of events that makes me late for my own wedding day. I am a fallible human being and I know how much more infallibility it would make TANG-0000 to perceive himself to be. He is not a full machine and I worry about the part of him that contains our humanity. I know he truly cannot grasp the concept of life and the progression that leads to the prevention of even the slightest incursion upon a given species. He is programmed with his objectives and within these objectives he finds his reasons. Within his reasons, he finds his own humanity. He does not have the capacity for faith. He has the capacity for belief in a task better accomplished. We did not focus on any perfection when it came to TANG-0000; we focused on standards such as ISO 9000 as much as was allowed by our budget.

Currently, TANG has virtualized into another scientist and engineer from France by the name of Alphonse Levreau in the year 1988. It appears that he is a chemical engineer by trade who has studied rocket propulsion systems at eSA as well as NASA. As he virtualized into him, TANG made extra certain that his vital signs were cleared because the gentleman has had some health issues, something that TANG-0000 picked up upon first materializing. It turns out that Dr. Levreau is fine for right now. Sampling and sample collections gathered from this host showed valuable information that could have been used in previous missions with previous hosts. The propulsion information that has to do with NASA is what TANG is sifting through and methodically discarding because he is looking for something specific (propulsion tables from NASA are being kept in the virtual history cache as evidence of this trip), something that could be used to design and construct a better propulsion system for Virtual Genomic Travel. His time is almost up with this host as he periodically measures Dr. Levreau's blood pressure and pulse. He de-virtualizes as he awaits his next instructions.

Bioethics Committee Visits Super Atom Smasher

I received an emergency call early this morning, February 14th, on my cell phone by Dr. Hourdeau's senior manager. He asked me to come to work two hours in lieu of my shift to discuss something of a personal nature. I did not know immediately what it was about, but I had a good feeling I would figure it out on my way to work. The truth is this: I had never really met the top management at eGSI and I never meant to rub elbows too many times with one of them because they were not considered part of my division. I am always courteous to managers who clearly wear a secondary ID badge and I always give them the time of day. This was unusual to me and I wondered if I had done something wrong on the premises of eGSI or since I had returned from the first de-virtualization. I met with Pierre Chevalier at 6:30 this morning to find out what the problem was. He was not pleased when I walked into his office. It turned out that the media should have never recorded what it did the day that TANG-0000 de-virtualized. In fact, as intriguing as TANG-0000 was to the American Journal of Science, it was not that intriguing to other groups of people and entities. He said that there is a journalist working for the Paris News Daily who knew about the genetic splicing that had gone on in Georges' house when TANG was being designed and built and had interviewed his mother for a few minutes. Someone had linked this information to George and I, but not Petra. The entity that did not know about it yet, but could soon find out was the european Union's Bioethics Committee. That same top management would not be resting easily if that happened. I had been warned and Mr. Chevalier had been served with a warning too. He specifically wishes for me to tell Petra and Georges. Georges was visibly upset. He knew his mother was a bit older and becoming senile. There was nothing more conclusive that we could think of except to keep it under the table as long as we can. We could potentially lose TANG- 0000 and this is the last thing that we could afford to do after having invested as much money as we had. The fact that an employee of eGSI was conducting private experiments with genetic splicing and in the same time period has access to the types of technologies and equipment at the installation which is Super Atom Smasher would be unacceptable to a committee which promotes and ensures bioethical practices. This could potentially have an adverse effect on eGSI's ability to attract future private investors. All in all, it would be a situation because of which I might have to leave and start a new life over because my contract with eGSI would be terminated. I saw Petra an hour later and told her what was happening. She shuddered as she heard the words that were coming out of my mouth. She looked at me with tears in her blue eyes and begged me not to tell the bioethicists anything about the sacrifice that we have made. She suggested that we say if asked that we had a side project that was complete. I replied that I was not going to withdraw TANG-0000 from his virtual travels even if my job was on the line. She smiled at this, saying that we would still have at least one income since she wasn't implicated in anything that might happen. She knew that some of the passion in our relationship hinged upon project TANG-0000. We would keep him in our virtual past for as long as we could. TANG gave our relationship an element of surprise. I had to brace myself for what came next from Petra's lips. That morning I found out I was a father-to- be. I found out that Petra had not taken her birth control pill for a matter of weeks and we had been together since then. My wife-to-be wasted no time in telling me that she had wanted a child for some time. She wanted to be a mother and thought that she was well prepared to be doing the dual role of a mother and a physicist at the same time. We had to devise a plan for the next ten months and set the date of our wedding in stone. We had to be even more discrete about what had transpired at Georges' house with his mother.

We also had to sift through information that has been saved and compiled within a master virtual history database. In addition, our work lives at eGSI Super Atom Smasher could not suffer as a result of this stress. He has to simply act effectively but be mindful of any health crises that Petra might have. I wanted a healthy baby boy or girl to be a member of this family. Petra is my family and one of the reasons I have to look forward to the day when I wake up in the morning. As the days go by, I remember snippets of activity and levels of consciousness that, when I was virtually embedded in the daily routines of people like Alexandru, Ricardo, cause me to remember details that make me wish that at least my brain had not been made virtual for periods of time during my virtualizations. Later in the day, while on my lunch break, I checked the synchronization point of TANG-0000. It is at 54.5%. He has virtualized into the body of scientist enrico Fermi's lab assistant Angela Girard on May 24th, 1948. As he attempts to run the virtual host health sequence program within her, she lets out a shrill shriek as if something has taken a hold of her. He waits a few seconds for his host to calm down. As she passes out, she is administered smelling salts that revive her within a few seconds. She calms down and exclaims that she feels better. Her pulse is now back to normal, her blood pressure is 120/81. Her other vital signs, including blood sugar, are normalized. She suffers from diabetes type II and sometimes has low blood sugar. As she bites into a Granny Smith apple, she is telling Dr. Fermi something about the last part of the last equation on his board. He notices and corrects his hastily made mistake. It was a factor of 16x, and not 256x. TANG turns on the virtual history database and switches it to its most sensitive level once more. He knows that Dr. Fermi contributed much to the development of nuclear and particle physics in the 1930's and that the information that he gathers about him will be used directly in stopping the deadly asteroid. He also knows that he was awarded the Nobel Prize for his work in induced radioactivity. The information is directly related to kaon decay and the ionization of metal in certain types of environments when building nuclear reactors. The situation in which this is occurring in is rather dire, but TANG-0000 is more mature at this stage in the game. He will get what we need and think about the consequences often when he is far away. He seems so far away from the truth, yet closer than humanely imaginable.

Economic Crises of the past and present

The recession of 1937 was called Franklin Roosevelt's recession. It was a different type of recession that what we are experiencing in the latter part of the first decade of the 21st century. It was a temporary reversal of the pre-war 1933 to 1941 economic recovery from the Great Depression in the United States. The reasons given for this downturn differ from one school of economic thought to the next. What it appeared TANG-0000 was headed for was the swinging 1930's, the era of illegal boozing and street wars among illegal immigrants and legal players. The date was November 8th, 1937; the time was 8:56 p.m. TANG-0000 was set to virtualize into a mobster leader in the city of Chicago who had been collecting alcohol revenues under the table and had not seemed to care how it affected his own neighborhood. He knew that he had to account for what he recorded and experienced here a bit differently. What he was experiencing was a slew of different emotions that he could not readily quantify. He was not a street villain, a crook, a concerned bar owner, a cop who was up to his neck in legal trouble, or an innocent child playing in the street. He was not Al Capone. He was a person who considered everything that he was doing morally justified and meant to create wealth and power, even though he was a criminal. He cherished his side of the story like last night's stale steak, as well as that expensive bottle of brandy that his grandson brought him on his way back home. He was in hiding from the police in an era when that usually meant losing one's life if discovered. He was a mobster during the Prohibition and he was running for his life. TANG-0000 tests his vital signs to be slightly abnormal due to his weight and the fact that he was a smoker. His pulse is elevated, his blood pressure is 134/81, his blood sugar is low, and his temperature is his sole normalizing factor (it turns out to be 98.9 degrees Fahrenheit based upon readings by the virtual host health database reader). TANG decides to test the architecture of this area of Pennsylvania as his host runs into an old abandoned warehouse while dodging the police. He has the cultures and mentalities of people to judge while he is inside of Peter Oakland (something he is not too proficient at) while he is observing other factors that the virtual history database is already picking up on). He doesn't know things that are as abstract as street culture. Luckily, he has a virtual history database and a chronological link to the World Wide Web. He has a wealth of knowledge on his hands and he is not afraid to use the technologies that are at his disposal. If anything, economic lessons that were never learned are being regurgitated now by the recording of past times and past flows. TANG-0000 courageously takes on his responsibility, his humanity being trapped by something he is not yet again. This is his social chronological position and he performs it well enough to fool space-time. In some ways, it is not the time to be this selective. It is time to be more selective and even TANG knows that he is a tool of his surrogate mother and surrogate fathers. He knows he is a tool of his cybernetic design as he gives this gangster a temporary boost into what could be the inevitable change in such a drastic differential that he needs in order to evade the police, with the vivid potential but no realistic chance of a paradox in virtual level IV. As the virtual history database scans for further evidence of historical discrepancies, it finds very few that would matter as much to our survival as a collective species. It finds police testimony records that differ by over three hours as to the time when they were taken. It finds reasons for broken traffic lights to remain broken due to budgetary issues at the Municipal Office of Chicago. It had missing records for certain people that the police had arrested and then immediately released. These police records were taken for some of the members of Mr. Oakland's racket and he knew that this had happened in an attempt by Chicago's District

Attorney to jail them all at the same time in the state of Illinois federal penitentiary. TANG-0000 checked his host's heath status and this time it was better than when he first virtualized. His pulse rate and insulin levels were normalized, with his blood pressure rate still elevated. He thought to himself that it should be easier to get out of this materialization because there did not seem too much else to record with the exception of atmospheric conditions. He didn't know how soon when a police officer approached from the opposite direction, ordering Peter Oakland to surrender. With all of his effort, TANG could not get Mr. Oakland to not reach for his gun holster. As the shots rang into Mr. Oakland's chest, the de-virtualization mechanism kicked in and the arrow of time altered TANG-0000 yet another time. He felt that the shots came a few minutes too late and that he could have warded off any harm by those very bullets. He had felt in a sense that he is invincible from the day he has walked and talked. Ultimately, even he knows that there are things that can harm his capacity to be indestructible.

The next stop on the fact collecting journey is near Moscow in August of 1928.

Fight or Flight

TANG-0000 virtualized on August 1st, 1928 at 8:08 p.m. into the body a Moscow mathematician by the name of Abram Dimitriev. He specializes in mathematical applications for the newly founded discipline within physics called quantum echanics. At this point in history, quantum mechanics is still newly minted and Albert einstein has just published his famous papers on unified field theory. The virtual history database has been scanning on a low frequency sensitivity for nuances that could reveal research that this gentlemen whom TANG-0000 was inhabiting was on the verge of discovering something sensational in the field of telemetry. His work had mostly to do with telescopes, in part, because the bulk of it deals with optometry. The Virtual History Database (VHD) was now set on 100% sensitivity, with a standard deviation of 0.005%. What he was discovering had to do with using the best possible resolution for a new telescope that the Russians were building in response to American research in erecting one into space. It is this type of competition that eventually leads to the building of superpowers in the east and West known as the Cold War, with the Soviet Union and its backing satellites on one side and the United States and its allies on the other. TANG-0000 knew not what conflict was and was conflicted by his very understanding of his discrepancy between human history and human progress. Our cybernetic traveler would be in other jams, but he had to understand a particular dialect of Russian that wasn't yet accounted for in the virtual linguistics database; he pulled it off quite well according to his own notes. TANG-0000 was getting to be an expert in gathering information from times beyond his own. He has begun to use more of his own vast computerized inference to calculate probabilities of where he will land next.

He can substitute entire manifestations of data in conversations with past personalities; he maintains conferences as an alpha leader should know how in any situation. He also has calculation capability beyond that of certain computers because he uses his human side to his advantage. While Dr. Dimitriev looks over his personal collection of telescopes, which serve as a great inspiration to his work, he senses a presence from within him that he cannot quite account for. TANG-0000 himself is aware of the looser co-relation of co-existence between this man and his own essence. The factor is 1:1.00000000000014, which means that the professor has more of a correlation toward Petra's side of TANG-0000's universal DNA sequence. This does not mean that the scientist can be cognitively aware of TANG-0000's existence. It just means that the odds that that probability is to occur have gone up tremendously with this particular host. After having collected the information that is necessary for further analysis, TANG-0000 awaits his next de-virtualization and de- moleculization. He is happier at this work than I ever was, although this does not preclude the possibility of even entering the newly minted space-time grid for myself. I am happy that he is finding his way around the virtual Multiverse as well as he has been.

Encounter with the Moral Authority

After I had been notified that I was being sought after by the Bioethics Committee, I was definitely at my wits end. There would be no understanding of what we have been doing here at the installation and outside of it at Georges' house. They had the power to pull the plug on TANG-0000, as well as to ruin any prospects of a normal career I have at eGSI Super Atom Smasher installation. They had the power to cause legal and other difficulties for myself, Petra Stravinova, as well as Georges Pouchet. I was about to try everything in my limited range of abilities to allow this not to happen. I also knew that there was no sense whatsoever in hiding. I contacted them and asked how I could help them. Aside from an alleged interest in what I was currently doing on the job, they inquired if I had a side project apart from my daily activities that generated revenue for me—revenue that could be taxable. I answered with a resounding no. I told them that my income at eGSI was enough to support myself and my future spouse if it ever became necessary. They persisted with some minor questions until they finally asked the unthinkable—did a recent side project of mine involve the use of genetic splicing methods that were questionable not only in France and Switzerland, but in europe as well. I had to answer that I had started a similar project in my spare time from my house, but have had to scrap it because of the cost- prohibitive nature of the project itself. I told them that it did not involve genetic splicing. They seemed to imply that I had stolen materials from the Super Atom Smasher installation in order to complete my projects. I told them that was not the case and that I was willing to co-operate with them or any other authorities to get this cleared up. I was not only thinking of my own career, I was trying to cover for Petra and Georges and their respective involvements.

They could have never gotten involved with something like this had it not been for me, at least not at this stage in their careers. They are talented and productive individuals and I did not want them to take even the slightest career fall because of my own extracurricular aspirations. I asked the committee representative if I had to meet with anyone in person. Her reply was that I did not for the time being. The involvement of genetic splicing was the main issue, it now seemed. I was going to have to regurgitate what I had done since the first week I started my employment contract with eGSI. I knew there was a chance they may even confiscate my equipment, the devices I used to communicate with TANG- 0000. TANG-0000 was a force to be reckoned with, yet even his historical role could come to an end if I chose not to co-operate with these authorities.

Universal Genetic Code

TANG-0000 had as close to a universal genetic code as I could have asked for in roaming around different times and different people. He did not have the ultimate universal code that I had been hoping to obtain one of these months through my research, the one that would enable configuration from an enigma state to any other configuration state of anyone who has ever lived. The discovery would be self-preserving and self-explanatory in that a Virtual Genomic enigma would be able to convert as needed his particles and end up in different points in the past. The discovery would have to happen as a result of exploring the virtual past in grid form. I knew that I could help save the world; I just did not know the exact means with which to enable this to happen. My endeavor was based on its fair share of assumptions. I had a ground-breaking idea and an excellent set of methodologies with which I commenced and maintained the process. The universal code is just that; it can adapt to the genetic code of anyone who has ever lived or lives in the past as long as the arrow of time flows in a certain direction. It can also adapt to intermediaries of Homo Sapiens, such as Homo erectus. This is the invention that people might remember me by, instead of the person who accidentally or almost accidentally blew himself up at the site of the Super Atom Smasher. Inside of the Virtual enigma, this type of protoplasmic DNA has infinite possibilities. It has other primary purposes such as enabling the cure of certain illnesses in human beings that have developed over the course of the centuries. It can tell us more about our own development and how we are linked to any phenomena such as the extinction of the dinosaurs or how we are linked to single-celled organisms. It may tell us more about the origins of life in past millennia and how we became the organisms that we are. That code is an rDNA code that serves as the communications network between our cells. It would communicate everything from what is happening to being the main communications mainframe in a time of Virtual Genomic Time Travel. Universal DNA, or perhaps rDNA, is something that is still out of reach to us, since the theories of how we historically relate to each other are not completely uniform. I had some explaining to do to the Bioethics Committee that had visited eGSI and communicated with me with regards to my side project, a project that had differed in scope from my technician's position. I had to eventually tell them that the DNA that was contributed to TANG-0000 came primarily from me, a relative nobody at the Super Atom Smasher. If my future wife and our colleague Pouchet decided to confess their involvement, it would be completely up to them. TANG-0000 had already linked more than a dozen other sites and relative points on the space- time continuum than I had in my three weeks while posing as a virtual genomic avatar. I did not know how I would be able to tell them and confess to my colleagues that it was out of a fear. I would lose my position for certain. I would not be able to continue tracking this cybernetic organism that we had all named after the tangents on the continuum that he had traversed in four-dimensional space. Petra knew and understood; she knew that I was protecting her as much as possible from the reach of these people who dictate the momentum of laws of ethics and moralities among scientists, as well as those that cross that world to other realms. I was not going to give up the love of Petra and my love of the scientific inquiry, having helped to design, build and equip TANG-0000 to find a solution that would help the world survive the already looming apocalypse.

History's Plagiarism

There are parts of early history has been a vast plagiarism, written by the dominant elite of the day, which has devastated lives, crushed hopes and dreams, as well as held the diary of Nature in its own esteem to be able to report history in a favorable way to this dominant class. There are parts of it that have contained half-truths, partial truths, and others that are more objective. The Virtual Genomic enigma (Grid) would have plenty of reviewing to do on an automatic basis if ever set up that way. It would be the auditor of history's half-truths and the reviewer of the truth in past history's inner womb. It would tell us what most of us have the right to know, as well as what we have the right to adequately and unconditionally change. Modern conflicts are many times contingent upon certain historical events being reported as such. The bulk of people, with respect to history, simply wish to know when it will be better so that they can get a taste of prosperity and democracy at work. Knowing historical truths is a prerequisite in having successful democracies. If we didn't have a way to ever find out, we would continue to heal the outer symptoms of all social diseases and debilitating conditions. Modern prosperities are there to hide the atrocities that may have been committed elsewhere and cover up that which is righteous and that which is historically and epistemologically true. I have often wondered what the true symptoms are of past historical societies, along with the respective developments of feudalism, industrialism, imperialism, colonialism, socialism, communism, and democracy. I have wondered if democracies have what it takes to take the world all the way in the direction of new global world orders. Societies, after all, are dynamic. There will be uproars over these words and whether or not they have any merits. My premise holds true and steady. I do not think that today's societies are just even in the face of modernity and modern technologies; it is necessary for me and for people such as myself to explore the past with a grain of salt. It is not always the dominant party, the party with the winning bid, whose stances are reflected in the historical perspectives that we have grown up with. Today's global news media is something that has a chance to turn fallible opinions around and must influence the differences between the concepts of just and unjust. It gives us these things somewhat based on their own net asset value. Would the real historical truth be something so horrific to bear? Would it be more than this Internet-savvy, interactive, gadget-wielding generation could handle? It might, depending upon whom we contact to ask in a survey or randomly show what actually happened if it were happening in real-time. Anything that is, as they say, out of sight and out of mind is irrelevant. In a somewhat unrelated analogy, would not you wish to know if you have cancer as opposed to cancer-like symptoms? I would like to know the whole truth, even if I could not handle its implications and even if I could not immediately benefit from it.

Bioethics Committee Visits Egsi again

On the morning of May 15, 2012, the bioethics committee visited Super Atom Smasher facility once again. They came looking for two other people this time, one of them being Dr. Hourdeau himself. The other one was Georges Pouchet. I nodded at them as they passed me up in the hallway near checkpoint #56; Georges had a look of horror in his eyes as if to indicate that he was unclear as to what they wanted. We exchanged glances and it became clear from this that he had already known about the contact this agency had established with me. I gave him an empathetic look and wondered to myself if Petra was next since she was key to the existence of TANG-0000. I decided not to contact her myself today even though I know she was aware of the possibility. We had taken a silent oath to ourselves not to talk about project Gamma-Gustav unless the highest authorities came looking for us. It seems as if they have. I sincerely hope that she will be able to avoid the interrogation that I had to experience the other day. I don't pray that often these days, but I am starting to wonder if right now would be a good time to start. even as I think, I am picking up synchronization alerts from TANG- 0000 and wondering how my "surrogate "son is doing. He had materialized into as far back as either one of us had; into a Swiss merchandiser from the 1860's. I knew he would authentically pick up anything as allegorical as a hiccup and everything important that he could in order to transmit it to his base. As I watched Georges round the corner, I figured I would ask him what it was about a little later. As I finished my rounds at the checkpoints, I decided that I would eat lunch somewhere a bit more modest today. I was still worried even after a few minutes of having seen the two of them walking off into the distance with representatives of the bioethics committee. I had a Caesars salad, half of a pastrami sub, as well as a fudge brownie for lunch. I remembered I had to change a variable in the synchronization acknowledge process, something I had been forgetting about but had remembered when I thought of TANG-0000 again. I saw Georges walking back the same way he came and decided to try to say hello. He did not have a happy look on his face and acknowledged that they wanted to know about anything to do with our "side project" at his basement. I already had told him I would only acknowledge one that I had at my house and that it involved my DNA. He said he and Dr. Hourdeau were threatened with lawsuits if this happened again. He also was quick to remind that Petra had not been summoned to talk to anyone regarding TANG-0000 or any potential side project that anybody could have going on at their respective domicile. I gave him as much empathy as I could and praised him for not revealing more on the event that may change the way we think of an ordinary event forming. I now knew Petra was to be next and I felt that I shouldn't warn her, but then again, who would if I didn't? I walked over by her designated area to see if she was there and, not finding anybody, walked over to the cafeteria. There was someone sitting there and it happened to be her. As I approached rather cautiously, she smiled and looked rather glum. I already knew. I asked if she was alright. She nodded, saying she was, all things considered. I gave her a kiss and asked if she wanted to talk about it, citing Georges' afternoon as well as that of our senior engineer. "No, not particularly", she said, almost holding back a tear. She knew and was completely compliant in being in all of this with us, but she couldn't help but notice how calm I was doing relative to everyone else that had been notified and warned about any side projects. I told her I was shaking the first day, but that I simply could not reveal the inner workings of TANG-0000 and have all efforts that were put into it collapse at that conclusion. She said she was upset because she was threatened with her job being terminated if she didn't speak up. "I did speak up and I told them the job involved genetic splicing, gene manipulation, as well as research in the house of a colleague. I did not tell them anything about the phases that we had to go through in order to get TANG-0000 off the ground." I told her if she was questioned again that she should tell them that I put her up to this task, and I told her I would tell Georges the same thing. "Georges would not go for it, I'm sure," she said. "We will see this through, Alen, she exclaimed, "For whatever happens this thing is bigger than all of us put together. I am not giving up on this now. BTW, I love you more than the moon loves the sky," she said as she kissed me good-bye. I stood there for a moment, waving after her. I did not expect that last comment, but it is always good to hear. That is the woman I love and hearing words of love never gets to be to tiresome. I wonder if we would ever get tired of each other when we were married. That date was coming up sooner than I had expected and we have not shopped around for tuxedos or wedding dresses either. A few seconds later, she is still present in me; her beauty makes me flabbergasted. I think the world will be a more beautiful place to live in just because of individuals like her, individuals who know how to make a person feel at home, individuals who know how to make the rest of us feel safe in our natural environments. I don't think we could ever grow weary of her even in a million years. I dreaded not to feel or try to put myself in her shoes and to ever wonder if she feels the same way about me. I was a one in a million but, then again, we all are at some point or another. every star has its place to shine at least once, very brightly and very indulgently.

Asteroid Fast Approaching

On May 21st, 2012, a wedding engagement party was held for us at eGSI. It was a surprise that was directed in part by Georges himself. I had grown to feel that the employees of eGSI were my extended family. There was Pierre, Hans, Klaus, Matilda, Catherine, among many others. Dr. Hourdeau was absent from work that day. There were also several people from the installation's administration there and they shook hands with Petra and I. They had heard about our engagement through Georges and had decided to make the party a surprise. It happened at the end of one of those days when the workload was fairly busy, but we got it done on time and in time to write our reports. Georges himself came in and said that my presence, as well as the presence of Petra, was required. When Petra and I walked in at about the same time, the room was dark. Petra said, "Hello?", and the room lit up with a roar of laughter and the screams of surprise emanating from the room. Petra later said that she had never quite felt that her heart was going to stop until the moment she heard the first shrill "Surprise!", which came from Matilda.

Matilda was a foreman who worked in Thermodynamics. She had grown fond of Petra, through whom she had heard about me. She was chilled the day it looked as though I had committed suicide and come back within a matter of a few hours. With over seven months to go until our actual wedding, we were both shocked and thankful of the surprise. The cake was delicious and the punch was very tasty. It was a wonderful way to end any work day and I was once again glad that I could consider my fellow employees my extended family. I had even told my mother and father about them. My dad was very proud of me, although he used to always try to hide this emotion in order to entice me to produce work with greater efforts. To him, smart work combined with as much effort as possible, coupled with minimal praise (expected praise) was that secret combination that produced results in life. I had done something in life that was very praiseworthy, but was unable to understand the full details of it myself without resorting to an outside perspective. To explain it to him would essentially take half of another lifetime. It was going to be more than seven months from now until I finally met Petra's parents, Alexei and Rada. Petra has told me so much about them that I cannot wait to tell them how much of a privilege it is and how much I love their daughter. I don't think there are too many marriages that are a match made in heaven; Petra and I occasionally have our differences. I love her. I love her company and her beautiful personality. She deserved the praise she received from people, especially from me. Right now, the threat of the asteroid had not waned significantly and I had to make sure that we didn't lose our investment in TANG-0000 and that the successes we have had continue to multiply. The latest news from yesterday claimed that the tangent of NT9 had changed slightly more toward the orbit of Venus, but it was still close enough to our vicinity to be indicative of what might happen in less than one year. What had to be done needed to be swift and achieved vicariously in less than one year in order to stop the devastation of a very virile and productive life force on the surface of the planet earth. So far, the Bioethics Committee has not determined the existence of TANG-0000. If they do, they will have a difficult time in trying to stop the time traveling cybernaut. All of this is going on as we are still trying to find the universal genetic code that would allow the Virtual Time Grid to be established virtually alongside any relative point in space-time. With the assistance of TANG- 0000, we may be getting a bit closer to that code every minute he travels the fourth dimension in this current Multiverse. Aside from this excitement, I am going to get myself a little more of that tasty punch, as well as a slice of cake. I still can't believe they decided to throw this engagement party. I am happier by a little bit that I am here every single day. I still cannot believe I became this fortunate with this company. Oh well, now it is not merely up to TANG; it is up to me not to squander something that takes some people a lifetime to accumulate. I shouldn't look back at those times when things were going more difficult. Instead, it is full speed ahead with Petra, who is to become my wife on December 31st, 2012.

Different Concepts of Antagonism

Antagonism appears to take different forms when living in a certain realities. The antagonism I felt from the world had much more to do with certain drivers and instigators than built up pressures from societies that I have lived in. What led up to an attempt at an invention was something that was quite expected in a sense, yet not the true instigator of what could ultimately be fame (even if my colleagues and I chose this for ourselves individually and as a collective). The reasons are sociological. The reasons are numerous. The reasons are about seeking acceptance and independence at the same time.

When the pressures of antagonism combine to form something that is otherwise unbearable, one must take a different route to explain certain decisions in life. Time is seemingly always on the brink of new realities and new discoveries; the discoveries are ours to bear and glorify. The antagonism that I feel comes from within me and it very swiftly time-progressed; the progression stops not to ask who or what I am and how I am doing on a given day. Some say that being a good listener is the best trait any human being can have. I would much rather interject that knowing when to stop listening as an even more important characteristic. Self-preservation is of the utmost importance, but being an active part of the collective, be it as an introvert or an extrovert, is more about social survival and the survival of the individual. Antagonisms lead to action, which inevitably lead to inventions that need not make sense to the present generations in which they appear. Inventions need not necessarily lead to the advent of new types of prosperity, for these types are always on the brink of new economic waves and, sometimes, a harsh impact on socioeconomic flows. Money flows along with the chronological flow of tachyons in a certain direction; it may not take more than a rational level of perceptiveness to figure out what many have known for centuries. It is up to us to resolve this sense of antagonism that is, in any event and at any rate, a process of equalization. It is process of something in abundance flowing toward something that is labeled and demarcated as something more scarce. We are missing the purpose of this if we do not acknowledge the insight. The insight that I have gained by not taking my eye off of the marker has been invaluable, it has provided a comfort against those times when antagonism has taken its toll on my very soul. The insight is happiness that is not equanimous; it is variable and has to be sought thereafter. Happiness is as elusive in genomic travels as is the final destination—it is there because of a more narrowly defined purpose which can never define happiness in a fixed realm. The prize is not the destination, it is the insight that is sometimes fleeting in other realms of life and living. Life is full of antagonisms and reason is not always there to smooth the edges. When it seems that you have all of the solutions, another antagonism provides reproachable evidence to the contrary. It is a form of exo-reality that provides itself as an alternative to insanity. Life would be insane without these riddles from beyond the void.

Love can be looked at as a series of equations that do not always conflict, yet need to be periodically adjusted in order for the processes to flow smoothly.

The Prophecy is upon us

The prophecy that some have called upon for centuries may be finally upon us. People have been finding out about the asteroid NT9 and a panic has just begun to ensue as a trickle on the World Wide Web about the potential Armageddon, the end of Days. The end of the world to them may be approaching rapidly. Meanwhile, shortages of food are being reported in certain countries that are trying unequivocally to stop the spread of disease, hunger and rioting over things that some have taken for granted. TANG-0000 has traversed four centuries in a quest for answers and information from past times that might be able to help modern humanity cope with this threat on the other side of the Solar System. The asteroid is still hundreds of thousands of miles away, but people are already taking notice of the news and what might be done to contain one's own misery. People are no longer batting a light eye to this situation. TANG-0000 should be returning to eGSI very shortly to report what he has seen and what he has collected and gathered. Today is June 2nd, 2012 and I am very anxious of what I have been hearing in the synchronization acknowledgments. I await his return with great troubles on my mind. If there was ever a time to tell Dr. Hourdeau about the project in full, this would be it. Petra disagrees with me; saying that TANG-0000, as advanced as he is, needs more time to collect and gather in order to contribute to the redemption of humankind. Georges thinks that we should hold off until September of this year in notifying anyone of TANG-0000's existence. I believe Petra might have the most moderate ground to stand upon with respect with what to do. Nevertheless, I told them both, I wanted to give TANG-0000 no more than 60 more days to gather, since a solution to blasting the asteroid in a peaceful fashion would only disturb those who are eagerly awaiting the prophecy of the end of days. I had heard about these times from a very early age and I know what a state of induced panic can do to people. Panic dictates the overturning of any leftover rationale until it is dominant. I did not think this is what needs to happen for people to realize that we can survive. The news was otherwise no more eventful that it usually is, with certain things like terrorist attacks, four- engine planes landing on one engine, or monumental discoveries that may even further revolutionize humanity's understanding of itself. It was time for the Virtual enigma to shine if there is even such a thing. I knew TANG-0000 was not going to come up short. The truth is, did I even know what coming up short in this case means? What does it mean? It unfortunately means that humankind could fall short of stopping the asteroid that might be deflected and pulled around by the disproportionate meshing between the gravitational pulls of planets earth and Venus. On the final swoop, in the worst case scenario, it would land somewhere in the Pacific Ocean. In the very best case scenario in would almost skim the earth at any angle and simply disrupt the tides of the oceans. The prophecy was almost upon us. It is up to news sources and interpretations of data from TANG- 0000 to stop this calamity. He has certainly grown in relation to when he was first created, although he can never be of a different size and proportions from the day when he was conceived. He will slowly mature, and eventually, his BIOS will have to be replaced. All in a day's work for an amalgam of DNA, metallic and plasmodic parts that has a guaranteed life of three centuries. He has recorded things I could have only dreamed of in my state of chronological lucidity and flight. I hope in the very least global authorities can shoot the menace down from the skies, that ravaging asteroid which is a fairly astronomical in size compared to us (estimates now put it at size factor of 30.075 km). I believe there is a better way and it involves levels IV, V, & VI of virtual technologies that have been employed in the creation of TANG-0000 himself. We now need to be working feverishly around the clock to determine a way around this universal threat to humankind, the kind that only materializes every few million years.

The Decision is made

While we are desperately awaiting the return of TANG-0000, the thought occurred to Georges in checking the virtual database records that were available to him from my brief voyages by my permission. He had known some of the outlines of where and when I had traveled, but he had not known one thing that was a crucial factor: the information gathering differential in calculating elasticity in the genomic continuum. He was looking for the possibility of more manned travels by one of more of us into the continuum that might bring about our imminent disaster or our immediate salvation.

According to Georges, it went without saying that the complexity of the atoms within a human cell was much more manipulable than the dense properties of titanium. The variable part of TANG-0000, in fact, was his close-to-universal DNA, the proteins that make his fibers even remotely human. If TANG-0000 ever needed any assistance out there in the virtual space-time environment, it may be now. Georges had spoken to me on several occasions about similar issues and knew how I felt about "purely manned missions" that did not involve TANG-0000 by himself, knowing well what had happened to me over a year ago now. I told him that the customization would have to work differently if any of the three of us decided to join the race against time. George readily admitted months ago that the odds of obtaining "crucial information, or raw data" from TANG-0000 alone could only be differentiated by his speed and capacity itself. He suspected TANG-0000 was going to need help even if in the form of individualized missions. I pondered on the issue for a few minutes while putting down the last bite of a doughnut. Petra was not ambivalent, yet she tends to agree that when there is work to be done, it needs to be done not only through all means, but by all means and everyone possible. I asked what they thought Dr. Hourdeau would say about this. Georges was silent, then said that he had spoken to Petra about the issue and that she agrees with him. In fact, their idea was to leave nobody of the three of us waiting and to ask eGSI's management to provide the facility with three separate checkpoints, mine of course being the infamous #56. I looked at them both, including Petra who had now walked up to the conversation from her checkpoint, if only to determine how serious they were about this. If they were consenting, I was going to have to overcome my fears of letting loved ones go before the blasting beam of the Super Atom Smasher. I agreed with them that this is a situation that I did not necessarily wish to confront, but it looks as though recent history has left me with little other choice and I simply could find no other alternative. The three of us agreed today to tell the management of eGSI, including Dr. Hourdeau, about what we had been working on in detail and to ask for permission to use four checkpoints on the facilities, with four other colleagues actively monitoring our individual progresses. Tomorrow is August 1st, 2012. I must first await the arrival of TANG-0000 at checkpoint #56, in order to determine if his self-correcting algorithms are functioning correctly. This will be the first day of the beginning of a new era for us at eGSI, a day which will determine not only the accuracy of scientific postulates set up by me and my colleagues, but a day that will determine what the rest of the decade holds for humanity. It was with uncertain steps that I left eGSI that day and kissed a smiling Petra, who had always wanted to feel the excitement of cellular separation while standing on a podium. The odds of her actually feeling this sensation look fairly high.

The Re - Virtualization of Tan G-0000

TANG-0000 arrived on August 2nd, 2012 at 10:38 a.m. His spectacular entrance was overshadowed by the daily news and the expectations that the asteroid NT9 would be arriving sooner than expected in this part of the Solar System. The asteroid would be arriving in the vicinity of planet Mars in 27.45 weeks. Our trio had already been to eGSI's management that morning and had consulted with them in a serious sense what it is that we had worked on and why the issue was contentious enough that we had not been able to be as honest as possible with them sooner, starting with Dr. Hourdeau. The news had overshadowed our conference in a different sort of way, for Dr. Hourdeau was facing budgetary cutbacks for this very reason. Nevertheless, when we presented our outlay of activities and our charted expectations, we were not met with the kind of resistance that we expected. Dr. Hourdeau was the first to agree that this wasn't the best example of using resources at eGSI, but added that people such as Petra, Georges and I were the future of this installation. He said he had faith in us to make the best possible scenario happen, in the past and now. To convince the management was to have the ability to telepathically move a mountain. We were not giving up though, especially after the warm reception we were given by our colleagues. After coming to, TANG-0000 (Gamma Gustav) greeted us in five languages and waited in the chronology debriefing room. He had collected volumes of information and we were not simply waiting for the download to cease. We were concerned and curious to see how he had advanced and what he was now like. He was still the most crucial piece of the puzzle. He had visited twenty eight countries through his virtualizations, materializations, and de- virtualizations. He was speaking 39 global languages fluently, going as far back as the 13th century. He referred to me as "SD

1", to Georges as "SD 2", and to Petra as "SM." He knew who we were and what we were like the moment that he had de-virtualized for the first time. He could sense the tension in the room when the room started to fill in with our colleagues who had never even met him until this point. Now they seemed to understand better what the scope and methodologies of our mission was. The information Gamma Gustav bore in his virtual files was massive, it filled volumes of books and amounted to the size of several small libraries. The employees at eGSI seem much better now and they vowed to help save humanity in any way that they could from this asteroid. Five of them volunteered immediately to help administer the processes of de-virtualizations of myself, Georges, and possibly Petra. After the internal downloads were complete, it was no easily surmountable task to sift through these piles of raw data that had been accumulated inside of TANG-0000. Gamma Gustav had been gone for the better part of six months of this year, attempting as many diverse collections and gatherings of information as possible in his still limited hard disk capacity. The task was left to two teams of six to sift through and organize; it was also decided that Petra would stay here at eGSI monitoring the synchronization attempts from the past once Georges and I de-virtualized, de- materialized, and virtualized elsewhere in space-time. If the asteroid was to be stopped in a purely scientific way, we needed human power and computer capacity, as well as swift global leadership. We also needed probabilities in our favor and, if we guess estimated anything, for the estimates to be right on target. Gamma Gustav himself was not to leave anywhere for the next month, primarily because of maintenance and psychological testing. He had a strong human component and he knew it. We had to give him rest if we were to send him out to the last leg of his voyage, a journey that might even involve virtualizing through his own standard duration into the future by about one minute. We did not wish to engage in this because he would never return intact after this futuristic quest. He would remember nothing because the CMOS battery in his di-lithium heart would then hold nothing but a blank slate, ready to start anew.

George Pouchet Virtualizes

George Pouchet had never been so afraid in his life, but he knew what had to be done. He knew he was going to de-virtualize and de-materialize into a space-time collector through the pages of chronological history. His virtual DNA file had been created, tested and retested. He had the recurring fear that what happened to me would ultimately happen to him. Coincidentally, I recovered fairly quickly and returned to work. Georges began to recount his family lineage in determining where he might end up in his virtual voyage through the abyss of space-time. He knew he wasn't Slavic and that the histories of different people have much to do with the history of nations. He was of French and Spanish ancestry. Things were not only different; they were exceedingly different in a cultural and historical sense. As reluctant as he was to do this, he was as ready as he would ever get. We had all been granted permission from our upper management, as well as the go-ahead from Dr. Hourdeau. The countdown was set for T-minus 15 minutes as he said a prayer for a safe trip, a trip from which he wouldn't soon recover from. The flash drive that contained his virtual DNA file was inserted into mainframe #48; from which the countdown began. This time, there was no need to lock the login screen, for we had obtained permission, if only for the sake that we would help create history in a vacuum. Petra and I were there for the duration of the countdown and we held his hands while his virtual outline covered twice as much database capacity as my original experiment had afforded me. This mission was not only about saving and helping people, it was about true friendship. It was about something I wonder if I had even known prior to working at Super Atom Smasher. It was about loving those that are near to your heart and never forgetting to show your true emotions to those that are not so close by. If only I could have known then what I know now, I'd be better prepared. So Georges will know it too. He will know what to collect that makes sense for later analysis, what makes sense for personal perusal, and what makes absolutely no sense and may as well be extracted and discarded as garbage. We stepped away at 5:04:45 because we had to administer the concentric charge, something that I couldn't do when I first virtualized. I looked over at Petra and gave a long silent look. "You are wondering if this is really the history that has to be written in our times and you wonder why now and why in such a way," she said softly. I looked over to Georges who seemed happier now that he saw the two of us talking about something else. The 'why' part of the question could be answered easily enough—it was because this time around at this point in time at this particular place, we were all involved with this thing called timeless fate. We were here to manipulate it. We were here to make sure that something that had never happened before under human supervision can actually happen. We had decided that it was moral because of all the lives that could be saved and because of the vast benefit to humanity and science in the same time frame. The clock was at 2:01:24. I changed the level and intensity of the beam on the blaster and resumed in looking at the condition of Georges at the given time. He seemed fine considering that he would catapulted long and far and to the very spot where he could provide the most merit. It was now T-30 seconds. And 25 seconds, and 20, and 14, and 10 seconds until his virtualization—9,8,7,6,5,4,3,2,1, 0.8, 0.5, 0.2, 0.1—we have de- materialization. Georges was gone. He affirmed beforehand that he would send a synchronization acknowledgment as soon as he could and we knew he would base it solely on his reliability. Petra shed a tear and remarked how lucky she and I both are to know him. I hugged her and acknowledged. The next step would be to utilize the already created virtual-Petra customized DNA file. She would be leaving in an hour, based on the equitable schedule that was established by Dr. Hourdeau himself. I escorted her away to the cafeteria and we had some water and grapes, in addition to some fresh Swiss cheese. She was not terrified, yet she could not help but re-live the fear that she felt when I virtualized for the first time and returned in the span of a few hours. She knew the method had been refined by Georges and I and that we had just utilized this in lessening his own pain. Still, there was something so unnatural that she felt about the whole project. I understood completely. The time was coming when I would have to pose the exact question to myself in all honesty and hope to get an honest answer. If I could not answer myself as honestly as I could, how could I answer honestly to God in the event that something went wrong?

Petra Stravinova Virtualizes

She was as ready as she would ever be. After all, we were to be married in a few more months and we both wanted the world to be rid of that horrific threat from the sky. The food helped to settle her stomach and we proceeded to mainframe #48, where we plugged in yet another flash drive in the mainframe. This time, the virtual genetic settings (the customizable DNA virtual file) belonged to her. The outlay of proteins and of the code was as uniform as it could possibly be. One thing bothered us both, especially me. Despite her pregnancy she had said that she volunteered to go for the cause that this represented. A family physician had even warned her to quit working one month before this day. What bothered me is that our baby might come in the way of us trying to act as super hero authorities in saving there world. Reluctantly, I am allowing her to do this in the hopes that the baby will not be born with an unknown defect that a pediatrician will have to treat, with the hope that it is treatable. Her virtualization will happen randomly and will not affect the nourishment that the baby receives in her womb. I was afraid that the baby might be born with the condition of spontaneous virtualization. We have decided to pray for the best and time her arrival back onto #48 in a few minutes to see what would happen. The countdown was set by me at T-minus 5:00:00.

I held her hand at the first three minutes of that countdown, the last two minutes I spent waving at her, smiling and telling her while silently moving my lips how much I love her and to hurry back. In an instant, she was virtualized and gone. I am praying the state of level V virtuality will protect her and the baby. Whether she would be brought back in a matter of minutes or hours would be the destiny that is foretold by the click of a computer mouse. I love her, I truly love Petra and I long for the days when these types of problems are in our rear view mirror. I could not wait to be a father, the kind of father that she has had and the kind of father than my dad has been to me.

Petra Returns

Within thirty minutes of her virtualization, Petra had returned and, apart from a slight feeling of dizziness, said she felt fine and able to walk on her own. I nevertheless escorted her to the cafeteria, where she rested and immediately had a glass of water. She claims she had recorded all of the data in the host that she had inhabited, but when it came time for her to virtualize again from the person she was in, the jolt brought her straight back to the podium. I asked her how she was and how she thought the baby was. At the back of my mind was the question of how long she resided in her host's body. She told me that she was fine and she thinks that the baby was unaffected. Apparently, the baby was the reason the conjecture held her back, since the file had no accounting of the baby as a separate entity. Babies typically develop quickly and something in the womb translated into something foreign in the genetic code on the virtual enigma file. She was brought back in one piece and that was exactly what I hoped for. She felt a bit guilty that she couldn't help more. I put my hand on her stomach and kissed her, saying "You are not to try this again under any circumstances unless it determined that you are not pregnant and you have permission from our upper management. I care about you and you showed bravado today." She smiled. "Actually, I just wanted to see how this felt and I did. I would not want to even try that again unless it was absolutely necessary. I love the bravado you just displayed," she said and almost burst into laughter. "I will go to the doctor one more time to see if the baby is progressing well." I nodded and smiled. Now, the person I had to worry about was Georges and to get back into the groove of things that goes on in this company. I had schedules to meet, machinery to inspect, procedures to check off on, and people to acknowledge. Georges is hopefully doing fine and handling himself well in past flows of time.

More News on Asteroid nt9

It happened not a moment too unexpectedly. The new co-ordinates were that the asteroid had bridged the orbit of Saturn and was headed in the immediate direction of our planet. I knew not how to gauge the path by way of complex trigonometric tangent, as I was studying the printout with a colleague from the next department over. He was not sure why the initial announcement came in the form of news that NT9 would be headed in between planet earth and planet Venus. He thought that there even might be a chance that the asteroid bypasses us altogether, although there must be a reason why it was defined so narrowly in the beginning. I concluded with him that the tangent it was taking through the mass and clouds that consisted of our Milky Way was probably the reason, primarily the reason lay with the gravitational and mass distributions. There were some slight changes, but if the current progression held still to within one standard deviation of mass distribution, NT9 was still heading between earth and Venus. I walked off with the chart after having thanked the colleague. His name is Fritz and he works in the Department of Theoretical & Applied Mathematics. We need people with his natural knowledge of super symmetry mathematics if we were going to stop NT9. After this errand, I passed in front of mainframe #48 in order to ascertain the synchronization acknowledgment between Georges and the facility. He seemed to be doing just fine and it appeared that he had finally left the 20th century in the other direction. This was as chilling as it was exciting to me, for there are always risks present in Virtual Genomic Time Travel. Georges himself was no more immune to them than I was, nor was Petra. She will be taking her maternity leave in about two weeks and not a day too soon either, for she was starting to show in a pronounced sort of way. She had not been the type to keep secrets from me, but she had found out the sex of our baby and wouldn't tell me for another month or two for personal reasons. She actually was a bit like other women that I knew; in a sense, she liked to keep some secrets from the significant other in her life to make their intimate and sexual life more interesting. In the case of gender, she was afraid I would have wanted the opposite for our firstborn. She said she would tell me in a month, after she confirmed the news. I assured her that I would love the baby as a father should regardless of the sex of the infant. She knew I trusted her and was there for her no matter what. She almost laughed as she watched me squirming out of the corner of her eye as she told me the news. I thought of it as something to keep me going until we find out news that is even more recent about the asteroid's path. Right now, I had to ascertain by importance all of the data that has ever been brought back from the genomic void and look for patterns that would reveal on the basis of significance something by way of a series of scatterplot diagrams, but also by way of statistically regressing and progressing the event which would allow us to know where exactly this asteroid comes from and what the mass is that will be coming our way. In a progressive sense, we had to know how quickly the asteroid is gaining in momentum. In a regressive sense, we had to use any information that was gathered using Virtual Genomic Travel. We were being faced with the first "astronomical" challenge of the 21st century and we were almost on top of things. Political occurrences in other parts of the globe were proving to be more complex than we expected. Petra promised to read these issues herself while on her maternity leave, while waiting for our baby. She had a better understanding of politics for she had once majored in political sciences.

Receipt of Signal from Georges

At some point after noon, I received a scrambled message from Georges, who had been trying to e-mail me from the current space-time location of his host in France; it was turning out to be no easy task. His e-mail had bounced around mail servers and returned to him via his virtual host database because of missing virtual elements and components in the Internet backbone of the time. I suspected he was trying to send the message through the host's server computer and the e-mail speed component was off. In a few minutes, I received the message. The message was that the asteroid was expected more than three decades ago and that the host has been researching a top secret computer server in order to try to crack the code in order to know how it would be handled. He also stated that he was hanging in there after what happened. He recommended that Petra not be allowed to help on any future missions in order to avert the potential personal tragedy. I had to silently agree. My little stowaway might not have been the reason for Georges' e- mail trouble, but was certainly going to wreak havoc when born, whatever its gender. I was expecting a boy, and she wouldn't explain why it wasn't a girl. In her words, it was something cultural that I simply wasn't attuned to. I acknowledged the sync and proceeded to check more of the data that had been downloaded and brought in by TANG-0000, who was walking around telling a joke or two to the young engineers who were brought in on college internships. He was different today in that he didn't have the Data aura of him; it was almost as if he was just a regular person who had regular goals, pains, joys, anguishes, and deadlines. He really did not have any deadlines.

The three of us had created life with a purpose and he had fulfilled it in a spectacular way by engaging in Virtual Genomic

Time Travel. He could easily blend in as one of the crew, Mr. Gamma-Gustav could. A few minutes from now, he will not be as talkative. He was just trying his social suit out for size, for size in an intimate social setting. The other thing that Georges was trying to imply was to have as many people help with the data analysis as possible and that the process would turn out to be as tedious as hell. Now that I am looking at the data, I can see clearly what he is talking about. To organize it would almost take a whole new level of virtuality and that is something we do not have time to develop in this circumstances. I am employing the use of fourteen data sorters and data analyzing software that will determine what each bit of data is best suited for. In this fashion, any way that scientific records themselves can be updated with help us in combating the oncoming problems with NT9. Any kink in any particular type of software can be resolved without the need for any more Y2K's, or any more uncertainties over the stock markets wild fluctuations and gyrations. We had come more than half way across the finish line and we are progressing well. I have at times had to assume the lead of the head coach in leading the team to victory, even if this is not supposed to be my main job description. I am thrilled with what I now see as possible, yet not ecstatic with everything that has been accomplished. even though things will need more than just patchwork, the updated level of chronological knowledge will now start to function at a more progressive level, in terms of levels of research that would have otherwise easily required a decade or more, in a matter of hours. It is being done in one year's time and, if we only had the time or experiential knowledge to backup how far we can safely go back in the course of one direction and return to safely change conditions that have led to this unsafe world that we call home, we could do all of this in minutes. We have the technologies to make this world bigger, stronger, and bolder.

We could also make it safer while we are at it.

A Call from my Proud But Concerned Parents

I received a call from my parents in the United States last night; my mother was worried sick and wanted to know how I was doing with my work. She was also anxious to meet Petra and couldn't wait to. My mother's name is Milica. She has decided that she wants to come to France and spend some time with her future daughter-in-law. If I didn't feel that Petra might be a little uncomfortable with that notion, I might have asked Petra myself how she feels about this idea. Petra had told me she didn't mind the company, but that she wasn't sure if she would be good company since she has been starting to experience mood swings, as is typical in the middle stages of pregnancy. She said she wouldn't mind the help if she could have time with me until the wedding. She didn't consider that to be a request of selfishness. She was very eager to meet her future mother-in-law and enjoyed the opportunity to speak to her the other evening over the phone. Petra has stated before, and I know this for a fact, that she is very fastidious and tidy and hopes this is something my mother doesn't mind. My mother has said that it would make her year to see Petra and to get to know her before our wedding ceremony in late December of this year. She looks forward to the visit to Paris and what she missed out in her own honeymoon by staying in Croatia. As for the data sorting and sifting, there are still mountains upon mountains left to sift through before the equalization starts to take effect and discoveries and phenomena that were simply or even deliberately forgotten get a new lease on life. The database server softwares are making the task much more manageable and, having said this, we might have over half of the original data from TANG-0000, from Georges, and the one-host trip that Petra experienced done in a week's time. I hope this is the case because I wouldn't mind spending some time with both my beautiful mother and my gorgeous fiancé. I wanted to tell my mother so much about what was going on at work, as I used to when I had hardships at school. This time, the stakes were a lot higher and I didn't know how much I could tell her and not get in trouble for doing so afterwards. I love my work and it truly shows. I love my personal commitments as much or more. I love Petra and I love my mother Milica. The thing I probably love the most on an on-and-off basis is the art of self- discovery (if I can apply it to something I have discovered about the world around me first). My paternal values as an alpha male kick in when it comes to protecting those things that I love, those people that I love. I strongly believe that things work that way for many young men, with either similar or dissimilar mentalities. In the case of TANG-0000, his alpha male tendencies are overshadowed by his bionics. He is the retriever of information that holds the key to past flows and tribulations in the localized part of the universe that is human history. At this time, I was not sure if I wanted my mother or father to directly meet TANG-0000, although I looked at it as somewhat inevitable especially if I planned on having him attend our wedding and since he was to be there socializing with the other guests at that time. I know they will be astonished and not as much dumbfounded as some of the others. I had to start to utilize him as a distraction away from the things I was doing in Virtual Genomic Time Travel, which I was afraid people would be asking me about left and right. I was not out to completely save the world from something that is needs saving from; I was out to give my contribution in the only set of ways that I knew how to manage. TANG-0000 was a Virtual Genomic enigma and I have already asked him to focus on things that he has seen in the installation at eGSI.

Georges Sends A Second Message

By this time, Georges had managed to send a second message in which he warned me that he had accumulated information from as far back as the 16th century. At some point, he said, he was not sure how far back he could keep going until he reached a point where he wasn't sure of the relevancy of the information that he was bringing back. I knew the feeling well and I had a feeling that we were to be seeing Georges return within a week with an absolutely packed virtual organizer that he has been packing since he left. If all of the information was that relevant, it simply would not require sifting through. Then again, if we knew the immediate relevancy of something, there would not be the need for anything less than a process of non- arbitrary virtualizations. It would be so exact that it may make what were doing not look like total nonsense; it was the exact opposite of nonsense. We are trying to save the world in a sense from an oversized chunk of rock and we hope that any other entities, countries and leaders that wish to contribute or simply know more about this should not be intimidated in finding out just that. This oversized rock could bring huge tolls upon global communications and the world population as a whole. I wish I would send him a message in the other direction, but since I couldn't control what he was gathering and collecting, I didn't want to confuse him. Suffice it to say that he had gone a long way back into the past of eGSI or anything else that we know today. We would know exactly what he brought when he virtualized and materialized next month on the podium near mainframe #48. His logs will be packed and his gathered information from the past will be unsorted and unorganized. He will have much of it to bring forward. It had not been decided yet, but Gamma-Gustav (TANG-0000) might make one more virtual voyage yet in order to smooth out any transitions in data and to bring a conclusion to the type of data that is needed in order to stop the burgeoning threat from the skies. He had had enough time to socially progress and to see exactly what he needs in order to bring the deck of cards even higher than necessary in order to bring the goal within reach. All information meant something different in the time that it was gathered than in the present time in which we ourselves were located. That same information in the present could be used in tandem with other, more "current" information in order to adjust settings on blasters within NASA or eSA that would keep the largest size of the blasted asteroid no more than the size of a baseball at Wrigley's Stadium. Although it looked more and more farfetched, the idea of creating a virtual representation of the asteroid based on the setting of the space-time that the asteroid "occupied" at some fixed point and sending it between earth and Venus as a sling was still in the running. We did not know whether or not we would have the information to be able to carry out this type of operation. TANG-0000 would have to go in search of things that are somewhat specific to this mission and return in mid-December in time for the wedding. I think he could pull off whatever Georges, Petra, and I could not. I think he is more of a man than when he was first built. I believe in his integrity, his construction, but more importantly, in his morality. He lacks certain types of moral connotations that most others have. He will always be unique with a low emotional intelligence that couldn't be measured anyway because he was not born. Should he falter, there might be other options, but there would only ever be one TANG-0000. Given that the data that he brought back is just now starting to be utilized, he has surpassed our wildest dreams and the dreams of anybody at eGSI. He has not only began the dream of building the Virtual Genomic Grid, he has been the first traveler of it (with the exception of his co-creator, myself). I will always feel pride in the historical feat that we have all tried to accomplish, as well as personal satisfaction that it was me that accomplished this, and not somebody else. TANG-0000 will look for data clusters within the last two hundred years and will have a much better idea of what he is looking for this time, as opposed to tree and soil sample data in Portugal in the late 19th century.

Georges Re -Virtualize Sand Re - Materializes

Georges re-virtualized and re-materialized on September 15th, 2012 and was very happy to see his own fingers again, as well as his own reflection in the mirror. He greeted Petra and I with a hug and the words that it was good to be back. He shook Gamma-Gustav's hand and asked him if he was ready to take over for a while. Gamma-Gustav nodded. "There is a place in Spain where I was visited that might be able to afford us more information on the ethnic concentrations of certain minorities as considered today. There was also a monastery where information was kept, information that I didn't quite have access to at the time," replied Gamma-Gustav. "Soon I shall give the world more TANG-0000!" he declared. He lived for the travels of Genomic Time. He knew by now what to expect and what not to strive for. He was a celebrity and, unfortunately, he was starting to realize the meaning of the word. In the meantime, Georges sat down and told us of his wanderings throughout the Human Chronological Multiverse. He said he could not be happier with what he gathered, he just wished there was more substance in the last few legs of the journey. He felt as though every time we were out there, that there is no information that seems less relevant until after one has collected it. He knew the kind of deadlines we were under and that we had to do something in order to sustain ourselves, our project, and the world at hand. There is unfortunately no training for this sort of travel; one must educate oneself as much as possible about the perils and about the punishment of not taking away from it what you could have. One must also be better suited for the next chance, the next journey. We could have personally spent several years in perfecting Virtual Genomic Time Travel as a method of collecting data and information; instead, we have been remanded to trying to get incrementally better at it every time in a short period of time as a trade-off between using it and not using it. There are learning curves; they are just tougher to measure than with most things for which a learning curve can be devised. A minute later, TANG-0000 returned and said he would prepare the usual podium for tomorrow for when he again set out to try to find some information where he had once been in the form of a Spanish sheep herder named Rafael. He had anxiously awaited the arrival of Georges and the time had finally come.

When we asked him how he was doing otherwise, he replied: "I don't really have time for that right now, but since you have asked, I am doing fine." He was beginning to understand the implications of failure a bit more and did not in any way wish to be a part of that verbal equation. He knew he was supposed to be a grown man and that he was conflicted with the fact that his surrogate mother and one of his surrogate fathers were getting married in twelve weeks. He wanted that one special present to them to be the ideal information that would help save us all allegorically and metaphysically. He was developing a will and, quite frankly, it frightened his surrogate mother. "Alen, I did not think it was possible, but Gamma-Gustav is maturing." I knew about it. I knew we would have some developmental issues to tarry, but not any that involved a grown cybernaut and an intrinsically teenage boy. He was a young man now. I offered the best advice to him that I could. "Gamma- Gustav, do not always expect praise when the job is not done. I know if anyone can get this job done, it is you. The praise and the self-actualization come later on down the line." He turned around and shrugged. "I am doing it, am I not? I am not really looking for praise. What I need is to be acknowledged more often. I do not need daily praise, but simply to be acknowledged as part of the team. I am a part of all three of you, and even this place of employment called eGSI!" As TANG-0000 walked off, Petra could have cried because a part of her was in that man, a part of genetic make-up and she understood him when he acted like that. In a nonchalant sort of way, he was allowing her to prepare for her own motherhood, the real thing, none of which were easy for her in this transition toward the next stage of her life. As TANG-0000 is ready for tomorrow, so she considers herself ready for the next few weeks in which she will stay home and rest and do some work around the house. If she has to, she will take a synchronization acknowledgment from TANG-0000.

Tan G-0000 Re - Virtualizes and De - Materializes

At 7:45 a.m. Meridian time, TANG-0000 prepared to de-virtualize and de- materialize again. He did it in such a way that nobody even knew he was gone by the time there was no trace of him. He wanted to be the phantom virtualizer and to be present in the continuum to which he himself believed that he belonged to the most. I came to see the tail end of the de- materialization flash by mainframe #56. I didn't even get a chance to wave before I started the last leg of sifting through the remainder of the data that was brought in by all four of us. I knew we might come up lacking, but as it turned out, we were doing better than I thought with regards to complementing existing knowledge of what we intended to do with the incoming asteroid threat. TANG-0000 and his last round of virtual genomic travels might just put us over the information target that we require in order for the NASA blaster to be employed. This blaster had a concentrated beam with a radius of 12 kilometers. It was extremely precise and was already being built in a designated area in Arizona where tacticians would have a clear view of the asteroid in the night time sky. The goal at hand was an update so important that the blaster will practically build itself. I saw a good bit of detail in the host health database files; files that were to be made classified in order to protect the identities of our hosts. They would have a hard time pursuing lawsuits in court because of technicalities but I would want to bring lawsuit if I were one of these people. I am not however and the use of their genetic codes has proven invaluable beyond belief. The "Blaster Beyond Belief" would literally construct itself if the information that we have gathered proves to be invaluable to earth's defenses against the asteroid; the update process was going on already. It was heeding nothing but the self- correcting flows of space- time in the artificial construct called the continuum. At present, looking at the newspaper, even the lettering looked like it was moving, as if it was a different edition than had been published this morning. Certain things come unaltered and possibly unalterable; other things can be altered at will with the right tools. I sincerely believe that the alterations of Virtual Genomic Time Travel will be the alteration that will have changed history and historical flows for the better. For the better, in a relative sense of the meaning of the word 'good'. The "Virtual Impact" scenario was getting to be less plausible, yet not completely ruled out of the question. The chances of expecting the type of alteration upgrade needed in order to turn the earth into a virtual planet and the asteroid into a virtual chunk of burning rock and metal were slimmer and slimmer; in fact, the levels of virtuality that were required to map the entire planet and the rock that is headed toward us are off the charts. The levels of virtuality had gotten as far as Virtual Level VI, which was in its core design stages. For ever development on the grid, there would eventually have to be another level of virtuality built in order to keep in touch with the "continuum masking process, or better known as the space- time cloaking process." In addition, the science talents here at eGSI and elsewhere had to know how to sort, organize, file, and utilize "past data" that was to become the crux of our defense system at eGSI Super Atom Smasher installation, otherwise known as Super Atom Smasher. The asteroid now had a little less than seven month before it was in our part of the Solar System. It would be approaching the rim of this system in about 3 months and, at that time, we need to have all of the necessary data prepared for our own defense systems not to fail. I would not like to see our defenses fall flat like a deck of cards when we have put many hours into mapping the genetic time grid, building and utilizing TANG-0000, as well as mining history's past flow records.

The Universal Code of Virtual Genomic Travel Unraveled

What might come to mind when one utters the words "universal code" is the genome itself; many of our humanity's best discoveries have been made within four to five years ago. The universal code of "virtual genomic time travel" includes not just strings of A,T, C, & G, but the underlying baryonic material itself organized in a virtual hierarchy, subsequently equated to a virtual allele. An allele represents singular or multiple forms of the same type of gene, relating to the mechanisms that make virtual genetic travel not only subject to imprecision, but also to egregious mistakes. This is what has gone on for months now at Super Atom Smasher and is what made Petra's attempt at virtual genomic travel so dangerous the other day when she could only be borne by one host because of her natural state of pregnancy. She could not travel very long as Georges, TANG-0000, and I had and felt very depressed afterwards. She is now home cooking, trying to find things to do during her maternity leave until I get home, usually much later these days. She knows being a mother is hard enough as it is; it looks like our baby will be born with a kind of recessive "spontaneous combustibility" gene, veritably from me, on the paternal side. It is a boy and this type of rare recessive gene seems to occupy people in certain ethnic genomes. The frequency of my virtual travels makes the condition even more unique. We have been trying hard to figure out a name for our unborn baby. I prefer to think that type of naming happens best in the delivery room. In our own way, we have to help stop this asteroid in order to be able to even ensure a better tomorrow. even though we differ as to what the baby should be called, one of my favorite names is Todor. The process of planning that guides us forwards as a principle of natural science is a universal code of conduct, along with rules that have to be either followed. Sometimes it feels like following those rules brings us closure to pain and feelings of ill-willed perception of our environments toward us. We don't exist to provide ourselves with concepts of beauty and elegance; we exist in order to unravel deeper meaning, to separate, and to connect ourselves. Our perception of existence can be sometimes to go our separate ways from our partners and friends of choice. even though I needed to give Petra space to grow apart from me, it was my natural tendency to be by her side. I love her. The elegance of the genetic code itself is a Pandora's Box itself; with my introduction of Virtual Genomic Travel, I had to be the one who involved those past tendencies with historical data that might have been better off left untouched. The puzzle in this case does not further relate to the genetic code itself in any customized sort of way, it is a maze of human will, emotion and intent. It is the process of saving a file configuration that has much more than an extension at the end to allocate to the computer what type of file has just been saved; it has a configuration of life looking out at you when you see it in a list of files, a list of files that could fill all the known hard disk space in certain time periods immediately preceding the one in the year where we are living and working on one of the most delicate, and at times, trying discoveries that has even been made. What makes it so trying is not the nature of the discovery itself; it is that one of the options that the survival of our species depends upon. The code itself would have been more universal from the start of humanity, but the odds that this ever happen depend on the odds of nature ever giving birth to the correct number of scientists and enthusiasts who will tirelessly work on decoding something that is simply a difficult enough puzzle in itself. Not to mention the collective supercomputing power available in the aggregate. Humanity has the tools to accomplish this very proficiently and efficiently. Who will be the lucky individual who scores the prize of discovering the genetic sample from which we all may originate remains to be seen.

Georges' Discovery Within the Collected Data

Today is October 15th, 2012. Georges had been sifting through some of the data that he himself had collected while in the form of a Virtual enigma, while he had been residing in an Anglican host. The discovery that he was looking for had to do with botanical arts in 18th century in england. As he came close to finding what he was looking for, he remembered the host whom he was inhabiting at a certain time and chills went through his body. The host was more disheveled than anything he had ever seen as himself when he looked in the mirror. The host's name was Brian and it couldn't be expected more than those days. Georges remembered the incident when his robe nearly tore on a stubborn, low-hanging branch by a nearby chapel; he was temporarily de-clothed and nearly burst into laughter. He regained his composure, continuing the mission. He finally found the data and the chart that had been saved as a specimen and a token of that trip. In this chart was contained something crucial to the development of genetics as a field in those times. He brought it to my attention while I had taken a break after having inspected eight of our last used mainframes near the collider. It had to do with what had been discovered by Mendel with respect to peas; this one had to do with corn and it was extremely accurate and detailed for those times. Georges' recollection was that it was a farmer who did not know what it meant when he drew it, but he thought to himself while next to Georges' host that someone of nobility should see it. I nodded and it filled my heart with nostalgia when I thought of the number of people who were talented in those days, but were simply passed up because they didn't belong to the upper echelon of society. People sometimes who see intricate drawings, shapes or even illustrations in their food or in the nature of their work, such as carving, cleaning or chopping wood may either be having a religious experience or may have been enlightened in some way or form that the epistemological mind cannot completely comprehend and does not have the notion to even start from, but it does happen. He continued filing while I drank my iced coffee, something that I had gotten into habitually that gave me a refresher boost in the afternoons and simultaneously affected my moods in a positive fashion. While I looked over Georges' shoulder, I could not help but wonder how Petra was doing at home by herself. She had complained last night of a stomach ache and had gotten up frequently. She said it had nothing to do with the baby and went back to sleep. I decided to call and find out for certain. When she answered, she was cheerful and remarked that she was cooking a special dinner for us tonight. I could not help but marvel at this woman for telling me this after not even having answered the question of how she was doing. She said she felt better and she couldn't wait until it was all over with and she had given birth. I told her I know that feeling somewhat, although not quite from the perspective that she was coming from. I told her that I love her and that I would be home in approximately two hours.

Synchronization up Date from Tan G-0000

I walked in through the door at 6:15 to see Petra sprawled out on the floor. I rushed to her aid immediately to uncover that she was still breathing and that her forehead was a bit hot. I was no doctor, but I tried to rouse her in a manner that might not disturb any injury. She started to rise by herself, but I put my hand on hers and kept her down for a second. She didn't remember how she wound up on the floor and said that she didn't feel injured. The only thing she did recall was a spinning effect that was going on in the background. I started to panic. I asked if it hurt anywhere and she said 'no' in a low voice, but said that she still felt like she was spinning. I called for an emergency ambulance and, while we were waiting, I asked her to describe what had happened when she got off the phone with me. She said she finished cooking and then sat down for about five minutes. When she got up, it felt like she was virtualizing and de-materializing for a split second. She then thought it was just a dizzy spell and proceeded to sit on the floor until she just passed out onto the floor. I asked her if she felt any other pains. She said she felt fine otherwise. As the emergency personnel took her into the ambulance, I told her I would be right behind them when they arrived. In my own mind, this did not make much sense since she didn't even seem or sound sick when I hung up the phone earlier. Nevertheless, we had to get to the bottom of these aches, pains, dizziness, or whatever else really might be wrong. I sullenly followed the ambulance driver about 6 miles down the streets until we pulled up into the emergency room. After I arrived, I waited in the waiting room for over an hour until the physician came out to introduce himself to me. He told me that our baby was going to have to be delivered on a C-section tonight if there was any chance that Petra recovers from whatever she was suffering from. I asked if she was conscious and when I was told that she wasn't, I gave my consent only in the event that her life was in danger and if the baby's life was in danger. I was angry at myself and if something happened to either her or the baby, I would never forgive myself for allowing her to become virtualized. Five minutes later, I was visiting her in the room in which she was staying and I started to cry when I heard the first thing to come out of her mouth. She said that if there was no way for her to get better and save the baby at the same time, she did not want to live anymore. She then echoed my own worries that this might have occurred because she had traveled through time in order to be inside of the body of one singular host.

She had not been the same since that day. When I asked the question if she was in pain, she told me she really wasn't, but the doctor thought this would be the best thing to do under the circumstances, especially when she told him that she works at eGSI inside of an installation. He took a precautionary measure, something that changed the course of Petra's life. Within the hour, the procedure was complete and the baby was resting peacefully asleep inside of the artificial womb some might call an incubator. Petra was feeling much better and would get to go home the day after tomorrow as a precaution. She was not supposed to lift anything heavier than 3 kilograms for the next few weeks until she was fully healed. When we asked to see the baby, we were told we might have to come back next week until the baby has acclimated to his new environment. I knew without looking that we have a beautiful baby boy who might have been inadvertently exposed to his mother's and his father's work a bit too early. He was growing faster by the hour and Petra and I both feel that something at Super Atom Smasher may have caused this. This means that Petra's uterus might never be fully healed to conceive another child in the regular way. We had to choose the baby's name for naming purposes and she went with my suggestion from before: Todor. After we left the hospital the following day, we took a peak into the nurtured environment room where the incubator was and got a glance at him. He definitely had her mother's eyes and his dad's hair was already coming through. Soon Todor would be home and Petra's maternal instincts would fully take over. As of now, she is on official maternity leave from eGSI. In five more minutes, I received a synchronization acknowledgment from TANG-0000, meaning that I had to go back to the office to send off the official reply.

More News from Asteroid nt9

How would it look if I didn't occasionally have the answers that were necessary within my role at Super Atom Smasher installation to properly function? It would not look good at all because I am being promoted to foreman technician in two weeks, according to Dr. Hourdeau. He said that I had earned it and that he loved having me aboard at eGSI. The following morning, I showed up about five minutes early and had forgotten one of the auxiliary access codes. Luckily, I had the ever so postured technician's manual that I clutched and brought with me almost everywhere I went for the first six months. For the most part, it never left my sight. Unfortunately, Dr. Hourdeau saw me looking through it and remarked that this better not happen again. I told me it wouldn't and that a code had just slipped my mind. He understood and within a grin congratulated me on my promotion. I thanked him. I was still shaken up from the incident with Petra and our baby even though it looked very likely that they would both be fine. It was too early to test, but it did look as though young Todor has some time of degenerative chronological disease that might cause him to spontaneously bounce through time when he is older. I went about my routine and was quickly getting the hang of it when the phone rang. It was Petra and she wanted to know how my new duties were coming along in her absence at the installation. I told her that they were going well and that I had better not talk long after having been notified of the promotion. She told me how adorable little Todor is and gave me the news that he would be in the incubator for at least six weeks. I told her that I had figured it would be at least a few weeks, but not as many as six. "At least," I added, "you both are doing much better than when I discovered you on the floor." We both breathed a sigh of relief and I went back to work, trying to familiarize myself with my new routine and memorize anything that I could possibly memorize. At eleven o'clock came the news; NT9 was approaching ever so rapidly and it was heading more incrementally in terms of a tangent toward earth than it was toward Venus. This was a bad sign because it meant that the asteroid might not actually head toward our neighboring planet. Based on solid prediction through extrapolation, this wasn't yet ascertainable. It looked like the Doomsday scenario was solidifying itself every second of every waking day of my life. It also looked as though I would be working overtime in lieu of these new events for eGSI Super Atom Smasher. I wish that Petra was able to make a full round with a couple of chronological hosts and, in a sense, that she was able to leave her duties behind as mother. I knew what I was thinking and immediately dismissed it, for my wish was not within the realm of the possible. I had been taught the difference between what is probable and what is possible long ago and in this case the probabilities that Petra could even think of virtualizing and de-materializing to help secure at least Meyrin from an incoming disaster were slim. She had to be with our baby. I couldn't wait for little Todor to come home; as a first time father, I was very excited about the prospect of a newcomer to the family. I was also ready for my fatherhood duties of picking out clothing at merchandise stores, cooking, changing diapers, bathing the baby, singing to him so that he can fall asleep and talking to him to build up his language skills early on. The few degrees closer than the estimated tangent shifted in the latest asteroid chart estimate would be enough for me to miss out on a few activities at home, and Petra knew this. She knew she had chosen wisely when she offered to take the longest maternity possible so that the baby could have a better chance of being cared for when she eventually returned to work.

Synchronization Acknowledgment From Tan G-0000

On September 28th we received a synchronization acknowledgment from TANG-0000, which confirmed new data from the eight new hosts that he had found himself inhabiting for the past several weeks. In the process, he had managed to collect certain invaluable information that was necessary, if for no other purpose, to continue to build the virtual time grid into which we would all have an opportunity to venture one day. We were getting closer to knowing what lies dormant, packed and untouched in this past century alone and what to do, when we came close to Doomsday, what to do with the asteroid NT9. The asteroid was over six and a half months away from coming in close contact with earth. Petra was resting when the synchronization came in and wanted to know how Gamma-Gustav was doing. I told her he was on this eighth host and had managed to send us another e-mail as well. She laughed. "What will it take to save the world from us, Alen," she said, giggling. "I mean, I know we mean well and that the world could use more individuals such as you. What do we know on how to stop an asteroid that is over 30 km across?" I didn't know what to say except that, the way I saw it, whether she meant it jokingly or nor, the world did not need saving from us as long as we have a game plan and as long as we stick to goals that we can set in a short-term, medium-term, or long-term fashion. Petra wanted to know how is it possible to take an accounting of the rate of overall global technologies for such a thing as an asteroid obliteration and of the differential between what it actually is if this progress does indeed update itself. I told her that the differential was in the recorded data that was collected and brought back, as well as in the predicted progress of the asteroid blaster than Petra herself had heard of, and in the actual progress that has been made on it since its inception. It was slated to be ready a whole five weeks after the asteroid was to pass in between earth and Venus on a sling shot. If our continued efforts had any impact, then the result would be the blaster being ready on time to blow that rock out of the evening sky on April 18th, 2013. It should be quite a sight. even TANG-0000 exclaimed that he wanted to be somewhere nearby to witness history in the making when that wide ray brings down the Doomsday traveler. His e-mail more or less quantified the collected data in encrypted format and told me from which host what data belongs to or resulted from. I was very pleased with this thoroughness (something I think he takes after his surrogate mother in), as well as his analytical behavior (something that must come through the most in my part of the overall genetic sample). If anything, I think he gets a lot of patience from Georges, from whom he also received part of his humanity.

Unexpected News from Georges

Tomorrow morning, I received some unexpected news from Georges, whose mother passed away over the weekend. She had been 71 years old and had become somewhat reclusive for the past 15 years. She even stopped attending bridge on Wednesday evenings with her group at the old folks home where she herself had lived for six months before she had moved back in with her son. I had always liked her from the time that the three of us, Petra, myself, and Georges had built TANG-0000 in the basement of his house in Meyrin, and frequently told Georges to tell her hello when he got home to her. He was very distraught, especially having lost his father several years ago from unexplained circumstances. He would now be the sole resident of this building and it was a very spooky feeling to have a place of a particular size to yourself after you have shared it with people for whom you cared or even if it was exclusively a love interest. Georges did not have a love interest and it seemed to me that he didn't try nearly hard enough to get someone. He could have been married by now, but he often claimed that he did not know how he could be married to anything other than his job. Petra had even tried to hook him up at one time with a friend of hers several weeks ago and he actually went out on a date and had a good time. I talked to him for half an hour this morning and he said he wasn't feeling well. When he had gotten home on Friday, she lay there lifeless and there was nobody that he wanted to call at the time except his sister in Switzerland. The funeral is being arranged for Wednesday of this week. He even said he might be leaving work a little early today to be with his sister, who was staying at his place. I comforted him for a few more minutes, then went about my duties. I had to inspect twenty more mainframes for fallibility issues, as well as functionality issues today. Later on in the day, I called Petra and told her what had happened with Georges' mother. She felt bad and wanted to do something for him, such as bring him dinner one night for him and spend some time over there at his house. I told her we might do that on Thursday since the funeral was on Wednesday and that it looks like he needs a few days to himself. In the meanwhile, I had a chance to analyze more of the data that TANG-0000 had sent us and it was beginning to appear that the differential progress was beginning to shrink from a solid "1.00" to a "0.854." This was a good sign because it meant that NASA would have a chance to test the asteroid blaster before the device was utilized in pulverizing the asteroid NT9. Overall progress will have been stimulated. I e-mailed TANG-0000 in return, praising him and telling him to keep up the good work in collecting any data that may be of any significance (unless, of course, it had to do with the personal lives of the hosts themselves). He later acknowledged the message and thanked me. He knew what it meant to us and what he meant to me. He could do things in the genomic continuum that I could only dream of and was very obedient when it came to following instructions. Now if we could just make that differential decimal more of a 0.65 or 0.60, we may have just succeeded.

Visiting Georges

On Thursday evening, we rang the doorbell to Georges' house while we waited at the door in the quiet Meyrin neighborhood. He answered graciously and thanked us for coming over, as well as for the food that Petra and I were bringing over, which included baked turkey, tomatoes and sun dried basil covered sweet potatoes, and rhubarb pie. He was still very depressed, although he tried consciously not to let it show with us there. He talked about all of the beautiful vacations that he had in France and elsewhere when he was a child and he went with his mother to various parts of this great country, as well as other parts of europe to spend summers and a few winters. At the time, his mother was already divorced from his father, and he instinctively spent more time with her than he did with him. He visited Bulgaria, Spain, Norway, Germany, and Slovenia, among other countries. It was in Spain at the age of 15 that he first got the idea of studying physics when he went to college, physics at a quantum level. He led a pretty sheltered life at times according to his own recollection. He loved his father, but his mother would never let his father back into his life for too long for fear of losing young Georges' affection. It never happened anyway. He never lost sight of his father, who attended the funeral and had some beautiful words for his late spouse; they had barely been divorced and Ryan Pouchet had continued to take care of Georges and his mother. He said at the service, weeping that she was a beautiful woman and that he wished that she and he could have gotten along better when it counted for the sake of his young son, now a grown man. Georges had never expected to hear these words for himself in a public place and, at first, was very angry when he heard them. Now he vows that he will have a different type of relationship with his dad, regardless of how long they end up living. He considered his father a good father at the time and a decent human being, unlike some fathers, who simply walk off and in some cases even allow a step father to come into the picture. He was remorseful as well about some of the things he had said to his father when he himself was younger. We both hugged him and said that we would help with whatever we could. Petra suggested that we eat something before it got cold. After exchanging some basic information about TANG-0000, I informed them of my e-mail exchanges with him and how the process of chronological progress what becoming self-updating, as I noted in the case of NASA's asteroid blaster. I informed them that if the past data flows tend to trickle that we may have solved the apocalypse problem solely by employing Gamma-Gustav in the role of TANG- 0000. Petra wasn't so convinced that this would last unless we kept the construction of the virtual grid going in the not-so-foreseeable future. I knew what she meant and so did Georges. In other words, how would we be able to save the gains that come from this exchange of past unincorporated data flows. The data would have to keep flowing in order to avoid a differential paradox in the flows of information itself, at just the right rate. In the meantime, while we were talking, TANG-0000 had left another synchronization acknowledgment message in which he estimated that his presence in the space-time is becoming less and less obscure because he is no longer able to predict de- virtualizations or materializations with certitude as we were able to when he first started. He was probably going to be coming back either late in the evening on December 15th or earlier in the morning on December 16th, depending on the tachyon reversal rate in his traversal. After I had read it, I knew some different types of fine tuning were needed and that I could no longer expect TANG-0000 to do the bulk of the work. He needed some hardware tweaks himself and then I could release him for a more indefinite period of time, possibly for over a year, depending on what our cybernaut brings back in the current time period. For right now, the correlation of direct past information flows, as I had determined after I took the sync acknowledgment alert call, means that the correlation differential is 0.67, which means the correlation update between the blaster and Gamma- Gustav's activities is getting fainter and fainter, but his correlation remains strong and the blaster might now be ready before March 31st, 2013. As previously calculated, it means a whopping success in terms of expected standard deviation. As for any long-term effects or tweaks on TANG-0000, we could need to analyze his *universal* genetic sample one way or the other to determine what effect he was having with the differentiation of past information flows in the present and his inability to predict co-ordinates for upcoming hosts in space-time. It truly looked like he was ready for some servicing in more than just the sum of his parts.

Tan G-0000 Returns from Genomic Space - time

It was December 14th, 2012. There was a little more than two weeks to go until our wedding in France and we had to make sure that we were leaving no loose ends behind to contend with later. We wished to get as many things possible, including finding a way for Gamma-Gustav to attend the ceremony. We ordered a tuxedo for him; it fit just fine. Anybody that we invited from eGSI already knew who he is and what he is about. Speaking of eGSI, twenty four people and counting have accepted our invitations to go to Paris to attend the wedding. At eleven o'clock, TANG-0000 finally virtualized and re-materialized into Gamma-Gustav. He brought back more information than what he had planned the other night when he synched with me. He was exceptionally excited today and knew what was coming up in two weeks, a regular trip as opposed to an out-of-reality, out-of-body, out-of-existence space-time voyage. He felt more human today than any other day since he has been programmed and living. He didn't even know how to fully express it. He was happy that his surrogate parents were finally going to tie the knot and was aware of little Todor. We decided to take Todor with us and make it an all-in-the-family wedding. Todor would be looked after by Petra's younger sister Renata during this trip. Petra herself was feeling up to the challenge but figured that is what she had a younger sister for, to take care of her baby when needed. That was more of a joke; the price of the ceremony hall rental, as well as the catering and the minister himself was upward of $30,000 (25,000 euros). We would be financially broken for a very long time unless my patent on virtual genomic time travel was proven to be a working theory with valid everyday applications. We would be able to recover on our salaries at eGSI Super Atom Smasher. It was almost as if we need a financial planner just to make it into our forties. We spotted TANG-0000 re- virtualizing and re-materializing at 10:54 a.m. Gamma-Gustav came up to us and gave us a bear hug, already reaching for the download function from his neural cortex in order to download the latest information into the cumulative database at Super Atom Smasher. He knew that this upload from his embedded virtual database would be the last download into our cumulative virtual database for a least a few weeks. He wanted to mature in a sense the regular way and have more everyday experiences as a human-based cybernaut would need to in order to continue to be functional as a cybernetic traveler in based in past flows out of the future. He wanted to meet some ladies and exchange phone numbers. He was at the stage in life where things are excruciatingly funny and utterly amusing at the same time. He was effectively on vacation and he did not care too much for what happened during this time. He understood now a little better what it was like to be human. Human to the point of annoyingly entertaining and only mildly flattering. He was Gamma-Gustav and TANG-0000 at the same time; nobody was quite him, and he could be everybody that history needed him to be. It is definitely a lot to go to anybody's head, let alone the head of a multi- functioning cybernetic being. He had also adopted the notion of being indispensable for at least fifty years, at which time he would stop being a child star and move on to bigger and brighter things. He had gained a strong sense of independence from myself, Petra, and Georges. In a sense, we had achieved the perfect worker, someone who knows his limitations but functions as well as his limitations can allow at all times. The only problem was that its trio of creators did not quite feel that way about him and knew his limitations better than he or anybody else did. After all, we designed him and had no more than one thing in mind for him. If he was starting to get tired of this routine, maybe we can find something else to do in the interim.

An hour for Wedding Bliss

It was December 29th and we had just arrived in Paris. Our wedding ceremony was going to happen in two days and we would all celebrate the coincidental arrival of the New Year, the year 2013. It was a year that would be marked by new beginnings, old endings, apocalypses, and futuristic endeavors. It would be marked by my love for Petra; it would be marked by my love of science and my ability to make it happen. It would be marked by the new arrival of Todor, a shining star in the Marinkovich family, a boy who might be plagued by a temporal disorder that kind that even his father has not seen. He is a beautiful boy who plays with his plastic atom nucleus models, stars and shapes and nothing could have made me happier had it not been for the image of Petra, smiling as she arose from our hotel bedroom for the last time as an unmarried woman. She never knew some of the luxuries in life that her friends in the Kremlin knew; she was not poor but was not wealthy to the point of flaunting it. She was from a middle-class family and this type of thing had a different meaning in Russia than it does in other countries. She grew up happy yet she felt as though something was lacking from her life in that there was a void that needed to be filled. She had dated three guys before she had decided that she ought to 'marry herself ' to her work. It worked fine for a while, at least until the day she became aware of me. That was the day that I decided to test my invention at the company that had just hired me; it wasn't as if I didn't know what the consequences could have been. I did it anyway and happened to have a conversation with Petra before I blasted off. She was now an inextricable part of my life and I wouldn't have it any other way. Somehow, that day, I felt as though I got a wild card handed over from the hands of Destiny. She had repaid me back since then a few times and in a sense not penalized me for playing cards. If it was she, then she had gone a bit easy on me and I knew some of my good luck (that I shouldn't think of a scientist) was going to run out pretty soon. I was hoping it was not going to be this weekend, not on the weekend of all weekends, the weekend when Petra finally becomes my wife and the weekend when I become her husband. I knew my days of solitude were vanquished when she came into my life; the trouble was, I didn't know by how much this held true. I was thrilled to meet my future sister-in-law Renata, who lived in Gdansk much of the year and part of the year in Leningrad. She was pretty like her sister and had a strong business demeanor about her that one could not shake after having met her for the first time. She could not wait to meet little Todor for the first time. "Isn't he precious?," Petra said. Renata held him all the way up in the air and declared: "You and I are going to be seeing a lot of each other little man. I will see to it that you are well fed, well cleaned, well groomed, and well rested. I run a tight ship, a ship where no pirates are allowed!" She immediately went to work to change Todor's diaper and to feed him his freshly prepared formula. Her maternal instincts were impeccable and, even though she didn't consider herself the mothering type, she indisputably was. In the meantime, I went with Gamma- Gustav to order some pastries for the next few days, something that nobody including myself had thought to do. I could see how Gamma could feel a little self-conscious from being in the vicinity of his surrogate father, in his ever glowing attire without cuffs. I thought he looked smashing and quite manly. I didn't even notice the maid that he had already made eye contact with and with whom he was flirting.

After placing my weekend long order for the pastries, I decided that I would leave here and return within half an hour to see if Gamma-Gustav was ready to accompany me back to the room. When I came back in twenty minutes, he was actually talking to the maid, making eye contact, smiling, and putting me to shame.

After all, he was a bachelor and was going to be accompanying some of the more seasoned bachelors to the bachelor party elsewhere, nearby the hotel. I made sure that Gamma-Gustav would get in and see the action for himself for a night that his human side would not soon forget. I also made sure that there was action going on there for myself, for the last night or two as a bachelor that I wouldn't soon forget either. As I called for him, the maid was just getting ready for work and decided that it was time to say good-bye to him. She kissed him on the cheek and walked away smiling. She would most likely see him again. In fact, I'm sure he told her that he was cybernetic and that all of his parts were fully functional this evening. We departed and enjoyed the scenes of the hotel lobby here in Paris, breathing in the bustling downtown Parisian air. The whole while he told me about this maid that spent most of her shifts working on the floor that we were on, the seventh, including the eighth and ninth. He liked her a great deal and I could see that he wasn't going to leave her alone. I decided that I would try to help him make a friend any way he could, particularly since he was not designed for every spur-of-the-moment human activity. I asked him what the maid likes. He told me some of her favorite things in life included wine and bubble baths. She also liked classical music and grunge rock. I told him that we would try to pass by there tomorrow after the rehearsal ceremony and that he would have more time to get to know this maid. Her name was Francesca and she had flowing blonde hair and a smile that wouldn't quit. As we got back to the room, Todor was smacking away at the bottle that Renata had put in his little mouth, smug as ever. His diaper had been changed and he had been bathed. Aunt Renata was talking extra good care of him. She had often told Petra that she could wait to have children of her own and that she would just have to practice on her sister's children first to get the hang of it. She was joking and it is said that motherhood comes about due to an internal instinct rather than social circumstances. Those who are better authorities at motherhood and fatherhood themselves say that it is something that will wait until you are naturally ready; the problem can sometimes be bad timing or meeting the wrong individual. As mid-day approached, we amused ourselves with local Parisian cuisine and TV programming that features soap operas that I had never even seen. They are very popular in this part of the world. We nibbled on appetizers that came just prior to lunch and then enjoyed seafood platters that tantalized the taste bugs. The lunch was scrumptious and not lacking in any form. I was enjoying our time here so far. The dress rehearsal was coming up in three hours and it was about time to dress up for the trial run. Tomorrow is the big day and, if we could handle customizing DNA in a virtual format along with sending people through the genome back in time to before the birth of the relatives that led to their birth, I don't think it will take more than one try to get it right for the big day, December 31st, 2012. The night was ours after that. The bachelor party was to be held four blocks away two hours after the rehearsal itself. The rehearsal was the last item on the itinerary for the afternoon.

Gamma-Gustav had his sights set on one of the walk-in bridesmaids that happen to be none other than Francesca, whose acquaintance he had made this morning while she was on her morning break. The condo we had rented for the bachelor party was not meant to house half of the male population of eGSI workers; it was meant for no more than a dozen males, including myself. I had not made a commitment to myself that nothing was going to happen nor was anyone going to get too out of line during this party. I had already made the same promise to Petra and Renata. Gamma-Gustav was here. What is the worst thing that can possibly happen if one of your participating members is a cybernetic traveler through the human genome? If there is striptease, then look out for Gamma-Gustav, for he has the raging hormones of a seventeen year old and has never been laid before. Personally, I didn't know those capabilities of Gamma- Gustav too well since it was Petra mostly, and then Georges who designed those functions. It was a wild night and nobody got violated, including my commitment to Petra.

Here Comes the Bride, All Dressed in White

The wedding day had arrived and I had gotten up twenty five minutes late, which is typical from what I hear about many grooms. I compensated and cut corners with a few things as soon as I could in order to allow the remaining time intervals to even things out. It worked until about lunch time when my lunch didn't arrive in time and I decided to skip lunch and snack on things until I could get my hands on some solid food. I ended up with cheese and crackers. Then came a drink with Petra's father Andrei and a long talk about what we expected in life and how we were going to get there. I knew I needed to have the conversation sooner or later, so I told him about my invention and our creation Gamma-Gustav, whom he had the good fortune of meeting twenty minutes into the conversation. He was aware of both of our capabilities as scientists and warned against our individual prowess and competitiveness as scientists getting in the way of what appeared to him as the beginning of a very happy marriage. I assured him that was very unlikely to happen and that we had our ways of making things work smoothly and accurately when needed. I enjoyed his company and something told him I was going to enjoy him as a father-in-law. By that time, it was time to start getting dressed and groomed for the upcoming ceremony and I knew at that moment that Petra was already trying out her wedding dress. I told Mr. Stravinovi that I would see him afterwards. everything else that happened that evening was history: the wedding reception was more than beautiful, it was heavenly. The bridesmaids were punctual, the accompanying boys were timely, and the vows were exchanged affectionately. I swore that I would never falter in being anything but what Petra needs from a husband and a man. She vowed that I would always be loved, in good and bad times, as well as taken care of in times of need and distress. The ceremony was one of the quickest ones I have even been in; afterwards, the reception hall had enormous amounts of food. We danced for hours to music of various backgrounds, Russian, Spanish, American, French, Swiss, after which I got up and decided to give a toast to long life and my long life with Petra. I made no direct reference anywhere to the asteroid, although I am sure it was in the back of certain people's minds. It all wrapped up around midnight, until Petra and I could nearly walk from exhaustion. We went straight to the hotel room, which we were going to have to ourselves for one night. We had talked about destinations for our honeymoon, but had not planned any as of yet. We slept like logs until almost 11:30 the next morning. Gamma-Gustav had to come knocking on the door in order to awaken us. It was going to be time to depart in a few hours and Gamma wanted to tell me something about that girl, Francesca. "I approached her, "he said, "and leveled with her. I am not fully human. I am a cybernaut, in other words, a cybernetic organism." She wanted my number anyway, so I gave her the office number at eGSI. I told him it was OK just this once, but to never do this again. I reminded him that I wanted to talk to him when we got back home. He agreed. At about 3:00 p.m., we boarded planes to get back to Meyrin and elsewhere. Before I boarded, I kissed my mother-in-law Anastasiya and shook the hand of my father-in- law Andrei. I told them I was glad to finally meet them, as was Petra (who was still taking to my parents outside of the hotel. My parents, Ivan and Milica, had a blast and they were nothing but proud to meet their daughter-in-law. Now that everything was set and done, it was time to get on the road. It would be nothing but smooth driving from here on in for the next 10 hours with rest stops in between. The big day was finally behind me and soon I had to get back to my position as a foreman/ technician, something that had almost become second nature to me. I was worried about the exact date that the NASA blaster would be online in order to target the asteroid that was headed toward our neck on the woods in our Solar System. Petra was getting used to her duties as a mother. As for Todor, he was busy napping. He had had quite an exciting couple of days, but then again who hadn't?

Back to Work & Awaiting News on nt9

It was January 3rd, 2013 and it was my first day back since we had left to go to our wedding in Paris. After my mainframes systems check, I perused through the new data on the asteroid while waiting to receive the update. I noticed that the differential progress on the NASA blaster was coming along more and more incrementally and that it would be soon almost perfectly inversely correlated to the sorting and analyzing processes of the information brought to us recently by TANG-0000 and Georges himself. The correlation factor was 0.45 and that put the estimated date on the completion of the blaster to March 15th, 2013. This was indeed good news, but not good enough to celebrate. What mattered to me was if anybody had a contingency plan in the event that this course of action wasn't enough to destroy the asteroid. I had not told anybody about my total virtualization plan in the case of planet earth allowing the asteroid to pass through under certain virtual constraints. It might be easier to land a shuttle onto a moving asteroid than it would be to make an asteroid disappear in a virtual sense through the side of the earth. I knew that I did not have any contingencies for alternative flows of events, but I knew others had a few ideas that they were working on independently. I had my plate full as of today. Little Todor is playing at home with his mother and she is taking exquisite care of him, the apple of her eye. I had to call my parents later and apologize for not spending as much time with them; the circumstances at the wedding did not seem to allow it. For a short while it seemed like I could almost bend time to my will, yet I couldn't be more forthcoming with my mother and father about the details of the wedding until they arrived in the evening of the day that we all did. Virtual Genomic Time Travel was developing into a methodology of tracing past information to truths about actual past flows whether they were recorded, recorded correctly, or not recorded the first time. It was not meant to serve as a way to develop weaponry for any event or contingency. It has the opportunity to shine in a few more months and I will not be any happier if it just dissolves the asteroid into small meteorites that barely make waves. It will be a rainy day when it comes and I have been prepared for the event in case it happens sooner. I have even made alternate plane arrangements to move back to the United States with Petra and the baby, as well as Gamma- Gustav, if such a move would protect us from this awaited apocalypse. As for Georges, Pierre, or a number of other colleagues from France, I would have to say *au revoir* to them before-hand. I know when to bail and when it is not a wise move to do so. I am prepared for whatever happens. I am ready for the eventualities of this life.

Analysis off in AI data from Tan G-0000 Journeys

It was January 21st, 2013. Gamma-Gustav had decided he wanted to put one more voyage into the mix before we knew what we were up against. He had heard me talking about a contingency plan and he knew exactly what I meant. Sometimes I wonder if I had created a monster in a joking sort of manner. He plays with Todor every now and then and I think it hurts him to realize that his own "birth" was based on the equivalent of a grown adult male being born immediately into adulthood. He suggested to me that Petra and I tinker with the genomic proportions in his historical virtual database of human genomes to see it this might bring him in an entirely different direction this time. I advised against it and explained to him how he came about and what we were looking for; in fact, I know he was ready to hear the whole story. I just never knew when he was ready or when he had time. After having heard my rationalizations, as well as second hand information from Petra and Georges, he decided against what he was looking for and decided to get on the associated podium to checkpoint #48. He said he would definitely be back before March and he wanted to be informed of a contingency plan if any came of knowledge. I promised he would be among the first to know. As the timer finished counting down, I could not help admire the shining coat of metallic titanium that comprised Gamma-Gustav's skin and enabled him to withstand things in space-time that none of us could handle. I was glad to have helped design and invent the concept for TANG-0000. He was a good companion and I would definitely find good use for him once all of this is over. I personally felt that this would be over victoriously for most people that I know and many more that I didn't know. He meant too much to me to just allow him to wander the hallways of eGSI Super Atom Smasher and look for ways to strike up conversations and to offer tips to its employees.

The Day of Reckoning

The day was March 3rd, 2013. The daily update was in and the situation was clear. The asteroid was in range of earth and was accelerating at a speed that would put it near the atmosphere of earth within ten days. I told Petra about this as soon as I could and told her to keep her eyes peeled to the TV news. I told her that if we needed to, we would be able to board a plane to the United States that I had reserved prior to the beginning of the year. The asteroid was traveling at a speed of 11,549 km/hour, but picking up in speed as it approached the inner Solar System. The massive gravitational leverages of Jupiter and Saturn would cause the speed to be raised exorbitantly and, from then on, it was headed toward earth and Venus. It would probably retract upon passing in between earth and Venus and swing around for the direct hit. The earth was as prepared as it could possibly be at this point. It was now or never; I decided to ask at the meeting what could be done with the under- utilization of the equipment here at eGSI. I was reminded that NASA's blaster was among the only technology compatible with this type of phenomena which earth might have only encountered once before, or should I say, the dinosaurs. The blaster itself was located in Phoenix, Arizona and would be able to distinctly target the asteroid from the evening sky. The blaster would be online in three days. What a relief that was to finally hear!! I asked him to repeat these words and we all laughed. At least we have a fighting chance during these times when it actually does seem like these could be our final days. even though I felt like much of the work was done and that there was nothing much that I could do but to go about my daily routine and then go home, Dr. Hourdeau wanted me to stay here the evening that the asteroid was expected, which was March 13th. I told him I would and I asked if there were any other duties I needed to perform that evening. He said that I would be notified if the contingency of additional duties arose. Now I simply had to convince Petra to take little Todor to the United States if worse comes to worse; it would be known very early on which continent would be affected the most during the destruction of NT9. Petra cried when I told her as she certainly did not want to leave me behind while she and our son traveled to his grandparents' house in Kansas. She did not wish to leave me behind while we still did not have enough information to exercise the purchase of those plane tickets. She wanted the three of us to be together. As for TANG-0000 (Gamma-Gustav), he would be arriving very soon if fate is in any way slated with his existence. Most of the time when TANG-0000 makes a promise, it is based on solid calculations and, at least to him, tangible evidence. I knew he would pull through with something spectacular and surprise even me. I also know his arrival back at eGSI would not be completely based on his will to return prior to the deadline of arrival of NT9; it would be slated upon the corridors that comprise the virtual human genome.

Gamma – Gustav Returns from the Genomic Void

It was March 10th, 2013. At 10:05 a.m., TANG-0000 virtualized and re- materialized on podium #48, bringing with him a smile of glee. He knew from the first split second on that he had arrived at a good time and that the asteroid had not arrived but was very close. He had information that might directly impact not only the fate of the asteroid, but also the fate of future human evolution if the scientific community chose not to ignore the consequences of the information as delivered. The information was in oratory form, as well as in the form of pictorial depictions that could not be seen by anybody who has not already been in a state of virtual genomic time stasis. I led him away as soon as I saw him. I asked him what he had discovered that would be more informative or significant than the asteroid that would pass through this part of the Solar System in a bit more than three days. He politely told me it has to do with human evolution and the ability of humankind to predict the gradual process of natural progression of human societies in a four-dimensional sense. When he confirmed that the blaster was operational, given the information that was in his virtual collections database, he vowed to attempt to encrypt this data more securely than some of the other data that had been collected in the past year or so. This was very pertinent to what would happen to human evolution if societies continued the way that they had in the last few centuries, starting with the First Industrial Revolution. He had a very solemn look in his eyes, the look that was the only true characteristic of his human side. I showed him how to encrypt the virtual aspect of the data; he did the actual data encryption of the physical data. He was happy that he could arrive back so soon and told me he would be staying at eGSI during the asteroid event. I told him that I had been asked to stay late on the momentous night to keep track of the equipment and to track the trajectory of the asteroid up until the last minute. There were other employees near Super Atom Smasher that stayed by request and others that had volunteered to stay for the sake of staying and learning more about an event such as this that only occurs every several million years no more than once. In ten minutes, the data was encrypted as well as saved. He never had to leave after this, for the excitement was truly just starting to happen. Two days, one hour, 37 minutes, and 46 seconds to go until the projected catapulting effect from Venus sent NT9 in our direction. I was preparing to call Petra and little Todor and I wanted to say something positive about their preparations to go to see grandma and grandpa Marinkovich in the United States. Petra was not excited about leaving me behind and she made no qualms about the real reason: in assuming the worst about what might happen, being separated was the dumbest thing that we could be doing even if it was requested by Dr. Hourdeau himself, who has been very supportive of my efforts with virtual genomic travel and my efforts to keep me progressing within the company. It was about our baby. She knew at this point that we wouldn't have another choice to do this over, so she agreed to take little Todor and stay with my parents for a few weeks, or at least until the emergency is over and the world was able to ascertain the exact damages caused by this falling satellite. I told her I would miss her when she was gone, more than the lush pastures in Russia miss the rain before it even stops raining and how difficult accepting all of this really was. She knew what I was talking about and said we would talk about it more when I got home that evening. I knew she might have a surprise up her sleeve by the way she sounded before we hung up on each other, probably something that she just figured out that day and never knew might be possible until she thought of it. She is a versatile cookie and she knows her finances as well. In fact, the money that is jointly ours is hers to manage and take care of. That is how much I trust her. I would trust her with my life more often if I didn't know the outcome of my unusually unlucky trends and my quibbles with fate herself.

The Asteroid Approaches

The date was March 12, 2013. It was two thirty in the afternoon and we were getting reports of all types about NT9, including an overload of global media reports that were trying to minimize the potential impact of the asteroid itself. Many of these reports were intergovernmental reports about the projected damages and the environmental conditions that might arise if even part of the asteroid broke off and landed somewhere such as in the Atlantic or the Pacific, or worse, in a populated terrestrial region. One particular report predicted that there would be seismic activities in all parts of the world near the epicenter, some reaching nearly 13.00 on the Richter scale. As I skimmed through some of the more sporadic ones, I focused on reports that had to do with atmospheric conditions in the next thirty six hours, the cosmic pictures taken from Hubble last night, as well as the potential damage done to oceanic and terrestrial life, land, and crops in the areas where meteorites were expected to fall. It was spectacular and terrifying to the point where my hands started to tremble when I realized that one or two of these reports were made possible by TANG-0000 (Gamma-Gustav) in the past week's time that he virtualized and de-virtualized in making possible the mapping of the virtual genomic time grid. The asteroid itself was more tangible and coming very close to our planet as I conceived these thoughts, and this was even more horrifying! Other reports had to do with statistical inferences based on information as to what could happen if chunks of the targeted asteroid fell too closely to earth or our vast oceans. Georges walked by and asked if he could help and noticed the terrified look in my eyes and stopped for a second. He started to talk to me, but it was as if I was having a premonition based entirely on one of my own virtual genomic voyages, or simply another type of flashback. I showed him the reports and explained what was going on. He said he spoke to Petra and that they had packed and were heading toward the installation before they depart for the United States. I explained to him that I was strung out over the consequences that even a chunk of the blasted asteroid could have on any part of the globe, not the least of which would be the meteorological conditions in the upper atmosphere. He agreed and suggested that I put some of this paperwork down and take a breather. He acknowledged how much work I had done even since I started working for eGSI. We both agreed that the blaster had better work, otherwise parts of this earth were going to start to look like Armageddon in a flash. I suppose, I told Georges, I was having a flashback to my first virtualization that is recurring and I may never quite get over the feeling of powerlessness that I felt. I brought it on myself whether knowingly or not knowing. In reply, George referred back to the experiences all three of us, including Petra, had witnessed in our out-of-body temporal states and the wealth of information that was gathered through these outings, as well as the advent of Gamma-Gustav. We were on our way of linking the entirety of human history to a virtual grid that will eventually be able to be accessed from anywhere and anytime, once networked to the Internet. At that point, Dr. Hourdeau walked up and asked if we were doing well. When he saw that we were OK, he introduced a schedule for us to relieve each other into the night and had it posted in all hallways in order to avoid confusion as to who was to be there at any given mini-shift. We were normally closed at six in the evening for regular operations. We both looked at Dr. Hourdeau and saw the same concerned look in his eye. We reassured each other that it would be OK and that this was a good day for science notwithstanding the personal risks involved and the potential destruction that might ensue in parts of the world. Now it was up to the NASA Blaster to stop this asteroid as soon as it came into range of few hundred miles outside of the range of our global satellites. It was up to organized science to record the outcome.

Asteroid NT9 Blasted

It was five minutes before the turn of midnight on March 13th, 2013. Petra and little Todor had stopped by the installation last night to say good-bye for a period of about two weeks before going to the airport to catch a flight for Washington, D.C., which connected to where she and Todor would rendezvous with my parents. Petra was happy to be making a trip somewhere and was concerned about my health even more than Georges had been. I was sleeping alone in the house this evening, yet I was having trouble falling and staying asleep. At some point, I got up to fill up a glass of water because my throat was parched. When I came back to bed, I was almost wide awake. It was a classic nervousness that befalls many a scientist who decides to work in fields that are filled with intrigue, yet at times devoid of direct answers to phenomena. I had to be at work at six thirty in the morning and we had to run contingency scenarios that would explain the expected results of various alternative actions that could happen depending on how the asteroid was dealt with today or tomorrow, or the expected variance in causality- outcome recording. I knew how to go about recording it as a series of events, or nodes, in an interconnected system that needed to be viewed holistically or individually as the sum of the parts, not including the synergistic effects that come about as a result of this phenomenon. We had access to vast amounts of information due to six private servers, not even including the World Wide Web; yet we were still short of certain information that could only be provided by running these contingency scenarios, for instance, what would happen to the asteroid and the awaiting earth in the event of a direct hit on NT9. What might happen if the asteroid is hit in any other place than in the most vulnerable place while going at the present rate of speed encompassing the effects of earth's gravity? What is the actual shape of the asteroid and how hot would it get upon brushing up the side of our planet in the direction of Venus? What concentration and properties must the ray have to be able to even have an impact on the asteroid? At what time would the beam have to specifically target the asteroid so that so that no other satellite, artificial or not, might get in the way? How wide the asteroid is in kilometers and what is its composition? All of these are variables that must be included in each contingency plan to bring it away from the alternatives in which it poses a threat to earth. either way, I couldn't sleep worrying about the possibilities that could happen and worrying about the worst that could happen. I was worried about Petra and little Todor, who by now must be in American air space. The part of me that already missed my wife and my child was the part that worried the most. even the allure of continuing the challenges that we had overcome in these past few years was not enough to keep me from stopping and wondering about the consequences of tinkering with variables that were just now becoming more manipulable, variables that may have in some ways contributed to knowing what might happen on this momentous day. Or the next. I was thoroughly excited and completely exhausted at the prospect of what we might discover. On the other hand, I was terrified enough that I simply got up on my own, without the aid of the alarm clock, and started to get ready for what was to be one of the longest days of my life. These days have never been more in sync with one another since the advent of TANG-0000, yet a large part of me was un-synchronized and out of touch with reality. I needed to be the economic unit of this household for the next couple of weeks, making my own lunches and dinners, or finding a way to get take-out food. As I showered, I noticed the change of the seasons clearly for the first time as another spring was almost upon us. I hoped (as a scientist I still retained some hope at times) that this year was not going to be an apocalypse year and that it happens some other time; if it is even meant to happen, let it happen when we are much better prepared to confront the problems and issues that accompany such a massive, life-threatening occurrence that the dinosaurs themselves were in some ways no worse equipped to deal with. even with our life-saving technologies, we could be in jeopardy in a few hours from a natural occurrence, the kind that never shows up as the reason for indemnification in insurance policies as anything other than an act of God. After breakfast, I arrived at eGSI at six twenty five, only to find a handful of regular employees there. The atmosphere was neither chilling nor warm within the room, yet I could tell that people were tense and it is very hard to speak to people when they tense up due to something that might involve you as well as part of the final outcome. Then again, are there any final outcomes in the study of cosmology? We are all part of a recycling of living and non- living things that cannot be simply replaced or renovated in the forms in which they were created. We live, we exist, and we may definitely be threatened by things that we don't understand, nor that we can always insure against. We were all once parts of the same primordial soup before life had even evolved on this planet and some other planetary bodies where water was recently discovered. everybody was going about their business so attentively that I immediately returned to the reports that were generated yesterday. I glanced at the bulletin to see that I would be there past 7:30 in the evening, maybe close to 11:00. I had prepared my lunch and was starting to feel hungry already when I saw some of the other installation workers chowing down on sandwiches and soups. I decided to wait and to finish looking at the reports from yesterday, following which I was to ascertain any discrepancies between yesterday's news and today's realities. Knowing was not doing or executing something in particular in this case, for it took an active machine to be able to act like a dynamic motion mechanism. I finished the old reports and sought out reports that were coming in this morning, reports that had the position of NT9 plotted out, as well as its velocity, and space-time based approximation to our planet. There were only two in the general bin today, and none in my own bin where I collected my own office mail. They dealt with the constancy of target, the target in this case being planet earth, as well as the composition of the asteroid itself. The reports are dealing with speeds that were not breaking any records, but were constant enough to put us in a lot of trouble if we were not staying in perimeter with the variables that could change on a moment's notice. The asteroid would be outside of the physical range of our satellites within four hours and NASA was currently testing the blaster in a series of experiments dealing with accuracy at very long distances. I was ready to provide information on any variable component that could be found in all contingency plans, information that had to be accounted for first. The first blaster test was fired at 2:00 p.m. It was fired virtually near the vicinity of where it was targeted to be this evening. It was successful, with the firing intensity normal and effective. Time went by slowly as I accumulated more reports on things that differed between the reports themselves and reality itself. Finally, it was announced on CNN, among others, that the asteroid was finally in range and that the officials at NASA were waiting for about 37 minutes and 47 seconds for NT9 to be in the exact range. The countdown had begun. In that period of time, Gamma-Gustav walked by and decided to watch the broadcast with me. I told him not to forget that, no matter what happens in the next half hour or so, we did everything that we could to lessen the impact of this threat on peace loving societies everywhere. Almost as soon as the interval was up, the fiery asteroid was in range of NASA's blaster. A ray was fired at the location in expectation of the asteroid's movement. It exploded in midair so violently than even Henry Volk had to stop his broadcast to look over to the screen behind him. It was successful; the asteroid had now been broken into four smaller chunks and this is where any data that we had accumulated at eGSI was "too little too late." Up until the point of impact, any data that we could have provided through virtual genomic time travel would have been extraneous. Now it was useless, since four smaller pieces were falling toward different locations and one meteor shower was headed in the general direction of the Indian Ocean. One part of the asteroid was headed 125 miles away from the Baja Peninsula, another was headed toward 37.00 latitude 45.00 longitude in the Atlantic, and a third was 229 miles east in the direction of northeastern Russia, while the remaining piece was headed toward the eastern Pacific. They would reach earth in a matter of seconds. This was the outcome that everybody who knew about the asteroid had been waiting for and it would make the final determination of who was to be affected. Global suspense abounded. Global governments and militaries were quick to react and I believe that this is the synergistic effect that I did not count on from the very news of NT9. We needed time to be able to evaluate the gravity of each individual situation.

Turmoil from the Break down

The fifteen minutes had passed. The tsunami impact was almost felt and it was headed in the direction of western coast of europe. We were just waiting on newscasts, internal, or external reports from the relative impacts from the respective asteroid chunks. We were flabbergasted at what we had seen on TV a few a minutes ago and had to work overtime to be on top of the situation. Intergovernmental agencies evaluating the situation were in touch with the BBC. Tireless efforts were made to contain the impact of the wave. Other agencies and multiple news media coverage continued to assess the developing threats from other locations. It was as though earth was being attacked by extraterrestrials. I wanted to call Petra so badly to see if she was alright, but there simply was no time. We would know more about this later in the day and tomorrow as reports starting to file in. They are coming in by the thousands at this point. I decided to call Petra and Todor sometime after 7:00 p.m. Petra had been dying to hear from me, but it was my mother who advised her to wait for a call from me because of the global events. Petra acquiesced, patiently waiting as she let out a little shriek when she finally heard my voice. They were OK. My mother and father were also concerned. Almost immediately I had to hang up the phone when Dr. Hourdeau came in to check on the reports status. I told him that I was getting to the reports as quickly as I could in order to ascertain where the damages were the highest. I told him there were damages reported in Russia, off the coast of Baja peninsula, as well as in the Pacific, but that some of these reports were still incomplete and that I would require additional time. He was worn out with the entire experience and hoped that this didn't happen again in his lifetime. I agreed. I was partly in my own thoughts, partly elsewhere, wondering how the strategic split of the asteroid could have occurred to lessen the impact on human life and property damages. Dr. Hourdeau left without saying another word. He knew I was exhausted and that I would be going home. As I thought about the gravity of different situations around the globe, anywhere where parts of the asteroid fell, I couldn't help but to wonder if Petra, Georges, myself, and others could have done more to counter the effects of what awaited us from the dark evening skies, had we had additional resources. It goes without saying that our achievements with virtual genomic time travel were monumental. I suppose the question is not pertinent to what else we could have done, but what we could do in this relative moment in time? Options are somewhat limited, and one of the best possible scenarios has been incurred. The asteroid has been blasted out of the sky and its remnants have fallen. How many times has this happened in human history? We might never know if not for the eventual setting up of the virtual genomic time grid. Now that disaster has almost occurred and proven to be a miss, we should focus our efforts on what we can do to avert similar tragedies. We need to learn from this event as much as we can. We also need to unravel and map the past flows of human history that would enable us to know not just the continuity, but the overall development. As I turned my attention back to some of the more recent reports, I noticed that over 130 people had been reported missing as a result of the chaos. Over five thousand people had taken temporary refuge in churches and shelters and many more were not accounted for. As for property damages, reports were coming in from various parts of the world in the form of tsunami alerts. Blasters on the Baja peninsula had managed to split the chunk of NT9 that had headed toward the Pacific, lessening the chances of a tsunami wave. In Russia, a mega blaster struck the meteor into pieces, three of which landed in the Pacific. We had not received any reports on this fallen piece yet and we were not sure of casualties or property damages that may have occurred. Petra was concerned about her family in Leningrad and had been trying to call them a number of times to no avail. All she could do at this point is wait and watch the global news outlets in search of a familiar face or any information regarding that part of the world. She cried and told me she had not spoken to her father since the wedding and just wanted to tell him that she loves him. She wanted to tell her mother to stroke the hairs on his graying head and to pray for us all, for this had the sinister fearful feeling of being Armageddon. I never for a minute thought that the scientific community had exhausted all options in terms of casualty and damage reports in various countries. My view was that there was something localized that happened, or might still be happening, that caused the asteroid to break away from its companions.

Casualty & Damage Reports Continue Top Our in

The date was March 14th, 2013. Reports have been coming in from far corners of the earth, including southwestern Pacific, which was faced by enormous tsunami-sized tidal waves. Similar sized waves were noticed west of Baja. Russia finally got news to the rest of the world that it was able to obliterate the chunk of asteroid that hovered over its airspace for what seemed like an eternity. Its casualty report was 29 people, all of whom happen to find themselves out in the open and had no material way out. The wait was over and a few other places in between may have experienced a death or two related to meteor showers, but it was not directly due to a larger chunk of asteroid NT9, which had now been downgraded to dust and fallen meteorite bits. Things were already starting to get back to the pace at which they were flowing prior to the announcement of the existence of NT9. even the Super Atom Smasher installation itself looked differently the next day; people were getting back to their regular routines at work and were being given instructions on the modeling of the Chaotic Inflation theory within the center of the collider. I knew that my days of virtual genomic time travel would dwindle after this and that I would have to find something interesting and invoking for Gamma- Gustav to do because he was not employed at eGSI, did not have a purposeful function for the company, and periodically did get in the way of others who were distracted by his looks. He was not banned from the property, but he had to be accompanied at all times in order to be maintained and closely guarded. Petra and baby Todor were coming home in a week, which meant that I was to be home by myself for a while. It had become lonely in the house without. I missed the privacy I had in being able to leave Gamma-Gustav here at the installation, but I knew I would eventually have to find him a permanent home in another part of town or be able to donate him for scientific feats and explorations of space-time in string theory as well as four- dimensional time travel. I could not trust him enough to leave him unattended and not have Petra come back to work after having difficulty in finding an appropriate babysitter. Things were normalizing and Inflationary Theory modelling was just one of the group projects that had to be postponed. The study of super massive black hole singularities remained another important venue for research and exploration. For me, apart from my everyday routines, one remaining side project remained—it was virtual genomic time travel in a universal sense. It may not have practical applications during my lifetime, but I know with the right formula and the right purposes it might have limited applications in verifying existing history records, as well as being a gauge of actual human progress in scientific terms. I had to try everything I could to actively promote this application and the working theory of virtual genomic time travel in order to keep up the need for Gamma-Gustav as well. It may not hurt to fully explain this to the european Bioethics Committee in order to not get blasted by lawsuits. I am determined for Gamma-Gustav to have a home and I am even more determined to have a platform for pitching a theory that purports an existing reality under certain circumstances.

Bioethics Committee Re Visited

Today is March 17th, 2013. I had heard from the european Bioethics Committee several months ago, during which time Petra, Georges and I were busy working on Gamma-Gustav (TANG-0000). They came by eGSI one last time to have a formal hearing with me in one of our presentation rooms and I naturally complied. Petra had not yet returned from the United States; it didn't really involve her directly anyway. Gamma was my project from the beginning even though without the help of Petra and Georges he wouldn't be a reality. Their chief complaint was that I used genetic material in such a way to create artificial intelligence on the property of Lucy Pouchet, Georges' late mother without being in compliance with a number of ordinances in the city of Meyrin and without a permit to do so. I agreed to the fine with the request of extra time to pay for it and I asked for half an hour of their time to state my case to the officers. They agreed, upon which I proceeded to tell them about virtual genomic time travel and the limitations of using people who are living and belonging to any particular ancestry. I told them of my background in college and they seemed to understand. I described the stages of our planning, designing, engineering, and constructing TANG-0000. When I explained why I used my genetic material, one of the officers stated that it was not illegal to use one's own genetic material for any other purpose than to clone. I corrected him saying that this was voluntary and that my two peers had gladly contributed their own genetic materials, with the exception of Georges who eventually gave in. They had nothing to charge us with and I tried to pitch the usefulness of Gamma-Gustav for an observatory or a scientific consortium. It didn't quite work that way, they said. I thanked them for their time and proceeded to get back to work. I had wished to be completely truthful without violating my companions Petra and Georges. I knew the truth when it came right down to the fundamental truth: Gamma was mine, although in part he belonged to them as well. I assured him later that he would have a place one day when the both of us could collectively engage in virtual genomic time travel and continue to map the chronological grid of human history. I know what it is like when you are left out and had had experiences such as this at M.I.T. I also knew that Gamma-Gustav did not reason or think in the same type of logical fashion as most of the human minds that I am accustomed in dealing with. Petra has already agreed to split the fee for the Bioethics Committee. Now what was left over was to find a research laboratory for further exploration of the time grid with the same essential setup as eGSI. I knew it would be hard to find, but not impossible. Meyrin is not a small town and I might even attract a couple of veterans from eGSI to come help us as an auxiliary project. By now I knew what I was getting myself into. I had received exposure at Super Atom Smasher. Now I needed to put this experience and expertise to good use for myself and the good of humankind on my own terms. I certainly would attract some partners, one of which already was Petra Marinkovich. Georges has implied that his bread and butter salary would still come from eGSI, but that he also wanted to participate in the project that I was suggesting. Both Georges and I had certain locations in mind and, as we got raises in our salaries in the future, could perhaps afford to split the rent of some of these empty laboratories. This way, we would be able to avoid any future fees to the european Bioethics Committee.

The Independent Virtual Time Grid

The date was April 17th, 2013 and the laboratory search was coming along. We had been to a very diverse cross-section of Meyrin and beyond in the hopes of finding something that some "borrowed" equipment from eGSI would turn into a medium sized installation. Gamma-Gustav would be able to continue his voyages through the virtual genomic space-time. I would have ample time to continue my research into the applications of the genome in traveling through space-time; I certainly would have time to break down the analysis of what I had discovered already about modern earth's bout with a full-blown asteroid. Petra would be absent from eGSI and from this project for another few months and, by then, she will have found a babysitter that would enable her to return to work and to return to our side research. She has had a wonderful string of weeks to find out what motherhood was all about and has been itching to return to her workplace. I could understand the feeling and I welcomed seeing little Todor trying to walk on his own. He is in many ways an ordinary toddler and his mutation condition had not "kicked in yet" and, according to the doctors that we have seen, he was probably going to be considerably older before anything like that even happened to him. Petra still blames herself for what had happened; I told her things would be fine and everything with Todor or an eventual condition would work out. even if he were slightly older when it happened, my research might allow some form of alleviation from this degeneration or mutation that we had been expecting since Petra first engaged in virtual genomic time travel. The primary mission went on as planned; I would take turns in the interim to help out, while Gamma-Gustav (TANG-0000) would be ready to explore times and places that no human being or cybernetic traveler had ever explored before. If the funding were ever there we might even contemplate an upgrade to TANG-0000. He has said that the double-helix itself packs a "doubled punch"; in the same fashion, two cybernetic travelers working in tandem might lead to a more efficient process of mapping the virtual genomic time grid. His grief about being one of a kind stems from the inability of others to understand what it is to be organic and cybernetic at the same time. He is, after all, human to a large degree, the degree that allows him to understand his cybernetics counterpart. In addition, little Todor might one day want to pick up where we leave off. I can look at him and already tell that he possesses the "curiosity" and "follow-through" genes. He struggles to stay on his feet, yet looks up to estimate how many more times he could do this before he finally walks. I imagine him being the same way when he grows up; after all, he has his mother's and father's lineages to draw from genetically. He has our determination and our eyes. We need a place that would be suitable for him as well. In order to locate a lab that is feasible, we have to narrow the location down to something that in appropriately in the middle of the part of Meyrin where Super Atom Smasher is located. Renting the lab might be 20% of our combined salaries, not including any bonuses that we might receive for work well done at eGSI. We are looking for something of at least 3,000 square feet, or about 278 square meters; something large enough to house our quantum accelerators, our mainframes, our laser emanators, our laptops, and our borrowed equipment from eGSI. This something could be a home away from home in that it can house a fridge, a pool table, a small bar, a kitchen, a restroom, and a reading room, a work study, aside from the aforementioned equipment. The lab needs to have the right lighting ambiance and the right touch that only a woman can add to a furnished residence. For aesthetic reasons, Petra is in charge of decorations and arranging furniture and equipment; I have the final word on where the work equipment finds itself in this spacious domicile. Georges claims he might know just the place to look for such a domicile and that he might know the landlord well enough in order to get a good deal on the first three months. The lease is something we are looking to lock in for a year and, from thereon in, negotiate an affordable rate at which to lease this property. We have to look harder, especially ever since Paris has been hit with a real estate crisis at the beginning of this year. When we find the place, we can begin to celebrate a new era of research between old partners, as well as old cybernetic friends.

A New Home for Old Research

Today is May 1st, 2013. With the help of Petra and Gamma-Gustav, we have located a new laboratory for our virtual genomic time travel experimentations. With the help of Georges and Pierre, we moved the equipment that we were to borrow from eGSI in the hopes that it would one day pay for itself. We were not technically stealing it, but this process started from borrowing the high concentration beam and the mainframe from the first time that I traveled through the genomic space- time by myself. We went on our lunch breaks, and found the parking to be suitable to the time of day. Later that evening, we finished the setup and how the three of us wanted this mini installation to look. We were pretty satisfied with everything but the color of the walls. According to the lease, we could not change that portion of the domicile nor extend our preferences in any way that would alter the lab space. We were finally here! We had our very own lab, upon which setup we sat down to toast to new beginnings, good research, exploration, and old friends. Pierre was expressing an interest in this setup and said he might request a Friday evening off every other week in order to see what this lab was all about. We explained to him that we would have to revise the scope of the projects conducted here based on our own hours at eGSI Super Atom Smasher. I felt he would be an excellent hire for busy times and I knew that he had practical experience in quantum mechanics and string theory applications as of recently that I couldn't begin to explain. The one thing that I was bringing to this table was an underlying knowledge of quantum genetics that would be the basis for nine out of ten of our endeavors; my colleagues have their respective specializations that would allow the progress to move forward and backward. We have to be frank, progress does take time and time is something that is of the essence. It is something of our essence, the essence that determines and frequently alters our respective DNA's. It is the continuity of our respective specializations that will keep this laboratory, and others, going in the pursuit of human and other ultimate truths. Pierre would be a welcome addition to our existing team, but it was ultimately up to him whether he wanted to join us. After the toast, we returned to work and continued the working day at eGSI Super Atom Smasher; I finished the routine inspection of the collider today, while George, Pierre and Petra finished their respective itineraries for the day. Once I got home, Todor was well fed and asleep; I lay down Petra for a quiet couple of hours that we haven't had to ourselves since before Petra took Todor to the United States six weeks ago around the arrival of NT9. She was refreshed when we got up and remarked that I had made good love to her, with the exception that my mind always seems as though it is somewhere else. I nodded and agreed that I had a lot on my mind, with the advent of quantum genetics as a field as well as my little boy Todor. He has started talking a little bit and frequently tells his mom 'daddy'. She told him that the nature of the work that his father does require him to mostly be in one place and that his daddy loves him very much. He seems half satisfied with that answer, chewing on the toys that we bought him, crying as he has just started teething. He had no known condition as discernable, as I have said before, but he seems distraught by phenomena that wouldn't be nearly as fascinating to many other kids his age. Petra was the first of us to go to bed and had remarked that I am wired enough to stay up all night at the rate I was going. I knew she was about half right and that I didn't seem to care not so much because I wouldn't eventually compensate. I didn't care about structure as much as Petra does when it comes to important chores and the utmost fundamental parts of life; albeit, I did care. I cared for my body and any nightmares that I had accumulated after my initial travels through genomic space-time have been diminishing greatly in strength. How did I know who was going to be the first to get up out of bed? The reason lies in whom I normally see when I get up, go into the bathroom and gaze into the mirror. It was now always me and it was me for now since I planned to do further virtual genomic time voyages that seem absurd to most people. To me they inextricably link history and progress. They link them in such a way that we all can alter progress and continue to be ourselves in the morning.

Amidst A Sweltering Turmoil

Today is May 17th, 2013 and I have just gotten used to the dualities of working both at eGSI Super Atom Smasher and at the rented laboratory. In a sense, it was the same thing as working in the basement of Georges' late mother's house; in others, it lacked the same type of privacy, which we were going for when we decided to rent it. It had the amenities that we sought and was not lacking in size or ambiance. The equipment that we both purchased and borrowed from eGSI consisted of six accelerators, a mini-collider tube, two sub-atomic recorders, a medium sized laser, as well as two mainframe database computers with podiums attached. This equipment cost a few million dollars, some of which had depreciated immensely. It still worked and functioned the way that it was intended out of the factory. I knew we might be better off if we had a genetics room and I would know at that point if I wanted to keep this lab and keep it up as a secondary work area. A feminine touch of Petra could bring this lab to life even more than just the individual occupations being performed here. She was the one who could breathe life into these rooms as a woman. As I arrived, Petra and Georges were already there, attempting to find a way to activate the accelerator while it is attached in just the correct way to mainframe #1 and its adjoining podium. I helped to inspect the installation and had confirmed the positive hook-up and configuration just as Gamma-Gustav was entering the door from the next room. Gamma-Gustav needed recharging, but he is eager to set off again as a virtual genomic time traveler, looking for a way to help the humanity that brought him into being as a semi-human/cybernetic traveler. He walked in, looked at the podium, inspected the mainframe, looked at the configuration of the room and announced that he is ready to depart once more. As the countdown was secured and our goggles were fastened, we talked amongst ourselves about what happened in our individual routines at eGSI, with the exception of Petra, who still had a few months to go before she exhausted her early birth maternity leave. With the sound of Georges complaining about a simple problem that could have been avoided at eGSI at mainstay #57, Gamma-Gustav de-materialized and de-virtualized. He would be picking up somewhere different this time because of the arbitrary change in settings since we moved this machine from Super Atom Smasher to our new location at this laboratory. In the meantime, Georges and I wanted to talk about genetics in a quantum sense, a sense in which nobody alive really knew the exact effect on the human brain or body, let alone the human genome. He started to re-route power a bit away from the quantum pod over to the other equipment which we would be testing soon as well. After having just tested one of the accelerators, we tested the other five for accuracy and functionality. Georges and I tested for voltage regularities two sub-atomic recorders, the laser and the collider tube, miniaturized as compared to the main one at eGSI Super Atom Smasher. Petra was alone by herself for a minute, inspecting what part of her salary was going toward different items in her budget after she returned to work. She thought of a few things that she could do in order to make it more aesthetic. She suggested to us that she bring some artificial plants or flowers that might make it cozier that it otherwise appears to be. She thought of changing the wallpaper in one of the rooms in order to make it brighter and less of a strain on the eyes to work in this particular room, which I would have designated the 'quantum genetics room.' I told her to do what she thinks will make it a more productive and efficient workplace and to employ her female touch to the situations at hand where she deemed them to be necessary. I also told her that she might need to consider getting home for the sake of Todor, since he was asleep in the main office and needed to be put to bed for the evening. I knew what I wanted to do; the issue was now how to obtain the working materials that would make this dream of mine come true, to make it a working reality that would employ my methodologies in an economic way.

Petra Returns to Work

It was June 15th, 2013 and Petra gave me some good news this morning at breakfast: she would be returning to work on July 1st because she feels like she has located an affordable and, more importantly, a trustworthy babysitter. I gave her a kiss in agreement and she told me she has been itching to do something with mainframes #1-25, which would be awaiting her at the beginning of her first shift. She was even starting to become seasonally depressed and I even suggested that there may be an option that allows her to return early and leave again if necessary, for emergency purposes, for instance, if Todor ever became ill. She knew what I was taking about and was very excited that she took this casual piece of advice. She would no longer be moping around the house when chores were over, with the urge to light a cigarette. She would be productive and happier than she has been in a while, with less excitement to last her much longer. She was never used to a sedentary lifestyle and did everything she could in order to stop from becoming this passive and emotionally immobile. I had to be at work at 7:45 this morning because I was running an errand for Dr. Hourdeau (he allowed the extra fifteen minutes on my time card). I was picking up some materials for the installation, some of which I might have accidentally taken for my secondary lab. I would definitely have to check up on the exact amounts because having Dr. Hourdeau part with too many pricey things from eGSI, such as those accelerators that are already functioning in our secondary lab in Meyrin. I had a good idea of what I could get away with and what I needed for the proper functioning of these secondary experiments. I arrived at 7:46 and my arrival was welcome by a few of my colleagues in the other part of the installation who had not even seen or heard from me since before NT9 had struck. They had heard about the wedding and, although they had not been able to make it to the physical wedding, they had purchased some gifts for Petra and I that we never could claim because we were not aware of them. I was grateful toward them and I invited them to stop by our house one of these nights if they had time. I gave them directions. As I brought the supplies in, I noticed someone lying on the floor, hunched over and clutching their stomach. It was a man in his thirties for whom I did not know if he was just visiting or if he worked for us. He was clutching himself like his stomach had ruptured. I called the hospital immediately and waited for them to arrive. As they were wheeling him off, he thanked me. He said he would probably be alright, most definitely now that he was so lucky that someone found him in the nick of time. I left to go about my daily tasks. When lunch came, I felt I should get a healthier lunch than I had been eating for a few weeks. I grabbed a tuna fish sandwich, with light cholesterol chips and a tall glass of iced tea to go. I didn't even know when I was going to eat and I had much on my mind from the day before and the ones that were coming. I knew I had to check synchronization with TANG-0000 in about twenty minutes, so I kept my hand on my wireless signal receiver in the event that it indicated a signal transfer. It did come, but not for another 45 minutes. I have to give him full credit for his consistency, though. He sent information from hosts that used to reside in Spain, Norway, and Germany. The last one was about a French host who lived in Paris 65 years ago; TANG-0000 virtualized into him and became a piano player for a while, learning the progressions, movements, chords, and melodies of an old expert who decided to become a professional in the night life of Paris, scrounging whatever and whenever he could in pursuit of fame. He picked up information about Alzheimer's illness, that the man had in the later part of his life, that prevented him from remembering a song that he had once wrote for an ex-spouse. He later remembered parts of it and began composing it anew. He knew that he had a memory illness and could not seem to overcome the desire to continue composing. It was one of those stories that used to make Gamma-Gustav tear up and cry, but he has been through quite a number of other people's sob stories and has since toughened up on the details of these stories. He knows his capabilities, what he is designed for and why he exists. He still desires a companion and I don't know if we had much better resources that we would be able to design one that would adequately suit his needs and his development. He is a good man if the label even suits him because of his added complexities. He loves little Todor in his own way and is fascinated with the way humans produce offspring that sometimes resemble them in such a petty way, or at other times bear no resemblance in the least to their progenitors.

Back to the Basics

Today is July 16th, 2013 and we have gathered in the lab after a relatively long day to try to map the main events of one long decade in human history, the one that had just transpired in a limited geographic locale between July 16th, 2003 until the present date. The time is 7:49 p.m. I am happy that we all are here because this usually signifies that something extraordinary has or is about to happen. We only have one accelerator working tonight and I will be stepping on the podium to test its capabilities with our database computer in order to test the quantum capabilities of our system setup. I know already and always have, when I was thinking of getting our own laboratory, that the setup would be more modest and humble than it was at eGSI Super Atom Smasher. What I didn't know for sure is that I would have items from the very workplace that I cherish and consider my first big break in life. I felt tonight to be the night that Petra would de-materialize and de-virtualize for the second time. She had requested it and had felt cheated when she wasn't allowed to virtualize any further than into her first host. She knew immediately it was because she was still pregnant with baby Todor, who was nine months and one day old on this very day. She knew then that she had to make a certain sacrifice then in order to preserve our life, our little baby. This evening, she stood on the podium, ready to be launched into the virtual continuum which has become a large part of all of our realities, including my own, hers, Gamma-Gustav's, as well as Georges. As reluctant as part of Georges was to continue with us, more specifically, these experiments, he had always been intrigued himself with the implications of the variability of human genetics, the genome and its role in society, as well as the inception of quantum genetics as a means of virtually traveling through time using a virtual genomic grid and a virtual enigma avatar. He had established a virtual grid connection himself, the kind that can only be built with Virtual V, and re-enforced with Virtual VI technologies. As he held Todor, he remarked that someone might need a diaper change in about five minutes, which is something I had been saving myself up for all day. I had never changed a diaper before and it was more natural to set up a certain level of virtual technology in the space-time continuum than to go near a diaper. I never knew babies could smell quite that way. either way, I passed the test, having cleaned my son's butt, having applied baby powder to it, and having wrapped the new diaper on securely. Todor was as happy as ever, smiling and looking for his mother in the other room. We examined the equipment, and then examined the connections to the mainframe, the power connectors themselves, as well as the embedded virtualization devices that were part of the power framework itself. We ascertained that the experiment didn't have to happen tonight, but we could start it anyway. Gamma-Gustav walked over, submitted a virtual genomic customized DNA file, then after the countdown, de-materialized and de- virtualized. He had been inside of a greater number than fifty five hosts in the total amount of time, not counting repair and maintenance time, since he has been designed and functional. He still had much time and much wear and tear to go through in order before we ever considered replacing him; in all honesty, we didn't know how to do it, but we were thinking of building him a counterpart for his voyages—someone that he could share his experiences with. If the assignment is not cost-prohibitive, we may start the new project toward the end of this year. This mostly depends upon TANG-0000's ability to map any other parts of the virtual genomic time grid. What he was saving for me when he came in only hours before the asteroid NT9 was the explanation in pure genomics of why certain peoples act the way we do when it comes to war and play, survival and letting go, as well as advancement and devolution. It is difficult for someone as diverse as TANG-0000 to think in terms of black or white, but he does seem to learn from his role models. He has a fairly diverse genome, but far from a genome that is universal that would be needed if we ever wanted to fully create a sample diverse enough to explore all of human history. We walked over into the next room to summon Petra and to see if she was ready. She was ready and beaming, for she would get to explore the space-time continuum like nobody else had before her, including myself. I knew she was happy and I gave her a hug and told her to stand on the podium. Her virtual genomic customized DNA file had been already gathered and established. After a countdown of thirty seconds, she was gone with the tachyon wind and in an exuberant swirl. I had to now track two separate synchronizations, but that was fine since I had Georges here with me, who was about to pour a drink of Crown Royal with me. He had no sooner stopped pouring the glass when Georges had a strange thought: he said he had thought about quitting eGSI and coming here full time if there was any government funding for a small laboratory such as this. I was shocked and did not know he felt this way. I told him there is usually some substantial amount that is always left over for smaller labs, but that I have not had time to ever begin to try to qualify for due to things that have gone on at eGSI, as well as home. I put my hand over his shoulder and told him to keep that thought, but not to quit his position yet since eGSI is the one thing that brings in income for him. He acknowledged that to be true and said that he would never do what he had done had I not come to work for eGSI Super Atom Smasher when I did. I told him I personally did not know what to expect from my first few days at eGSI and that I am forever grateful to have made his acquaintance.

Petra Makes as Tunning Discovery

Today is July 24th, 2013. I had been receiving a constant stream of synchronizations from TANG-0000 and received three more from Petra before she popped in on July 20th in the evening back at the smaller lab. She had visited twenty hosts herself in a desire to answer some burning questions about her past through those hosts, as well as the past of other people. She finally saw Todor again the next day and knew then what she had missed: the love of her son. She had traveled extensively and had recorded even more than I had during my first ill-fated genomic journey through space-time. She was weary, yet enthusiastic about the possibilities of her journeys which have led her to a greater closeness to her own husband. She felt emancipated in a different way today, since she returned to work on July 21st, having slept on the sofa in our private laboratory. She felt stronger and more determined to do her job more correctly if possible, and to test the resolution limits of her creativity when it came to conducting her everyday routine. During all of this, she was sorting her experiences in the space-time continuum with her thinking as a rational scientist and a rational, albeit emotional, human being. She felt comfortable in the opinions that she drew and in the objectivity of her recordings in the sample and collections virtualized database. She knew what to expect next time and she knew that she would have to find a way to account for Todor's behavior and whereabouts in a more systematic fashion. The greater closeness that she felt toward me was the understanding of the de-moleculization process and what the experience is like in spiritual terms. She almost did not immediately known how to handle that first non-destined host from several months ago that almost forced her to give up trying to be a virtual genomic space-time traveler. The nuances of existence, the resolution that one feels when traveling are hardest on the first attempt and when one realizes the wealth of excitement and enjoyment that he or she is experiencing and even bringing back, it becomes all the more easier to start to comprehend the vastness of space-time, even in our limited and localized part of the Multiverse. I love her and will give her anything she needs to feel happier and more independent. I know she can do much of these things by herself and that she is proud when the result is an independent victory, one independent of anyone else. even though social intelligence is a measure of how well people interact with each other in groups, I love Petra for who she is and for what the Virtual enigma can make her become. In this event, you are not really interacting with people of your own space-time. You are interacting with Nature's Diary and with the souls that lie within that still leave traces of existence within the cosmic radiation. The discovery that she made was one that confirms a discovery made by TANG- 0000 when he re-virtualized back at eGSI the day before the asteroid NT9 was headed our way. It has to do with tendencies of human behavior that are objectively based on ethnicity, race, ethnographies and other components of human existence that are protected in many contemporary societies; it has to do with social evolution and individual devolution. It has to do with the concept of group-think and individualistic thinking in the context of a more broader progress that is usually mathematically possible within certain constraints that act all at the same time. Time is a variable dynamic that never goes away and never ceases to amaze or intrigue the wanderer. The wanderer is me, the wanderer is you; whoever it may be, the reward is tangible in the least tangible and material way possible. She has confirmed the postulate that human society can mathematically dissolve over time in a linear fashion based on excessive information that cannot be recorded accurately but once through virtual genomic space-time travel— after this, it may only be transcribed. This is why she is transcribing and copying everything she recorded on her voyages in past space-time. This also has to do with whether or not information would survive the crunching effect of any black hole singularity, or would this be the downturn of society that depended on such information to survive what our singular earth just survived. Petra believes this is worth pursuing, in part because it reminds her in this sense of a postulate that was made by cosmologist Carl Sagan before his death. While she runs the variables in the supercomputer at eGSI, she is reminded of the many things that can cause an unresolvable paradox and would cause an altercation between our natural existence and our future as a species. In the very least, she is comforted with the fact that the paradox or conflicting realities will not directly influence anything that we are doing in this very moment.

Life in A Singularity

The date today is August 3rd, 2013 and I am at checkpoint #56 at eGSI Super Atom Smasher, the very mainframe that enabled me to discover virtual genomic space-time travel. It is secure, the routine is enabled for anyone with clearance and even the external framework of the computer and keyboard has been polished to a shine. I double check the programming routing and noticed that it has been changed since the time that I used it to virtualize into the body of Ricardo Johanes, the school teacher who posed as my first host. It had to be this way, even though my technique of virtualizing DNA was not only secured, but also patented now. It was something I had gone finally to take care of last month at the advice of Georges, who had been pushing me to do this for the last year and I kept putting it off.

I stared at the mainframe and wondered if anybody would ever mention it in a history book and considered asking eGSI myself if it were ever possible to setup space-time tours, on certain days (something like an amusement park). I will never forget the overall experience and what it was like for me when I left and when I came back to the same location barely 2 ½ hours later. I was expecting a call from the media any day now to describe my "journey" and to explain how I would have even attempted to conduct this experiment at the possibility of risking the lives of the colleagues in my vicinity. I became aware of the media pursuit a few weeks after my re-virtualization and re-materialization at #56 and had been avoiding them up until now. I did not want fame, or at least not yet. I was looking to tell my side of the story as to what happened the day I jumped, according to their own terminology, "jumped in a space-time sense." I definitely do not want my media testimony to affect my work in any way that would hinder any revolutionary scientific discoveries that might come up at eGSI. I wish to be as truthful as I can without going into to many details about a manuscript that I am currently writing that would shed light on the entire process, not just a fraction of it. I finally broke down and told them that I would enjoy being interviewed as part of the workforce at eGSI. My objective was not solely for the sake of fame, it was for the sake of understanding what I have uncovered with the help of Gamma-Gustav, Petra, and Georges; it was not a sheer miracle that we survived the wormhole that opened up the virtual genome as our researching ground. every invention starts with a defined thought and I was under no illusions that I would make any novel discoveries for myself when the day came that I decided I would blast myself from a highly-charged hydrogen particle beam at my primary place of work. In a sense, the entirety of the practical applications still eludes me in the sense that it is hard to see in a holistic sense what all could come of it. The term "quantum genetics" is not all encompassing in that it doesn't even include animal or DNA of another nature in this sense, but is based in part on humans with volitional power to travel into past event flows that may or may not have anything to do with them. My decision included my willful curiosity and my volition to act upon that curiosity in order to reap unseen benefits. So far, the decade that has just ended in 2013 has marked 3.859 years out of those ten mapped as part of the virtual time grid. The process that started with an exponent has been growing incredibly fast for something that is otherwise defined as timeless and humanly corrosive. Time connects the dots, it connects our consciousnesses, it connects our primordial wills. Space-time gives it a location to happen; quantum genetics gives it a scope, a purpose and a scientific definition. The remainder is the human will and the follow- through to make it happen. The point is that we will see them and interpret what we will of them. Depending on the person who stands as the interpretation of past times, we will see truths that can be verified by not just two, but a multitude of people. We have entered a new era of computing when the figures generated are not astronomical mountains to climb, but become calculations that take less and less of our times to analyze and attribute authentic values. The problem is not the lack of seriousness; it is as it occasionally has been the lack of reference point.

Another Synchronization Session with Tan G- 0000

Today is August 9th, 2013 and I have just received another synchronization signal from TANG-0000. He has mapped three months in what is the span of about one month that he has been gone from the private laboratory. Slowly but surely the process is beginning to unfold and the quantum dust is settling to reveal the complex intricacies of the beauties of space-time as we know them and as we are discovering them. With over four years of the space-time grid mapped in a virtual sense, the task is still overwhelming. I have often thought that the first ten years would be the most difficult to attain with respect to solidity and accuracy of data. With TANG-0000, though, any challenge is a good challenge. He is relentless. He is expecting a companion in the full sense one day, with the companionship being more of an element of USB standards than FireWire. He has friends, but he simply needs a companion that can understand his building needs, the needs that arise because of his innate human nature. The more I think about this, the more I feel I need to give in to his desire to have someone else in this life that is designed, programmed, and custom-built just for him. He had described certain events that were related to the United States between his host and a science conference in Toledo, Ohio as crucial to another bend, another set of nodes that lead up to one of the reasons that I decided to move from the United States a few springs ago. There was little threat of a virtual paradox, but I took the potential seriously and I messaged him to try to leave that host's body as soon as possible. It appeared that a professor of mine from M.I.T. had attended that conference. I did not wish for this to get messy. I knew I was going to go back very soon and that there was a chance that I was supportive of my own selfish motives to conquer this bend, this set of nodes. I had to see for myself how this was coming about so quickly and I knew

I couldn't do this very thing at this very time. TANG-0000 was very accurate, yet I felt that the statistical margin of error could somehow creep into his estimates as well. This is the reason, after all, that verification of the correct mapping of the virtual time grid was so crucial for history to reminisce. I also knew that I had been neglecting little Todor for a while and that I wanted to see him playing with his new toys, which were at the recommendation of his mother, various geometric shapes and sizes, nothing too small to swallow. The babysitter was at home when I got in and realized that Petra had left some dinner for me and had gone to the private lab, where she was to work on a quantum genetics thesis herself that could have some bearing on what will happen to our research in the next four to five months, something that might prevent us from de-materializing and virtualizing any more than we have to. She has said that she enjoys quiet activities better. As I ate my dinner, I realized that I had not seen Georges at work today and that he had not come by my part of eGSI installation to say hello. When I called him, he answered the phone immediately. He seemed fatigued and said he had not been in because he was sick with the flu and decided to call in. I told him I was going to our private laboratory and had intended to ask him to go, but now that I knew he was sick, I thought I should just let him sleep or go back to warding off the influenza that practically confined him to his bed. He said that he was feeling a little better and did not want to contaminate anyone else, but that he also wanted to meet me at the lab. He wanted to see what other alternate power configurations could be setup with the accelerators and why the accelerator did not work quite the same way from eGSI as it does from there. He said that he would be over there once he had had some dinner. I finished my own and, after having played with Todor for thirty minutes, was on my way. As I listened to the radio in my car, I received another synchronization in my car receiver from TANG-0000, who notified me that the paradox had been avoided and that the three months had been mapped very closely and accurately. I would now have to ascertain this for myself.

Virtual Genomic Travel Starts with Reverse Progression

Today is August 15th, 2013. I knew Petra's contribution to virtual genomic travel had been somewhat elementary in terms of the process itself. She had not revealed the details on what she was writing about and I knew it must be something that might coincide with what might be part of my theory or something that even conflicts with it. Her "thesis" was on the postulate that virtual genomic time travel happens with a reverse progression taking place first in order for the process to obtain information that could be set forth into past chronological flows. She did not wish to immediately reveal how or why she chose to write about this particular aspect of this theory; she simply came to the conclusion that the virtual fetal DNA file enabled the process to continue into what would eventually, in a split second, turn into virtual genomic space-time travel. This is exactly what would cause a paradox to be avoided in genomic travels, in a virtual sense. In a sense, true genomic travel would not happen unless this contradiction was ultimately resolved. The alternative would be for the DNA configuration file to be drawn, to flow to, the parent with whom the virtual traveler has more genetic likeness. In my case, the paradox that could have been caused by my parents being overseas at the time I virtualized/de-materialized was resolvable by this postulate and my stronger likeness to my dad led to my paternal co-existence with my father for a fraction of a second. After this, of course, the statistical margin of error came into play and I was no longer in paradox zone. So what if someone is the vicinity of either of her parents when virtual genomic space- time travel occurs? It simply means that the probability of paradox is larger and that the only thing preventing an actual paradox or triggering the virtual enigma is the virtual technologies employed that allow for the mapping of the virtual space-time grid in the first place. As I have said before, virtual technology levels range from I through VI are quite effective in allowing a traveler to perceive through the senses of the host the world that existed prior to the de-virtualization. Petra's experience with being pregnant with Todor and not being able to virtualize into the second host means that her virtual enigma could not full activate a second time because of her pregnancy, because of the baby's molecules, atoms, nuclei, and quarks actively getting in the way of the virtual enigma preventing a paradox, or even activating properly. Her parents were in Russia at the time of this occurrence. It took the process a second time of analyzing Petra to realize that she was pregnant and that there could be little room for a paradox inside of a paradox. This is what she concluded and wanted to present to me next week for a consultation or for an agreement. I could not give her full agreement on something that was so continuous that I have yet to describe it myself. In this case, the technology itself that is employed is the driver of prevention of paradox-like activity before and after the traveler's genomic space-time virtualization and de-materialization. I had to agree that that would have been the most classic case of paradox that there is, as well as the twins paradox. Todor was not expecting a sibling, either way, until we could realize if his DNA was going to be affected by Petra's decision to step into the accelerator of the genomic virtual machine.

To Dor's enigmatic Characteristic

It is September 9th, 2013. It is evening time and I have been playing with Todor while Petra and Georges have been at the private laboratory working on individual things. He is truly a beautiful baby and Petra and I have been tremendously blessed with his birth. even since he was born, I have been paying attention to any condition that could have evolved out of Petra's somewhat inadvertent yet careless trip through the virtual genomic space- time machine. Tonight, I have noticed what appears to be some evidence of what we have been afraid of this entire time. Todor is a very smart baby and we made sure to have this tested at a hospital more recently than his first birthday, which was last Saturday. He has developed a certain glow when he gets excited and I am afraid that he might have a sort of built- in virtual enigma that may cause him to become a "jumper". His parents are time travelers. For this reason, I continue to hope that Todor, if he jumps, will end up virtualizing toward his mother's side of the family. In this way, he will not be stretched or put in pain needlessly for something that is at this point as much my fault as it is Petra's. I know in my heart as well as my intellect that he will be a virtual genomic space-time traveler and that this might continue on into the progeny of Petra and myself. This "jumper characteristic" may prove to be useful to him in a sense and may not be a trait that stunts his growth; after all, it affects his entire body, not just his thyroid gland. He may not need an accelerator in order to 'leap' 80 years into the past. He has emotions that he must learn how to control and a pretty solid intellect that he inherits from both sides of his family. His condition might be considered a disability at first and he will have to be taken to urgent care the moment that it is discovered that this trait is endangering his life. I am not prepared to lose my son, no matter how ludicrous his capabilities are and what they mean for modern science. I hesitated a minute and called Petra and Georges. Georges answered the phone and handed the phone over to Petra. Petra was concerned and said that she was just finishing up what she had been working on. She said she would come home immediately. Before she even hung up the phone, she almost fainted. Todor was at the private laboratory and it appeared that he just appeared out of nowhere. He hadn't. He used the IP addressing of the phone and materialized in front of Petra and Georges next to the other accelerator pad, the one that Petra had taken recently. This was a grave situation and seriously baffling as far as situations go. How could he just appear? There was not virtualization present and he seemed intact. They called me back and asked me what I wanted to do. I opted to go down there to meet them at the lab. As I changed coats, I noticed something in my pocket. It was a new flash drive that I had purchased for the sake of customizing someone else's DNA. I had never really had anyone in mind before now. I decided that I had found how I wanted to utilize this flash drive —on my son Todor. Originally, it would have been suited for Petra who had already gotten her DNA virtually customized and mapped. Now I knew part of what I wanted to do. There was little left to do but to lock up and head to our private laboratory. As I drove, I cried. I didn't wish to see myself curse the day when I invented genomic virtual space-time travel, but it has arrived. I also knew it would have to be part of the solution to little Todor's problem. As I drove, I took a call from Petra, who was freaking out that Todor seemed fine, but was changing colors. I arrived to the lab in ten minutes and did not know what to expect when I entered the door. Georges and Petra were there and Georges was consoling Petra as the shining star lay on the ground, playing with his cubes. I could see that he was in a good mood by the way his upper lip formed an impatient smile. He was our baby and I needed to find a vaccine for what he had developed from both of his parents. It would not be easy and nobody in the room was a qualified pediatrician. I continued to probe until I decided to virtually customize his DNA. He squirmed and I knew that this was going to be a long night, at least until we could find a competent doctor to diagnose if he has a simple case of an aging disorder.

A Blessing in Disguise

Today is September 10th, 2013 and, after having virtually customized Todor's DNA for the first time, Petra decided to take him to the pediatrician. He did not squirm as much on the ride over there, according to her, but he did cry for a while, keeping his thumb in his mouth to keep himself occupied.

Petra was not as scared about what had happened last night as she was of what she was going to have to tell the doctor when they finally saw her. Her name was Dr. Adelheid Blosch. She remarked that he is very smart and that the aging disorder was not easily discernible from a number of other illnesses that could be the cause of his condition. When Petra asked if a follow-up appointment would be necessary, Dr. Blosch seemed to think not. She had said that she had seen cases such as this in parents that work around nuclear waste and nuclear radiation in general. Petra told her what she and I do for a living and Dr. Blosch smirked. She said that there was nothing else that she could do with the exception of recommending a specialist who specializes in combustible conditions that are related to premature or immature aging.

Apparently, Todor was not born with Benjamin Button disorder, but he had a type of disorder that cause his tissues to regenerate very rapidly at the cellular level. In scientific terms, something the doctor herself might not have understood, Todor is a jumper. Had he not be born on a C-Section, he might never have materialized as an infant and never re-materialized. In other words, the night he was conceived, my DNA had been impacted by the genomic virtual space-time travel. Petra's was impacted when she decided to try to virtualize and de-materialize while she was still pregnant with him.

Hence, our baby has a condition which would serve as a feeling of being cursed for life, but they may be a blessing in disguise in the event that he preferred to be alone. It would feel supernatural at first, but he has already made one jump and has landed in a room close to one of his parents. The chances that his birth is directly related to a real paradox are rather high. I am a small part digital, which happened to me the first time I virtualized and de- materialized. This was going to be hard to explain with respect to any of his class photographs in the future if he ever "jumped" while in front of his camera. I felt I was to blame and I hated myself. After all, the farthest thing I wished for in a progeny was a son who is a combustible genomic traveler. This is what I have and the next time that Petra, Todor, Georges and I are together, I will have him Georges take a photo of us. This might be the last time Todor is so readily available and the next time he is so young and disposable that he won't be "jumping" over in the direction. I wonder, could this really be a blessing in disguise, a good hand at the poker table? I am starting to wonder if Fate was a bit more than a call girl. I could feel Petra's anger at herself as well as the anger directed at me for having this happen. I told her that we will have to work this through because he was going to grow up on us and be able to control his combustibility far beyond ways that I can imagine. She was still terrified at the thought of her baby "beaming down" next to her in our private laboratory. She said she had almost stepped down on that exact stop when she saw a flash of light, a flash of brilliance that might one day dazzle the girls in high school. She was getting over it. Before she took the job at eGSI, she wanted her health to not be impacted, nor the health of any of her offspring. This has happened and I immediately promised her that if it took our research in a different direction, I would stop doing what we were currently working on. She didn't see a point and pointed out that we would soon marvel the scientific community with what we have discovered. Todor as a baby has been the product of an eclipse of virtual and real paradoxes. He was not going to change substantially in the most likeliest of senses. I knew he would have hardships as a result and I knew that I would be with him through thick and thin as a parent. I knew Petra was with me 100% of the way. Our work continues the way it should and we continue to map the virtual genomic space-time grid.

The Virtualization of All Virtualizations

Today is September 21st, 2013 and Petra, Georges, and I have come in from an all-night work load at the private laboratory. We are tired and we all plan to turn in early this evening. This has only happened twice with respect to pulling all-night shifts; one of those times was during the NT9 threat. We spend much of the time customizing Todor's virtual DNA file, with all allocated sequences. He has combustible DNA that 'jumps' on its own within the configuration that he was born with and was taken to the incubator with. Had he not been, he might be a living virtual enigma with no control of his destiny or his travels. In this small but significant way, he has the opportunity if addressed correctly to control this order/ disorder in order to live a full productive life. Petra and I love him more than we even know, knowing that he is also inadvertently a product of the love of science and adventure. Petra still blames herself, but is taking precautionary measures not to have him pop up at eGSI Super Atom Smasher. Something that we devised at our private lab will help control his jumps and his urges to jump. It is a timer that is preset to manage his food cravings and his baby desires to leap. It helps control his intrinsic motions, his metabolism, as well as his material kaonic breakdown, which is the reason for his spontaneous jumps. He has not had any major jumps since the jump to the laboratory the other night, although he has had some from the nursery to the living room, from the kitchen to the dining room and back. He is spectacular when this happens because he is a cute baby and does not know what just happened to him. He knows when it is time for mommy and daddy to come home and when it is time for Hanneli, the Swiss babysitter who comes by on Tuesday's to be here; he gladly waits to be fed and doesn't usually complain much unless he feels he is being neglected. As I have said, these activities are something that he will not outgrow but his bodily instincts will learn how to manage and distribute evenly in his body as he gets older and more mature. The primary trigger seems to be heat and he had spent some time in the incubator after he was delivered. Today would normally be an interesting day if not for lack of sleep and the drudgery must endure in order to achieve those quiet mini successes in the course of the week. Petra and I both would replenish our sleep batteries when we got home that evening since we were taking a night away from the private laboratory. We had to maintain the functionality of mainframes, beam parts, lasers and laser parts today as if we had gotten a fresh amount of rest from the night before. I finished with my tasks around 5:15 p.m.; Petra was done at about 5:35. We went home together for the first time as a married couple, ate some old chicken and spaghetti dinner, rocked Todor for about an hour and ended up going to sleep about 9:45 p.m. We had had a long exhausting 48-hour time period and it had to be wound to a close. We would be up at 5:45 a.m. to start the cycle anew and to do the type of work that makes even mystery men ponder existence. The virtualization of all virtualizations was going to belong to our biological son, not our adopted Gamma-Gustav, not our cybernetic friend who serves us well and wholeheartedly.

More in Formation from the private laboratory

Today is October 1st, 2013 and we have been poring over reports that have come in from TANG-0000 and from previous reports, some of whom were obtained by Gamma-Gustav during the NT9 crisis. It is becoming clear that this information would have been very helpful in the time during which it happened or during which it was created in the virtual space-time grid. It also became clear that we might have been the select few of those people who preceded this information that has had the opportunity to manipulate and analyze it as if it were today's information used to make global logistic, economic, and otherwise scientific decisions. It was information that we could now punch into certain slots and to revise the equations that are lives are based upon, to make the kind of vehicles that do not break down, to make the types of foods that do not go sour or bad in three times as long, to make all sorts of decisions that could have revolutionized life back into the previous century. In a very short few days, I would have to summon Dr. Hourdeau to notify him and to see what function this information could serve. I knew better than to immediately include everybody and anybody from eGSI since the last time I almost had to have an interview with the Paris Scientific News. I have already had one and it is excruciatingly difficult to explain certain terms on the air about something as static as a camera which can be used to monitor and then as an aid to report our everyday lives. The dynamics of what I talked about needed a different set of terms and explanations the audience that was listening, who was a lay audience and did not know the difference between an atom and an allele. Dr. Hourdeau said that this information should be guarded with the strongest encryption and even a security guard; after what he just found out, there would be more people who would want to see it for themselves and to even sell it to third parties. "Good work, Marinkovich!" exclaimed Dr. Hourdeau. "We will have to see what else your private laboratory yields. We are not to use the eGSI Super Atom Smasher for any other types of activities other than those that were determined beforehand. Whatever else you discover will be a result of research from your privately rented lab." I immediately gave credit to two other people, Petra Marinkovich and Georges Pouchet. I also credited Gamma-Gustav (TANG-0000) for this information to be known so exquisitely beautifully. He is to materialize at the private lab in three days and I want to be the first to tell him that Delta-Zhana will be a project that we will start on next month and that she will be anatomically a female. With all respects of the DNA composition of Gamma-Gustav's DNA bank, hers will contain something more feminine that only Petra can produce. She will fill that void that bothers Gamma- Gustav so much in that his longing for an equivalent companion may soon come to an end. She will be the one that will analyze the information while he picks it and brings it back to the present.

They will also be handling independent virtual genomic space-time voyages at the same time whenever it becomes possible.

Tan G-0000 Returns From Mission

Today is October 4th, 2013 and TANG-0000 is destined back as Gamma- Gustav in approximately two hours and fifteen minutes. In the meantime, we are all at the lab, including Petra, myself, Georges, and Todor, who is sleeping in the nearby study. We are trying to figure out what we can do so as not to exacerbate Todor's condition as well as how to go about raising additional capital for the design and construction of Delta-Zhana. She would inevitably cost more money to construct, but it may only be dangerous for the sake that this time we might have to let the Bioethics committee know how and why we are looking to develop and construct a female version of Gamma-Gustav and, if we don't, then I get fined, along with possible fines for Petra and Georges. We had the initial investment formula, now we just had to stick to our budget and develop this female cybernetic traveler. With the two cybernetic travelers, we could map out up to two more decades in eighteen months. Of course, the larger the virtual grid becomes, the more maintenance it requires. By this time next week, the Unified Global Initiative will have reached the scientific forums of the world, those same forums that ultimately decide which issues have more merit than others in the eyes of the global scientific communities. The initiative is to create new types of businesses that revolve around virtual genomic space-time travel, businesses that take advantage of the disequilibrium in the tachyon paths of the past, the past flows of the present from the past, as well as the current flows into the future in order to create something from nothing. There can only be so much equilibrium in space-time that these businesses are actually feasible here on earth for future generations and are ecologically safe because of the emphasis on recycling and utterly obliterating things that even these days are not considered recyclable. I had thought long and hard on the initiative before I told Petra and Georges about it. It won't have to be achieved in 2032 after all. Within five minutes of that thought, I saw the familiar swirl and the particles coming together to re-constitute Gamma-Gustav and his built-in virtual databases. We rushed to greet him and to say "hello" to his materializing halo. He looked tired, but after he became solid, Petra gave him a hug, and I gave him a steady handshake. Georges embraced him like the 'godfather' that Gamma-Gustav could have had. He brought more valuable information with him. He started his briefing with a question about the fellow cybernaut. I told him we would be starting work on her this month. He was impressed. He asked if anybody had seen Todor and proceeded into the next room to say hello to him. Todor was already sleeping, so we all came back into the main office room where he uploaded his virtual collections and sampling databases, as well as his host health database, among others. The information finally concluded what was supposed to be an overall linked web of one hundred years into the past through random links and a full decade of virtual genomic space-time links in a carefully linked mini-web. Without knowing the exact date of the manufacture of Delta-Zhana, we could not know for sure how long it would take to genomically map one centuries worth of collective memories. With better estimates for parts, it would take 40% less material to create the time documenting companion of Gamma-Gustav, but the total cost would be 10% more than his had been. Looking at our cybernetic traveler, I would have said that the expression on his face is that of triumph, but it wasn't. I was the face of someone who enjoys doing what he does for a living, with meritocratic purposes in mind. He had the loneliest expression on his face since we had talked about his new companion for the first time. By now, he is used to getting by with what we provide him in terms of technology. He has only once asked if it is possible to know if the technology could be any more advanced. I told him the same thing I once told Petra, and during a separate time, Georges—the technologies have their limitations and are updated every so often to enable, but they are only as good as the program design is. If you build a building or a living quarters according to certain constraints, this building may only come out as planned if every detail is followed meticulously. He will soon be happy, I guarantee, after we have built her and he has gotten to know her as a cybernetic human being.

Gamma-Gustav will be taking the next two weeks off for repair, maintenance and relaxation. In the meantime, he will help to analyze much of the information that he brought back himself in order to help classify and categorize it into something useful for the twenty first century and for the creation of the virtual genomic space-time grid. We are making progress and this is what counts on a voyage toward something some do not even understand the concept of.

The Planning, Design, and Construction Phases of Delt A-Zhana

Today is October 14th, 2013 and Gamma-Gustav has been working the clerical/scientific job of separating, categorizing and classifying the "past flows information" that he himself discovered; it is an easier task that produces much less wear and tear on even a cybernetic mind. He will be going back into the space-time continuum in three days to continue to connect the milliseconds with the seconds, the minutes, with the hours, the hours with the days and months of past flow history. As for the three of us, Petra, Georges, and me, we are researching the best way possible to build a counterpart to Gamma-Gustav, to receive the highest quality cybernetic woman for the least amount of money invested. We've had to face facts: investments in materials and parts were one of the highest resource-draining activities in this field of science. Conformity to certain industry standards is of utmost importance. We could not continue to do this without verifying that we were conducting our research with adequate ISO standards. Georges has brought in a long time friend in these standards who has worked in various industrial and scientific settings. Ingrid Thomas has worked in installations such as eGSI before in her long time career and had noticed one or two things out of the ordinary, aside from the amateur setup; the electrical setup of our private laboratory was not set up according to standards, which we corrected. The next standard would have been a certification from the european Scientific Standards Organization, which we were not in a position to comply with now, but I promised we would do so as soon as we were in a position.

We were professionals in every other sense of the word. Mrs.

Thomas stayed for a cup of tea and left abruptly without knowing the exact nature of why we were using this private laboratory. She was not privy to know that this was the place that corresponded with mainframe #56 at eGSI Super Atom Smasher. As of now, we have to do whatever else we can by the book and not expose ourselves to being shut down because of noncompliance. As Gamma- Gustav sorted through the copies of the virtual data that he had collected during his latest travels in the virtual genomic space-time grid, I sat in silence with Georges and Petra, trying hard not to have to choose between a higher cost model of Delta-Zhana and a lab that can operate by the manual. It was a no-point breaker and we had to find a way to achieve both of these goals without reverting to going without—the cost/benefit analysis was a very difficult one to determine and we would have to find a way to keep things under a certain cost no matter what. Petra and I had to think of any potential medical costs for Todor in the future. This was our life. We had to prove everything that had been done at a Scientific Symposium in Paris on November 1st after Dr. Hourdeau took credit for the first instance of genomic virtual space-time travel happening at eGSI Super Atom Smasher. What we had to have ready were copies of virtual records that existed in paper form from other sources and other people, some of whom were are hosts in past space-time flows.

Scientific Symposium on new Technologies

The date is November 4th, 2013. The Scientific Symposium on New Technologies went rather well, although it lasted well into the ten o'clock hour. We demonstrated information about how virtual genomic space-time travel occurs by using a high quantum charge and a virtualized DNA file that is linked to the human genome. I told them of my early experiences and how I felt like I was looking out of someone else's body, as in the case of my first host Ricardo Johanes. I described how dizzying it felt to leave, de-virtualize and materialize into another host, or even to return to my own body. I had derived much experience at it, I told them, before the crowning achievement with my spouse and my best colleagues that resulted in Gamma-Gustav (TANG- 0000). As I led out our favorite cybernetic traveler, with Petra, Georges, and I already on the stage, I mentioned what happened to our son Todor and described what has happened to his molecular integrity when he get emotionally excited. I told him that this science is very important to me, but that the event made me wonder how to continue. As I got emotional, Petra stepped in and finished the rest, saying precisely what had happened when she tried to engage in virtual genomic time travel on her own. We both told the audience that we felt as though we have discovered something without regards for the dangers that might result in a virtual paradox, which begins at birth going the opposite direction along the thermodynamic arrow of time. We told them of Todor and his jumping condition; we told them how we believe his condition results from having both of his parents in a state of flux between different space-time points and being between two points of virtual paradox. As we left the stage, we received a round of applause, with the host saying "Now there is an example of an entire family who is rapidly engaged in the process of science in its core. They have already left a mark upon the newly minted field of quantum genetics and are swiftly cornering the world's understanding of the world of quanta and that of the nano- biotechnical. Be on the lookout as they do this again." Petra was glad that we went and said that this could help us achieve funding for our projects at the private laboratory, as well as recognition that might result in the same type of acceptance or funding. I was happy that I had finally achieved something I had always wanted to achieve through something less than notoriety, which is through acceptance in my field. I also achieved acclaim by being able to talk about my experiences in front of others in a given reality. I will always look for ways to be accepted and to contribute to the world in a positive way. The Unified Global Initiative was founded by us in order to advance funding to independent scientists in this world who haven't the means or capacity to inquire about funding on their own. The world was said to have been shrinking like a "global village" in the 1990s; now those connections between the most and the least fortunate continue to multiply and to establish themselves as oases of ultimate connections and grounds for the fruitful harvesting of meritocracy. The chemical bonds that underlie everything in this world underscore our efforts to bring the world into a stew of interdependent and understanding people in circumstances of which we have much in common. Petra commented on the way home that conventions like these are needed for people at a lower level than the global upper echelon of scientific discovery. I knew what she was talking about and that she didn't know how many science fairs I had attended or had exhibited in before I received the recognition of a lifetime tonight. I knew what recognition meant for other aspects of living beyond the sheer need for funding. It meant fame and fortune in many cases. The benefits of our fame and fortune were something that we meant to provide to anybody with an interest or with no interest in what we were doing. Our inquisitiveness is our guiding principle since we need to accomplish goals so that many more will know the truth about our surrounding world and the world within us that comprises all of us.

The Design & Construction of Delt A - Zhana

Today is November 18th, 2013 and we have already completed the design phase of Delta-Zhana and started the assembly of this female cybernetic traveler. Her genetic make-up will be spliced with other DNA that we have obtained with permission from a few DNA laboratories in this area. She will have skills that Gamma-Gustav himself does not possess, such as a more powerful internal processor and more memory. She will not be retroactively compatible with him in certain features such as database variability, nor her host database adjustment factor. The one thing she will share in common with Gamma-Gustav will be her general prototype. Her DNA mix is more universal than that of Gamma-Gustav, as stated, and will be more universal and add versatility to her virtual enigma. She will be a time warrior in her own realm and a proficient recorder of events that have already happened and need to be known. Her inside chamber contains virtual protoplasm, something slightly different than what is inside of Gamma-Gustav's internal bodily make-up. She is digitized and virtualized and has a vast scope of sensing as a perceptive young woman whose capacity to remember, collect and expound on data is equivalent to that of Gamma-Gustav. She is not the anti-thesis of Gamma-Gustav; she is an upgrade if there is such a thing in the human cybernetic evolutionary process. She is an improvement on certain things, yet it is too soon to tell if she is an upgrade or a more efficient model when it comes to reliability. As we were putting together her limbs, we noticed a glitch in the bionics of her left arm and decided to inspect all limbs as proscribed. We added the left arm last. The final phase involved making her feminine in all ways and making sure there was enough plasma for her orifices and what would be her reproductive organs were she a regular female

— with size C breasts, she astonished Gamma-Gustav and made him feel apologetic that he ever doubted my ability to deliver. After this evening, she was as good as completed. She had to be charged for 48 hours in order to fully be activated. We had to make sure she was clothed and well prepared for her activation as well as to meet her new mentor, Gamma-Gustav. It was not yet assured that he would take a liking to her, but we had to see. When I pulled up to the lab with him in the passenger seat, he asked what the surprise is and what was this important that he had to be restricted to the house for two weeks. When he walked in, she was activated and carrying on a conversation with Petra. I brought him in for the first time and they made eye contact. Gamma-Gustav shook her hand and they introduced themselves.

After 10 seconds, they knew everything about the other, without the use of cabling or wireless. It was an input method we had not quite tested before, but it seemed to be working fine. Later, I let the girls socialize as ladies, while the boys went to go spend some time with one another in the lounge. Gamma- Gustav had already taken a liking to her and was astonished at her capabilities when she began to list them. She knew she is superior in her own right to many of the very things he was designed and built for as well, but was programmed not to take a bragging right to them. He knew that he was not about to be replaced by her and that she was to be his assistant and student in the art of virtual genomic space-time travel. Overall, I would say that he is more than satisfied with the option that he has been granted. Our goal now is to map out what we have of the virtual time grid in terms of the more and more specific detail that arises when studying temporal phenomena. Our ultimate goal is to map the entire century by the onset of the next decade, something which is almost an insurmountable task for the present time and our present obligations to eGSI. Our goal for Gamma-Gustav and Delta- Zhana is for them to work as efficiently as possible as a team and as individuals.

Into the Vast Realms of Virtual Genomic Travel

Today is December 2nd, 2013. After having found out that Petra has received a promotion to chief engineer of her division, I was also happy to find out that Georges was getting a promotion in his division as head scientist in the Thermodynamics Department. I was to receive another promotion very soon and, from what I have heard, the management was thinking of making me a senior engineer in the division of quantum mechanics. Things were starting to work out in life. I was content in finding out that for a second time I was going to be a father; this time the baby was female. I was thirty eight and I was ready for fatherhood once more; what I did not know was if Petra was completely ready for motherhood anew, although she claimed she was. Todor was almost two years old and it seemed like our family tree was branching a bit, but what wasn't as quickly as I had hoped for was our virtual genomic space-time grid. In fact, we had everything from the present year back as far as the year 1983 explored and marked upon the virtual grid in relativistic fashion. What we were missing in many cases was the detail that came about when these events transpired. I knew I would have to return to some of these places that I initially mapped myself and attempt to perfectly specify what the core meaning of what we found is. I knew the private laboratory was going to be barely adequate for the time being and that, eventually, we would have to find a bigger and better place. Delta-Zhana has been learning the ropes and was becoming quite the time gatherer and collector that would soon begin to outflank Gamma-Gustav in her overall efficiency and her stamina. She was very easy to moleculize and virtualize, but she never quite remained anywhere long enough to maintain an adequate cosmic background radiation (CBR) link to the point in the space-time continuum that she happened to be visiting. The central value of the information that she brought back to later map the existing grid more than compensated for this lacking feature, though, and had she been the product of any more of a concerted effort of splicing, she would not be perfect. I was not looking for perfection because I know that there is no such thing that is human made. With virtual genomic space- time travel and grid mapping, I am not looking for flawless perfection with an absence of any mistakes. I am looking for something very close to error- free. I am looking for a structured collection of bookmarked data in the form of events, nodes, occurrences, and phenomena. This could encompass an entire century full of intricately woven space-time maps and information that could eventually be linked to the World Wide Web or Internet. Gamma- Gustav knows his flaws as well as I do and continues to efficaciously collect and gather data from past decades as a space-time traveler, while knowing that he has human-based needs and desires. One of those desires was someone like Delta-Zhana, who is a companion as much as a co-worker. She has become an impetus and a driver of him as much as the enigmatic nature of virtual genomic space-time travel itself. As for little Todor, he has yet to jump again further than from across the distance from the house and our laboratory, or from any point further than the two points that Petra and I find ourselves in. He has been a happy child so far, but I have wondered if there is a way to make that happiness last more and be even better for him. It is not easy for him being the child of scientist parents who have good parenting skills but do not always give 100% of the time when it counts, instead providing a babysitter. Considering he is about to have a little sister very soon, spending time with him these days will be a necessity that can no longer wait. He needs new toys and I just picked up three for him last week. Many of them he tosses to the side very quickly because he becomes bored with them. I like to think that they stimulate his mental development and that he will have many things to learn from in these earliest days of his cognitive life. even if the toys do not tickle his fancy, he still loves his mommy and daddy and, though we are trying everything we can to not be distant from him, a babysitter is a necessity that could not have waited when it came time for Petra to get back to the workforce, to get back to eGSI. She was going crazy for a time not having as much to do at the house, postpartum depression being the reason. either way, she now has her promotion and I feel that this is the only financial solution and it is not an unusual one to have both parents working in a household. If in my lifetime I could map fifty years of the virtual genomic space-time grid, I would be a happy person. If in some way, I could visit Russia a few times to understand some things from my wife's childhood that I do not understand, I would be a happy person. What would make me feel empty would be that unknown element that I am always looking for in the virtual data that Gamma-Gustav and Delta-Zhana bring back as part of their collections and gatherings from previous decades, the unknown element to our love going out like a part of a sophisticated electric car going out and being non- replaceable. I know what my life is and I am happy with where I am going with it, but sometimes I feel as though I am growing apart from Petra strictly because we have so many obligations and responsibilities that we have enough preventing us from spending as much time together. We are still in love and she jokingly says she wouldn't even trade me in for the newest model of Mercedes. She says it was Fate herself who brought us together the day I de-materialized and de-virtualized for the first time, yet it almost felt like a walk through the grocery store when everybody seems so preoccupied because nothing appears to be in the right place or the correct order. In all of the disorder, however discomforting it may have felt for both of us, there was an element of entropy, love and order that I still cannot quite explain. What I have stumbled upon, what I have invented I could not have done without my colleagues Petra and Georges, nor without Dr. Hourdeau. He was very upset the day of my stunt that he almost terminated employment contracts with five employees who were in the vicinity of mainframe #56 that day. I know he has probably had some regrets about keeping me because of personality issues but otherwise has great respect for me as an employee and as a colleague. I could not have invented virtual genomic time travel without the virtualization technologies that are employed every time an individual has utilized upon turning on specific operating systems. These included Virtual Technologies of the I, II, III, IV, V, VI, and VII order. I used to be very modest and I still attempt to be a modest man, but it has gotten more complex that I thought.

My research has become seemingly more arrogant in a sense because much of what I have discovered has been verified, but some of it still cannot be taken as scientific fact. There are other revolutions going on, including the revolutions of artificial intelligence, nanotechnologies, and supercomputing, among others. They are showing the way to the future, the future that hasn't been written yet but is visible from beyond the horizon. It is that close that my own blood starts to boil at the possibilities. It makes some of the phenomena I have seen meaningful as that cup of coffee that I enjoy daily or the walk on the beach in Santa Monica beach that I might have taken had I landed in that part of the world. My waves are slightly different, brain waves included. My future is different from yours in a multitude of different ways. We also have to make way for occasional waves of indifference that pass through us on their way to a more violent place in time that most of us want to stay away from because we have the notion that all people are ultimately family. It is our plethora of differences that can ultimately bring us together and what we consider social intimacy that can also tear us apart. It is our imagination that is the impetus to our creative id, the force that never leaves our hearts. It is our multi-sidedness that occasionally brings us around full circle to the place where we were born, the origins of humanity. Fear not the unknown for it is not a realm to be feared. The circle is yours to de-virtualize in. The possibilities are limitless and the rewards worth the wait!

www.ingramcontent.com/pod-product-compliance
Lightning Source LLC
LaVergne TN
LVHW040134080526
838202LV00042B/2908
* 9 7 8 1 9 5 6 0 7 4 9 3 2 *